It takes a killer ... to stop a killer.

That's how crime lord Armin Petrossian sees it when he summons Bonnie Parker to his palatial home on Christmas Eve.

Petrossian has personal reasons to take care of the serial killer known as the Man in the Moon. And Bonnie—a private investigator on the Jersey Shore who moonlights as a freelance assassin—seems like the perfect choice for the job.

But the Man in the Moon has secret accomplices who are playing their own deadly game.

And they don't intend to let anyone spoil their holiday plans ...

Michael Prescott is the *New York Times* and *USA Today* bestselling author of more than twenty suspense novels.

TEARS
FOR THE
DEAD

Books by Michael Prescott

Novels

Manstopper
Kane
Shadow Dance
Shiver
Shudder
Shatter
Deadly Pursuit
Blind Pursuit
Mortal Pursuit
Comes the Dark
Stealing Faces
The Shadow Hunter
Last Breath
Next Victim
In Dark Places
Dangerous Games
Mortal Faults
Final Sins
Riptide
Grave of Angels
Cold Around the Heart
Blood in the Water
Bad to the Bone
Skin in the Game
Tears for the Dead

Shorter fiction

Steel Trap & Other Stories
Chasing Omega
The Street
Die Wide Awake

Humor
(as "Owen Fusterbuster")

Die Stupid
Obamandias & Hildebeast

TEARS FOR THE DEAD

MICHAEL PRESCOTT

Tears for the Dead, by Michael Prescott

ISBN-13: 9781792695940

The essential American soul is hard, isolate, stoic, and a killer. It has never yet melted.

—D.H. Lawrence

Prologue

THIS IS HOW he does it, the Man in the Moon.

He never hesitates. He isn't that type. He has no fear, no slightest doubt.

He is quiet, and he is somehow invisible, never seen by anyone, even in the clear light of an October morning.

Does he choose his victims? Or is each merely a target of opportunity, anyone outdoors and alone? People argue about this. Experts differ. The consensus is that he kills at random. There is nothing to connect the victims, not age, not race, not sex, not occupation, not looks, not anything.

He kills the living to make them dead. That seems to be the whole of it.

This one in the park, the woman with dark hair who jogs in a pocket park alongside the railroad tracks, spouting feathery plumes of breath—this could be one of his.

She runs with her head down, watching the blur of her shoes over the rutted earth. She sees nothing around her. She is unaware of being watched.

His victims are never alert. They are dropped from behind, no struggle, no drama, only the momentary violence of an unmuffled gunshot. The gun is small caliber, a .22. The report is not very loud.

The woman has a fine, trim body under her orange sweatsuit. She runs hard, almost sprinting, with a fierce, tigerish determination.

There is no sound but her breath and her footfalls and

the distant clatter of wheels on rails. A train, coming. Not close. Not yet.

The runner covers another few yards of brown grass. She reaches the narrow side street, empty of cars, and turns toward the railroad crossing. She is a few steps from it when bells chime and warning lights flash.

She hesitates, jogging in place. Will she risk going across, or will she wait?

Somewhere a bird sings, and the tune is taken up by the train whistle, blowing loud and long as the locomotive barrels ahead.

Behind her, death rises from the underbrush, death with a .22 handgun.

The gates begin to drop. She comes to a decision. Ducking her head, she steps boldly onto the tracks. No third rail to concern her; the railway is not electrified this far south.

The whistle rises in pitch and volume. Sunlight glints on the engine of the train just rounding a curve, and on the barrel of the gun as it comes up. Two scintillant flashes in perfect synchronization.

When the gun fires, there is no sound of a report, only the wail of the train whistle achieving its climax as the woman falls prone on the wooden ties, an entry wound stamped in the back of her head.

She was given no chance to scream, but the train screams for her, a wild lonely sound, as it thunders headlong down the track.

1

'Twas the night before Christmas, and within the estate
Were some mobsters who'd whack her if she showed up too late.

As poetry, it wasn't her best work. Still, it might possess the virtue of truth. She wasn't entirely sure they would take such extreme measures to punish her tardiness, but they might. Or—and this was what had her a bit more worried as she lit her eleventy-millionth cigarette of the evening—they might be planning to whack her for other reasons altogether.

The big house was a modernistic pile, unsymmetrical and unadorned, crouching dark and still behind a high steel fence. She steered the Jeep down a long gravel road flanked by snow-tufted pine trees under a horned moon. At the front gate she tapped her brakes, rolled down her window to let in the freezing air, and heard an intercom stutter to life.

"Identify." The male voice, low and growly, was edged with a Slavic accent.

She stuck her head out the window, giving the camera a good look at her blue eyes and blonde hair, and spoke around the cigarette.

"Bonnie Parker. Your boss is expecting me."

She said it lightly, trying to sound jaunty and nonchalant. If she had to enter the lions' den, she could at least fake out the lions by doing it with a certain panache.

The screen went dark, and the gate whirred open, gliding on an oiled track. Motion-activated spotlights snapped on as she proceeded down the driveway. Dark figures moved among the trees, watching her. Sentries.

Her purse rested on the passenger seat. She touched it to feel the reassuring shape of the Smith .38 inside.

It was a definite risk, coming here. But it would have been an even bigger risk not to come at all. There were some invitations you just didn't turn down.

She'd been driving away from her office in Brighton Cove, pretty badly shaken by events that had just transpired inside. When Sammy—that was her phone, a Samsung Galaxy, yeah, he had a name, deal with it—when Sammy started jangling, she'd answered without checking Caller ID. The man's voice was unfamiliar, quiet, unaccented, serious.

"You have heard of Mr. Armin Petrossian?" She had. "He requests your presence at his home. Tonight." Why? "He will tell you." It was Christmas Eve. What if she had other plans? "Break them."

He recited an address in Swan Neck, a tony town where old and new money nuzzled cozily against each other—the family fortunes of the horsey set, and the freshly minted riches of hedge-fund managers and arbitrageurs. "Be here in thirty minutes." And if she took longer? "Don't."

It was remarkable how motivational that last word had been. She'd made it to the gate in twenty-five minutes. She hadn't even needed Rudolph's red nose to guide her. Her phone had GPS.

She was pissed off, though. Petrossian really could have waited until tomorrow. Right now, she had other things to deal with, unfortunately not involving mistletoe and spiked eggnog.

As if to remind her, Sammy started singing "Jingle Bells" again. In an uncharacteristic moment of holiday cheer, she'd made it her ring tone for the season. "Jingle

Bells" had sounded three times in the last half hour. She was thoroughly sick of it, but at least she hadn't opted for "The Little Drummer Boy." By now she'd be ready to kill Sammy or possibly herself.

She hadn't taken the first two calls, and she didn't take this one. It had to be Brad, and she just didn't know what to tell him. It had all gone down too fast, and now everything was ruined for them both.

And on top of all that, it really was possible that Petrossian had invited her here to kill her. She couldn't rule it out. If the *Die Hard* movies had taught her anything, it was that nothing good ever happened on Christmas Eve.

The Jeep rolled to a stop across from a floodlit stairway climbing to a canopied porch. Two silhouetted figures stood post in the doorway, motionless as mannequins.

She shut off the motor, stubbed out the cigarette, and waited as the Jeep shuddered and hiccuped, releasing several blats of noxious black smoke from the tailpipe before falling silent. The vehicle was on its last legs. Lately it had been making an even greater variety of strange noises than usual, including one that was an exact match for that YouTube video of a farting hippo.

Her mechanic had told her frankly that there was little more that could be done. The Jeep was not long for this world. At the moment, the same might be true of her.

She zipped up her fur-collar coat. With her purse slung over her shoulder and a buckle trim fedora sitting smartly on her head, she climbed the stairs. The two mannequins resolved into pale, close-cropped guys in their early thirties, her age. Donner and Blitzen, she dubbed them. Even in the December cold they were too manly for outerwear. There were no obvious bulges under their suit jackets, which only meant their holsters were well concealed. She had zero doubt they were carrying. Anything else would have been a breach of professional standards.

"Miss Parker," the taller one—that would be Donner—said with a nod. His voice, as flat and generic as a TV newscaster's, was the one she'd heard on the phone.

"The one and only. Looks like I beat the deadline."

"Lucky for you." Funny. She didn't feel lucky. "Mr. Petrossian is waiting for you. This way."

Donner led her inside. She noticed he didn't offer to take her coat. She followed him down a long hallway, Blitzen taking up the rear. It was like a fun little parade, if you ignored the atmosphere of creeping menace.

Her boots, knee-high over rolled-up blue jeans, clacked on the bare floor. The jeans were soiled and slightly ripped, not as a fashion statement, but because pretty much all her clothes, except the hats, were shit.

Piano music played softly over an unseen speaker system. Canned music, she was pretty sure, though it was possible Petrossian shelled out for a live pianist just for atmosphere.

"Nice music," she said.

Donner nodded. "Vivaldi."

"You know classical music?"

"Not really. He only plays Vivaldi."

"Huh."

Conversational dead end. Her knowledge of classical music was limited to watching the first twenty minutes of *Amadeus*.

"You guys got any idea what this is all about?"

Donner shrugged without looking back. "Talk to him."

He said it the way someone else would tell her to talk to the hand, if anybody still said that.

The living room featured an artificial Christmas tree with stylized silver branches and an Art Deco angel at the top, but no packages underneath. Though lit with tasteful white bulbs, the tree was invisible from outside, thanks to a window treatment of steel shutters—light-tight, fireproof, bulletproof, and probably bombproof.

Other than the tree, the house was devoid of holiday decorations. Devoid of almost anything, really. Bare walls, steel tubing, glass sheets, stone floors. From outside, it looked like an untidy stack of boxes. From inside, it looked like a utility tunnel enlivened by an occasional geometrical mosaic or abstract art piece.

There were no photo portraits, no tchotchkes and knickknacks, no souvenirs of the family trip to Disney World. Her own place, one-half of a duplex a long mile from the beach, was a crap hole by comparison, but at least it felt like someplace a person might live.

"What's the deal with this mausoleum?" she asked Donner as he guided her around a corner under a bank of bare lightbulbs in an unfinished ceiling. "Still under construction or something?"

"It's the Bauhaus style," he answered.

"More like warehouse style."

"The architect is considered a genius."

"If he gets people to pay him for this shit, he must be."

Behind her, Blitzen stifled a snort of laughter.

A nice house, some people would have said. Expensive, for sure. A good candidate for the Swan Neck home and garden tour. Bonnie didn't like it, and not just because the creepy industrial-style architecture was not to her taste. She was morbidly aware that the house itself and everything in it had been bought with lives of teenaged addicts, women sold into prostitution, tourists set up for kidnap or blackmail schemes, vagrants shanghaied into labor camps in the Caucasus.

It was a house of death and pain, even with the Vivaldi.

She reviewed what she knew about Armin Petrossian. It wasn't much, because not much had been reported. Born in Armenia, Petrossian first made a name for himself as a professional wrestler known as the Fighting Rooster. Presumably the name lost something in translation. His time in the fight game brought him into contact with an Armenian mob boss, Sargis Avetisyan. He was said to have worked as a hitter and narcotics smuggler before taking a shortcut up the ladder by marrying Kira Avetisyan, the head man's daughter. After that expedient move, he was put in charge of an export business, an obvious front for trafficking in drugs, weapons, and human beings.

Fifteen years ago, Petrossian, then thirty-five, emigrated to the United States with his wife. In the US he started other business concerns and displayed commendable philanthropic impulses. His present net worth was estimated at north of fifty million dollars. He owned, at last count, fourteen cars, three of which were Lamborghinis and one of which was a Rolls-Royce.

Basically, he was a James Bond villain. And while he had never been arrested, because he was too wealthy and well connected for the authorities to touch, nobody doubted that he was dirty as hell.

There was one more thing she knew about him. His nickname nowadays was Warlord. Which was a hell of a lot scarier than the Fighting Rooster.

At the end of the second hallway, Donner tapped a button for an elevator. The house was only two stories high, but apparently the great Armin Petrossian couldn't be expected to walk up and down the stairs like a commoner.

The doors opened, and the three of them got in. The cage lifted.

"That is nice coat." Blitzen spoke for the first time, his words heavily accented.

"Thanks. It's imitation fur, in case you care."

"I do not."

"Didn't think you would."

"You were at a party?"

"More like a date."

"We make you leave early." He produced a grin of astonishing stupidity. "Boyfriend does not get lucky."

"Hey, there's a first time for everything."

A moment passed in puzzled silence. Then the guy laughed.

"You make joke," he said approvingly.

"Yeah, I'm a real cutup."

She thought this might not have been the best turn of phrase. Note to self: when in the company of violent men, avoid words that suggest cutting things up.

The doors opened on an upper-story hallway, where another one of Santa's elves stood waiting. This one didn't trouble to conceal his weapon, a pistol-grip shotgun with a cut-down barrel. The kind of gun that could do some serious damage at close range.

He looked her over. Donner spoke a few words in what had to be Armenian. The man with the shotgun stepped back to let them pass.

Near him, a monitor was built into the wall, the large screen crowded with an ever-changing mosaic. Each tile displayed a camera angle on a different part of the house and its environs. Bright colors for the interiors, the monochrome of infrared for outdoors. Total coverage of the property, every approach and access point under surveillance at all times.

Donner led her down another hall. This one was carpeted, probably to conceal pressure-sensitive mats linked to an alarm system. Sprinkler nozzles were embedded in the ceiling, along with other doodads she recognized as gas dispensers. Yes, in the event of an intrusion, it was possible to release toxic gas into the corridor. The latest thing in home security for the super rich.

Halfway down the hall, she passed a hinged metal contraption hiding in a recess of the wall. It appeared to be a gate that could be manually pulled across the hallway and locked in place. Beyond it, plaster pilasters started appearing every six feet. She didn't think they were decorative. Most likely they contained caches of weapons that could be broken out in an emergency—small arms, shotguns like the one she'd seen, machine guns. Hell, maybe rocket launchers.

The house was a fortress. Multiple layers of security, growing ever tighter as you penetrated farther inside, and at the center, like the inmost figure in a nest of Russian dolls, was Armin Petrossian himself.

The last door in the hallway approached. It had no keyhole, only a biometric reader, no doubt keyed to Petrossian's fingerprint.

At the door, Donner turned to her. "You're carrying?"

Honesty was not always her policy, but it seemed prudent in this case. "Yeah."

"In your purse?"

"That's right."

"You'll have to surrender your weapon."

She stiffened. "Why's that?"

"Policy."

"Your employer called this meeting. I didn't ask to be here."

"So?"

She took a step back, including both her new friends in her field of vision. "I'm holding on to the gun."

The two men tensed. They were big guys, solidly built. She knew they'd made their bones by killing people. But she still wasn't giving up the .38.

Her best shot would be to strike first. Kick a field goal straight into Donner's beanbag and hope it put him out of action for a second or two, long enough to crack Blitzen's kneecap with another kick. Then put them both down for the count with blows to the head—and run like hell.

Might not work. Some people had a surprisingly high pain threshold. And she'd still have to deal with the guy at the end of the hall, the one with the sawed-off shotgun. Not to mention the difficulty of driving off the property before the rest of the security team converged on her. Even that Israeli chick who played Wonder Woman couldn't beat those odds.

Still, it was probably her only play, and she was thinking about trying it when the door clicked open, swinging inward in response to a remote command. A man's voice wafted through the gap.

"It's all right. Let her come."

A cultured voice, only lightly accented. Not a voice Bonnie would have associated with the Fighting Rooster, much less Warlord.

But it could hardly be anyone else.

2

SLOWLY THE TWO men stepped aside. They appeared a trifle downcast, as if they'd been looking forward to kicking some American ass.

"Go," Donner said.

Bonnie brushed past them, making a show of clutching her purse to underline the fact that they hadn't taken it from her. Behind her, the door eased shut, moving ponderously, a heavy slab—steel core, probably. More protection against bullets and fire and bombs.

The room was a home office, as starkly utilitarian as the rest of the house. An unshaded ceiling light cast a fluorescent glow over concrete walls, tubular armchairs resembling expensive patio furniture, and a massive glass-and-steel desk. There were no windows. She knew why. The impenetrable door with its biometric lock had already told her. This was Petrossian's panic room, his final retreat in an emergency.

She wondered where the weapons were hidden. There would be a gun in Petrossian's desk, obviously. Heavier firepower was probably concealed in secret wall compartments, or inside the large bar with its rows of liquor bottles on glass shelves. Gas masks, too, to navigate the rest of the house after the gas dispersion system had been activated. Night-vision goggles in case the lights went out—although there would be one or more backup generators, of course.

The only thing the room would lack was a security camera. The man in charge wouldn't want anyone spying on his inner sanctum.

She crossed the uncarpeted floor, approaching the desk. Behind it, in a straight-backed chair as tall as a throne, Armin Petrossian sat watching her.

He wasn't holding a gun on her, which she took as a good sign. That was the first thing she noticed about him. The second thing was that he was wearing a robe, plush and loose-fitting. It looked like cashmere. In his hand was a glass of cut crystal holding amber liquid and half-melted ice. He smiled, a genial host.

"Bonnie Parker," he said with a shade too much satisfaction. "I'm Armin Petrossian."

"Hey."

She refused to sound either friendly or impressed. She wasn't one of those idiots who idolized drug kingpins and white slavers. She'd done some bad stuff in her life, but nothing that could touch this bastard's résumé.

"Take off your coat." He gestured to a steel chair facing the desk. "Sit."

She tossed the coat on a glass coffee table and took her seat, holding the purse in her lap, the Smith readily accessible. She kept her hat on, partly to be rude, and partly because, well, she just liked wearing hats.

"Hope I didn't get you out of bed," she said.

He glanced down at the robe. "This? It's a dressing gown. Lora Piana. Do you know them? I like to relax in the evenings."

"Yeah, I get that. Sometimes I hang out in my underwear. Hanes. You know 'em?"

Petrossian's smile remained fixed on his face. A hard, cunning face, a face like a set of knives. "You're saucy, eh?"

"That's one word for it.

"What's another word?"

"*Bitch* would pretty much cover it. Why aren't you hanging out with your family on Christmas Eve?"

"My wife and young son are spending the holiday

with her parents in Armenia."

"Without you?"

"I have a very full schedule. I find it difficult to get away."

"All work and no play makes Jack a dull boy."

"I'm not dull."

Bonnie could believe that. "Okay. That explains your situation. Now what the hell am I doing here on Christmas Eve?"

"Is there somewhere else you'd prefer to be?"

"Pretty much anywhere."

"Can't you guess why you're here?"

"Possibilities have occurred to me. But I need more to go on."

"Perhaps I just want to do some business."

"My office hours are nine to five." She considered it. "Ten to four." She considered further. "Sometimes I don't open before noon."

"This is a matter of some urgency. And also some discretion. It was not advisable for me to visit you at your office."

His answer reassured her a little. It sounded like he wanted to hire her, which wasn't the worst scenario she'd envisioned. "What's wrong with my office?"

"The police are watching it."

"How'd you know about that?"

"I make it a policy to find out such things. May I interest you in a brandy?"

He could have interested her in several brandies, or better yet, several slugs of Jack Daniel's, but it seemed wiser to keep a clear head. "Thanks, no."

"Cigar?" He flipped open an ornate little box.

"What makes you think I smoke cigars?"

"Your namesake did."

This surprised her. "She posed with a cigar for the camera," Bonnie said. "Not sure she actually sucked it down."

That photo had hung on the wall of her office until some bad guys shot the place up. It was a reproduction of the most famous portrait of the original Bonnie Parker, Clyde Barrow's girl, of Bonnie and Clyde fame. People were always surprised by that photo, because the girl in it looked nothing like Faye Dunaway. She was small and bony and tough, with the wiry spareness of a chicken wing.

"You truly were named after her, then?" Petrossian leaned forward, flattering her with his full attention. "It's not a coincidence?"

"My father had a strange sense of humor."

"He liked outlaws?"

"He was one," she said curtly.

Petrossian nodded. "And so are you."

"It's not how I planned it. But I guess that's how it's worked out."

He sipped his drink, which was looking awfully good to her. "How *had* you planned it?"

That was an unusually astute question. She didn't know anyone in her personal life who would have asked it. Certainly not Brad.

"I'd intended to stay on the straight and narrow, be a regular private eye. All legal and by the book. You know, like *Mannix*."

"You're too young to remember *Mannix*."

"So are you." She knew he was about fifty.

"In Armenia they run all the old American shows. I'm more partial to *MacGyver* myself."

"Yeah, *MacGyver* was cool." In any version of this meeting she'd rehearsed, a discussion of classic TV had not come up.

"What made you deviate from the straight and narrow, as you call it?" Petrossian asked.

"Expedience. Some situations can't be handled any other way." She shrugged. "You know what they say. Necessity is a mother."

He laughed. "That's good. I'll remember it. What became of the father who named you after a criminal?"

"He got killed by some associates of his."

"It's so important to keep the right company. You've been through a lot for one still so young."

"Well, I never made it big on the wrestling circuit."

"Ah, you've read my bio. Those stories are exaggerated. I wasn't so big."

"Why'd they call you the Fighting Rooster?"

"From the way I would strut around the ring. It was my signature. Part of my brand, you might say."

"Gotta tell you, you don't come across like a pro wrestler."

"Perhaps the years have smoothed off my rough edges."

Or maybe, she thought, things weren't always what they appeared.

She had to remind herself that the man facing her was a monster. A very civilized monster, a monster who undoubtedly knew the correct wine to go with any meal and the correct words for any occasion, but a monster all the same. That cashmere robe–how many kids had gotten hooked on heroin to pay for it?

"I've heard a great deal about you, Bonnie," he said in the tone of a man getting down to business. "May I call you Bonnie?"

"Sure. Can I call you Armin?"

His lips pursed momentarily, a man stung by a small pesky insect. Then the smile returned, as perfect as if it had been painted on. "Of course."

"Great. Now we're besties. Before you know it, we'll be hanging out at the mall."

He took another tug at his glass, but the level of liquid didn't seem to change. She wondered if he was actually drinking, or if the cocktail was only a prop.

The whole scene had the quality of a performance. The office that was actually a stronghold, the house that was a fortress, the polite host who trafficked in heroin and death. Nothing about it was as it seemed.

"You've made quite a name for yourself in your sideline," he said.

"Nice to know people are talking. It's not like I can advertise."

"How many, shall we say, special jobs have you done?"

"By special jobs, I take it you mean hits."

"Yes. It's best to eschew euphemisms, isn't it?"

"That's what I always say. As for numbers, that's the kind of detail I prefer to keep to myself."

"Forgive me for prying. It's only natural curiosity. You haven't been very active lately."

This was largely true. She'd kept her head down for the last few months, ever since a particularly hectic weekend involving Arian Dragusha, a container ship, and her old friends Ed and Edna Goodman. There'd been just one special job, as Petrossian put it, in all that time.

"Maybe no one needs anybody put out of the way right now," she said casually. "Maybe there's been a general outbreak of fellowship and good cheer."

Petrossian nodded. "We would like to think so. And yet there are always enemies, aren't there? Lurking just outside the glow of the fire, like jackals in the night."

She decided she was tired of chitchat. There were several ways this meeting could go, and none of them turned out well. It was time to find out which unhappy ending she was headed for.

"Look, Armin, I don't know what you think you know about me. But you probably don't know the most important thing."

"Which is?"

"I'm not your standard gun for hire. Yeah, I moonlight as a shooter. But anybody I take on as a client has a legitimate problem the law just isn't equipped to deal with."

"What sort of problem?"

She used her standard example. "Say there's a woman whose ex-boyfriend has gone all stalkerish and is getting ready to pop. Nothing the police can do until it's too late. What are her options? She can run. She can arm herself. Or ..."

She let the implications fill the silence. A dead stalker was pretty much a nonissue.

"Are all your special cases so clear-cut?" he asked.

"I'm not sure any of them are clear-cut. There's always a gray area. I have to use my own judgment."

"You're judge, jury, and executioner."

"That's me. Triple threat. But always on my terms. And my terms"—she took a breath—"don't include working for someone like you."

His eyes slid half closed, the dark pupils nearly eclipsed by the heavy lids. It gave him a peculiar look, both bored and hungry. "Is that so?"

This was the dangerous part, what she liked to think of as asshole-puckering time. It was possible things were about to get real ugly real fast.

"I'm afraid it is," she said. "So it looks like we're wasting time here. I'm sure Santa's elves can show me the way out of your toyshop."

She started to rise, never taking her eyes off him. If she could make it out of the room, she might be okay. She reached for her coat ...

"How do you feel about serial killers, Bonnie?"

Petrossian's question stopped her.

"I'm against them," she said. "Why?"

"Because that's who I've targeted for a hit."

3

BONNIE SAT DOWN slowly. "A serial killer?"

She had to admit, the son of a bitch had gotten her attention.

Petrossian put aside his drink. "You've heard of the Man in the Moon?"

"Sure. He's done, what, five by now?"

"Six." His fingers drummed the desk, a soft, thoughtful patter. Long fingers with manicured nails and small black curls of hair on the knuckles. Fingers both elegant and bestial. "What do you think of his technique?"

"Simple but effective." She rummaged in her purse for her cigarettes. Lighting up might be a mistake; it would indicate she was planning to stay a while. But she couldn't help it. She liked to smoke when she was on edge. Also when she was relaxed. Basically, she just liked to smoke.

She ignited a Parliament White and sucked it down.

Petrossian was watching her. "And the man himself?"

"He's scum."

"I'm interested in a more technical evaluation."

"The experts say he must be a pro because he gets so close. One shot, back of the head, point-blank range. An amateur would lose his nerve, they say."

"Is that what you think?"

She shook her head. "I think he probably *is* an amateur. He takes the shots up close because he can't trust his aim. He risks getting spatter all over him, which a pro wouldn't ordinarily want to do."

"You don't agree that a nonprofessional would suffer a failure of nerve?"

"A normal person would. But a normal person doesn't go around offing random civilians. We're talking a straight-up psycho here. Or else ..."

"Yes?"

"Maybe not a psycho, exactly. Maybe just some regular Joe who's at the end of his string. A guy with nothing left to lose."

"That's very perceptive."

She inhaled an unhealthy amount of smoke before answering. "I could be wrong."

"You aren't."

"The way you say that, I gotta figure you know who he is."

"I do."

"Even though the cops and the feds are still looking?"

"I have connections in many places. I've made certain inquiries, with the inducement of a reward in exchange for information."

"Law enforcement is offering a reward, too."

"The people I contacted weren't the type to go to the police."

"One of his friends gave him up?"

"I'm not certain he has friends."

"Then who's your informant?"

"That's not something you need to know."

"How much was the reward?"

"Ten thousand dollars."

"Very public-spirited on your part. I wouldn't have pegged you as a do-gooder."

"I most assuredly am not. I believe I fit the popular conception of a sociopath. I'm indifferent to human life, as a rule. But there are exceptions."

"Yeah? Just what did the Man in the Moon do to get your blood up?"

"Do you remember the third victim? Her name was Rosa Martinez."

She remembered. She took another long pull on the cigarette. "From Algonquin, right? Ran a restaurant or something?"

He waved a hand over his desk. On the far wall, a giant flat-screen TV which had been displaying a map of the tri-state area shifted to a new image. A photo of Rosa Martinez. Mid-thirties, dark hair, big smile. Pretty.

"It was a catering company," he said. "I hired her for an event. We became friendly."

"How friendly?" Bonnie asked.

He studied her, his eyes unblinking. "We were having an affair. It had gone on for some time. Kira—my wife—didn't know. It would have ended eventually. I hadn't expected it to terminate so soon."

"You don't sound too broken up about it."

"I'm not the sort of person who gets broken up. Are you?"

"Not really."

"Have you ever lost anyone?"

"Sure."

"Did you cry about it?"

"No."

"Even as a child?"

She flashed on a memory of her parents, murdered in a motel room in Pennsylvania. Her fourteen-year-old self looking at the bodies. She saw herself as if from an observer's perspective. Her pale face tightly drawn in fury and grief. Her eyes wide, but not wet.

"Even then," she said.

"You're much like me. I also have never cried. I didn't cry for Rosa. I simply decided to avenge her death."

"Okay," she said, hoping she wasn't committing herself to anything. "So who the hell is the Man in the Moon?"

"This man."

Another wave of his hand, and the TV display changed again, becoming a wall-size blowup of a New Jersey driver's license. Staring into the camera was a weedy-looking guy, not young, with thin shoulders and a balding egg-shaped head. The name on the license was Henry Louis Phipps, and his address was 626 Lake Avenue, Brighton Cove.

"He lives in your town," Petrossian said. "You don't happen to know him?"

"I don't know too many of the locals. More to the point, they don't want to know me."

"You've acquired something of a reputation, I understand."

"I'm a friggin' pariah. How'd you get hold of his driver's license?"

"In this state, everything is for sale."

"Fair enough. What's the story on this guy?"

"He's nobody. You were right about him. Henry Phipps is not a professional, he's quite insane, and he does indeed have nothing left to lose."

"He got a record?"

"Not at all. He lived an entirely uneventful life—until recently."

"And all of a sudden he just snaps?" She checked the date of birth on the DL. "He's, what, fifty-eight?"

"Strange, isn't it? He lives alone, no wife, no children. He has no job, limited income, few if any friends. To all appearances he's an utterly harmless individual, as nondescript as a million other faceless men. And yet, rather late in life, he becomes a killer."

"Why?"

"Does it matter?"

"I guess not. You don't ask the snake for his life story. You just whack him."

"Aptly put. You'll take the job, then?"

She spent some time nursing the cigarette. "You sure you've got the goods on this guy? I mean, he doesn't exactly fit the profile."

"My informant had no doubts."

"In my experience, snitches can't always be trusted."

"He wouldn't lie to me. I made certain he was fully apprised of the consequences."

"Maybe he was willing to risk it. He might've really needed the cash."

"No one needs money that badly."

She wasn't totally convinced, but she let it go for now. "This is probably a stupid question, but why not go to the police?"

"No." The word was a sharp rap. "There's no death penalty in this state. If Phipps is arrested, he'll live out his life."

"In a cell."

"Perhaps he would be happy in a cell. A man can adjust to any conditions. Or perhaps he would be miserable most of the time. But one day something happens, something good. He eats a nice sandwich, maybe." His tone became less cultured, his accent more pronounced. "He has a beautiful dream. He sees the open sky. He jerks himself off—I do not know. But for some little time he is happy. For that time, life is good. I do not want his life to be good. I do not want him to be happy. Not even for a minute. I want him dead."

His face had gone pale. He sat very still, composing himself.

"Then have your people do it," Bonnie said. "You have plenty of guys in-house who can handle the job. I mean literally in-house. Like Frick and Frack outside the door."

"It must be you."

"Look, I appreciate the business and all ..."

"I'm not doing you any favors, Bonnie."

"Then what's the deal?"

"The deal is that my people know nothing of this. My connection with Rosa Martinez is unknown to my associates. I wish it to remain so."

"Why?"

"Perhaps I value my privacy."

"Try again."

She saw him breathe in and out, slowly. She was getting on his nerves. Not surprising. She had a way of pissing people off.

"You know something of my background," he said. "Perhaps you know that I obtained my present position through the good graces of my father-in-law. He remains the chief of our entire global operation. He's intensely protective of his daughter—my wife."

"You can't let anyone know you were diddling Rosa, or the alpha dog will start to growl."

Petrossian grimaced. "He'll do more than growl."

"By this point you could be strong enough to take him on. You know, if push comes to shove."

"Possibly. But I don't wish for push to come to shove. I met with my informant personally, and alone. I've kept my people out of it altogether."

"What makes you think you can trust me? Suppose I decide to squeal to the big man."

"There's nothing in it for you except the additional risk of attracting unwanted attention. One of my associates, on the other hand, could see a path to promotion within the organization. Even a chance to take my job, if I were to be—shall we say—deposed."

"Okay. I get it. Of course, you could take out Phipps yourself."

"I'm not a killer."

"You sure about that?"

"I've given certain orders, but—"

"You keep your hands clean."

"As clean as they can be, in a dirty business."

"You know, I wasn't bluffing when I said I wouldn't work for a narco guy."

"And yet you're still here."

"Yeah. Well, it's one thing for me to take out some other drug lord and help you consolidate your territory. Taking out the Man in the Moon ..."

"Rather a different story, isn't it?"

"I can't say I have any moral objections. Let's put it that way."

She wondered what Frank would say. Frank Kershaw, who'd taken her in off the street and raised her as a teenager. She thought she knew. More than once he'd warned her about the lines.

Kiddo, he would say, *there are lines you can cross and lines you can't. The first kind, you can cross back over. The second kind, there's no coming back.*

Working for a man like Petrossian meant crossing a line, for sure. The question was, could she come back?

Under other circumstances, she wouldn't have hesitated about taking out a serial killer. She'd already finished off two of them, and she hadn't lost a wink of sleep over it. She had no faith in law enforcement, no interest in due process. She was, as Petrossian said, judge, jury, and executioner.

Did it matter if she took the assignment from him, as long as it was a righteous hit? Maybe it did. Maybe forging any kind of alliance with Petrossian was a mistake. Once he had his hooks in her, he might never let go.

But this was her chance to put the Man in the Moon out of action. A psycho who shot little old ladies and people out walking their dogs and inebriated old farts whose worst crime was peeing in public. If she didn't do it, and he claimed another kill, the guilt would be on her.

And she had to admit that Petrossian was right about a prison sentence. Life in a cell was too good for Henry Phipps, assuming he really was the Man in the Moon. Any life at all was more than he deserved.

"All right," she said softly, realizing she'd persuaded herself. "I'll take care of it."

She stood up, and this time she did retrieve her coat.

"There's still the matter of your fee," Petrossian said.

"Forget it." Holding the cigarette between her lips, she shrugged on the coat. "I'm doing this one gratis."

"That's hardly necessary."

"No offense, but yeah, it is. I don't take money from drug dealers, no matter how high up the chain they are."

"My payment could never be traced to any illegal activity."

"I'm sure it's been thoroughly laundered. That's not what I'm worried about. It's profiting off some kid in the morgue."

"You put people in the morgue, and profit."

"Those people deserve it."

"Some might argue that a teenager who abuses his body with chemicals purchased on the street deserves what he gets. He's failed the test of natural selection."

"Kids have a right to be stupid. You don't have a right to make them dead."

"You have a finely balanced sense of propriety."

"Yeah. And it works out in your favor, 'cause I won't cost you a dime."

Petrossian nodded, accepting this. "How soon will you get to it?"

"Tonight, if I can. The longer I wait, the more chance he'll do somebody else. His timetable's been speeding up."

"True. Perhaps he's grown more confident."

"Or more crazy."

"I sometimes think there's a fine line between self-confidence and madness."

"Yeah. I walk that line every day. Nice meeting you, Armin."

"And you, Bonnie," he said.

With a parting wave, he unsealed the bombproof door.

4

HENRY PHIPPS SAT on the edge of his bed, a gun in his hand.

He longed to put it to his temple and pull the trigger. It would be so easy. His great escape. His victory. He had given others this gift. Why not himself? Had he not done enough?

But no. He hadn't. His work was incomplete. He had, as yet, acquired only two followers, of doubtful value. His testimony was only partly written. There was time left in his sentence. Additional days, weeks, even months to serve in the prison of this universe, before his glorious jailbreak, his final freedom.

Reluctantly he put the gun aside, storing it in the nightstand drawer, on top of the mapbook he used to plan his ambushes. The sites where he'd taken lives had been marked with sticky red flags. The most recent flag had been added just two days ago.

Not very long. But already he felt the itch, the need to do it again, soon. Tonight, even.

A killing on Christmas Eve. The idea intrigued him. But he was tired, and the night was cold. Tomorrow, though—Christmas Day. Even better.

Maybe he would do two. He'd never done more than one at a time. The prospect of a double sacrifice stirred something in him. Something like hunger, like lust.

But not like that, because his was a holy calling, a mission of universal redemption, with nothing corrupt or vicious in it.

Yawning, he slipped off his clothes and pulled on long pajamas, baggy around the waist—he'd lost a good deal of weight in the last few months—and a terry cloth robe. He padded around his little house in slippers and socks, turning off lights and checking to see that every door was locked. Before retiring, he checked the local news online. He found one story on the Man in the Moon that he hadn't seen before. It was merely a recapitulation of other articles, with no fresh information. He printed it out anyway, adding it to his collection, which had grown quite large, taking up most of the bottom drawer of the file cabinet in his study. A drawer that was always locked.

The collection was not a matter of vanity. He thought of it as an archive. Someone needed to keep a complete record of these early days. He had embarked on a momentous crusade, the true history of which had yet to be written. When it was, these preliminary chronicles would help keep the details straight.

The details, but not the meaning. This was known, at present, only to himself and those two others. But there would be more.

Lazarus was already in Henry's bed. The dog had taken to sleeping with him after Katie died. At first Henry had been grateful for the company. Now he found old Lazarus a somewhat disagreeable bedroom companion—the dog had a tendency to drool and break wind, and his breath stank of unmentionable things—but the habit had become impossible to break. Really he should have put Lazarus down by now. It would be a kindness, as all killings were. And the dog was old, half blind, entirely deaf.

Yet something stopped him. He found this strange. A weakness on his part, a touch of hypocrisy perhaps. But not doubt. Never doubt.

Though he lay down, Henry did not try to sleep right away. It was his custom to read in bed. For the past five months he had been reading the Bible. This was not a matter of religious devotion. It was more in the nature of a military campaigner's due diligence: Know thy enemy.

Tonight he opened the careworn volume to the Book of Job. When read critically, Job was a horror story. The creator of the universe allied himself with the prince of evil to torment and destroy an innocent man. Taken at face value, it made no sense. But if the reader understood that God and Satan were one and the same, all became clear.

Henry's favorite part of the book was the advice given by Job's wife, whose recommendation was to "curse God and die." This was a sound policy, expressive of deep wisdom, and Henry only wished Job had been sensible enough to follow it. His sufferings—and the story—would have been shorter.

The explosive clatter of a train along the tracks by his house diverted him from his reading. He did not need to check the nightstand clock to know the time. That particular train pulled into the Brighton Cove station at 11:13 every night.

Setting aside the Bible, he turned off the bedside lamp and lay in darkness, Lazarus huffing and wheezing on the pillow they shared. He thought about what he'd read. About Job himself, Job the man. Henry could relate to him. He, too, was Job. So were other human beings, all of them.

They didn't know it, though. Until this year, neither had he.

His life had taken such a drastic turn, one he never could have anticipated. Henry Louis Phipps, a multiple murderer.

Most serial killers, as he understood the matter, had been prone to violence from an early age. As children, they set fires and hurt animals. As young adults, they were in chronic trouble with school authorities and the law. They practiced voyeurism, stalking, burglary. When they graduated to homicide, it was merely the last step in a natural progression.

None of this held true for him. He had always been a gentle sort, mild-mannered. The kind of fellow who would hand out candy on Halloween while wearing a funny costume and whistling "The Monster Mash." No one would have pegged him as dangerous.

Over the past year, all that had changed. Losing his job was the beginning. Or maybe the beginning had come earlier, when Katie died, leaving him a widower, childless, lonely in the dusty house he never remembered to clean. But he didn't think so. Losing Katie had been hard, but he'd had the routine of his work to see him through. Dull work, balancing columns of figures, confirming and reconfirming the results—but it kept him occupied. Each day was another checkmark on a mental calendar, another twenty-four hours accounted for and done.

Then abruptly he was unemployed. Without a job, there was nothing to do all day. He made desultory efforts at finding other work, but no one was hiring, or at least no one was hiring him. He found himself reading the news. He had never paid much attention to current events. Now, having nothing else to occupy his mind, he studied the newspaper and certain Internet sites for hours every day.

The news demoralized him. It seemed everything that was happening was bad. He had never realized just how bad the world was, and how many bad people there were in it, and just how terrible life could be. Wars and crimes and natural disasters, famines and plagues and toxic foods, ugliness and hatefulness and spitting malice wherever one looked ...

The planet, the universe itself, seemed to have some fundamental design flaw. Nothing was as it should be. The wrong people always won, the right people were forever getting screwed. Stupidity was rampant.

Corruption was rewarded. Civilization was a tissue-thin veneer over savagery. Everything was shit.

He realized he had been feeling this way for years. He had not been entirely aware of it. In times past, snippets of thought had come to him: Nothing works. People are rotten. Why bother? It's a lost cause.

Many such thoughts, but they had never added up to anything. They were scattered puzzle pieces, Scrabble tiles unconnected into words. They had come and gone and come again, leaving him uneasy, frustrated, angry, but directionless. And now they would not leave him alone.

At times he thought he must be having a somewhat delayed midlife crisis, or perhaps he was going insane. But he didn't really believe it. To him, it was clear enough that the world itself was in crisis. It was the world that was insane. Just watch the news.

On a summer morning five months ago, shortly after his fifty-eighth birthday, he woke at dawn and had an epiphany. It was unexpected, as he supposed epiphanies always were. No signs had forecast the event. No earthquake or falling star announced it. He simply opened his eyes in the young daylight and lay in bed without moving. He lay there a long time. He watched the dust motes glitter above his head, twirling like dancers. He was tired. Not sleepy, but worn out, ground down, and feeling it right down to the bone. He had lived nearly six decades on this earth, and he did not know what it had been for. It felt pointless. It felt like nothing but pain.

The dance of dust continued. So much dust. Katie must have made herself crazy dusting this house, and he had never known. Now she was dead, and the dust remained. Had her efforts mattered? Had she herself mattered? Did anyone matter in the end?

It was a fever dream, this life. A madhouse of slaughter and stupidity, a cosmic accident—no, not an accident. It could not be. Something so vast and laden with malice, so complex, with so many subtly interlocking parts, could not be purely random. It had to be intentional. A plan. A deliberate and unfathomably cruel design.

He sat up slowly, the dust motes forgotten. He saw beyond them, saw deep into the essence of things. He saw things he felt sure no person had seen before.

The world had been made to hurt. Deliberately, with premeditation. Life, every life, was a parade of pains, each separate and distinct, like individual notes of music blending in the symphony of suffering that defined existence. Even transient joys and momentary respites were part of the design, a trick played on the naïve, persuading them to lift their hopes—a cup of water offered to a thirsty man, to be dashed from his mouth after the first sip.

And the master of this lunatic asylum, the god who ran the show, could be only a lunatic himself.

Light bloomed in him, a strange red-orange light that was not daylight, a surreal glow that suffused the room around him.

He *saw*.

The deity they worshiped, the omnipotent and omnipresent One whose praises they chanted in houses of worship, was a fake, a fraud, a sick joke played on mankind. God, *their* god, was a sadist, a cosmic psychopath, casting dice for human lives, chortling at human pain. A god who'd made the universe as a torture chamber and peopled it with an endless supply of victims. Be fruitful and multiply. More bodies to be stretched on the rack.

That great and shining light was all around him and within him. He had risen from his bed. *He had risen*. He saw the leering face of that monstrous god. It was the face of any small boy who incinerated ants with a magnifying glass. The face of every bully and degenerate and despot. He spat at that face, at that false god, deceiver and dungeon master, the immortal enemy of mankind.

There was a way to cheat the imposter god of his fun. The charade could not go on if there were no players. A torture chamber without prisoners was only an empty room. The way to stop the game was not to play. Not to let anyone play. With no more puppets, what would become of the puppet master?

He understood all of it then, the great secret, the problem and its solution. And it was so simple. To end suffering, it was necessary only to end life. Kill everything that lived, and there could be no more pain, ever.

He stood at the window, face to face with the rising sun, its light combining with his own greater radiance, his body aglow, his very flesh a flame of fire, his whole being transfigured in his glory.

From that day forward, he had been as one changed. He had a mission. He understood, with infinite compassion, that his fellow creatures lacked his insight. They clung to life because they knew no better. He must teach them. He must lead the way. He must show them that death was not to be feared but joyfully embraced, because death alone offered an escape from this living hell, victory over the tyrant that had crowned itself their god.

He must expunge humanity, one life at a time.

The scope of his work was necessarily limited. He knew that. He wasn't some crazy person. He couldn't actually kill *everybody*. But he could make a start, and before his departure, he could testify to his truth and share it with the world.

Others would carry on the work. What he began, his successors would finish. The truth, once known, could never be suppressed. The end must come, even if it took a thousand years.

He began to make plans.

In his garage he found the shoebox where he'd stored an old .22 revolver, left to him by his father. It was a Colt Frontier Scout, single-action, with a walnut grip and a blued steel barrel four and a half inches long. Henry hadn't used this gun or any other in decades; but shooting, it seemed, was like riding a bicycle: you never forgot how.

He expected the first murder to be hard. From books he'd read—murder mysteries, that sort of thing—he knew that the novice killer could lose his nerve, could falter at the last moment, and even after the deed was done, could panic or swoon. Nothing like that happened. The books had lied. Killing was not traumatic, and afterward there was no remorse. Carrying out the first execution disturbed him not in the least. He did it, and he looked upon what he had done, and he was well pleased.

His first sacrificial offering was a woman pedaling a bicycle through Gathers Park in Miramar. It was early morning. No one was around. She was not a young woman—close to his age—possibly attractive under her big floppy hat. He sat on a bench with the gun in his lap, covered by a newspaper, and as she pedaled past, he stood and lifted the gun and shot her once, at close range, in the back of the head. The bike canted, and the bloodied hat flew off, and she fell over on her side and lay there like a pile of old laundry. The spent shell case remained in the revolver's cylinder, and the bullet, as best he could tell, remained in her skull.

The shot had been loud enough to make his ears ring, but he was otherwise unfazed. He went up to her, impressed by the steadiness of his legs and the integrity of his digestion, and inspected the body, never touching it. He saw a flicker in her face, a last troubled flurry of thought, and then only the slack stillness of death. It was different from sleep, somehow. Not just because the eyes were open. He had seen people sleep with their eyes open; his college roommate had done that. This was not the same. There was no person there. That was the thing. No person at all.

He spent a few minutes looking down at the splash of blood in her hair, and at the spoiled hat and the slowly spinning tires of the bicycle, which squeaked as they turned and very gradually came to rest. Anyone could have come along and seen him. If they had, he would have shot them, too.

Do you see? he asked the trickster god. I saved her from you. I set her free. Others will be emancipated in their turn. And someday there will be none left. No toys for you. Playtime's over.

"Playtime's over," Henry Phipps murmured, smiling now, his head on the pillow, eyelids fluttering as he drifted into dreams.

5

BONNIE GOT HOME at eleven o'clock, parking on the street outside her duplex rather than in the garage. She wouldn't be staying long. She just had to pick up a hit kit.

At this time of year, the duplex on Windlass Court was a study in contrast. Her side was dark and unadorned. The side belonging to her neighbor, Mrs. Gloria Biggs, was a twinkling riot of holiday festiveness. Mrs. Biggs really got into Christmas. In years past she had graciously tacked up a few decorations on Bonnie's side of the building, just to spread the wealth around, but ever since Bonnie's unit had been shot up by overzealous gunmen, Mrs. Biggs had been less than friendly. In fact, she persisted in trying to unload her half of the building, though as yet she'd found no takers. Potential buyers were apparently turned off by the prospect of living next door to a known bullet magnet. That was the trouble with people in this town—no sense of adventure.

She tapped in the six-digit security code on her alarm system's keypad, let herself in, and went directly to her bedroom, where she unscrewed the vent cover over an air duct behind the bed. Hidden in the duct was a sack of goodies. The sack itself was perhaps similar to the one Santa was carrying over his shoulder as he snaked down chimneys tonight, but unless Santa had joined the NRA, he wasn't carrying goodies like these.

She opened the bag and dumped its contents on the floor, a spill of handguns, silencers, magazines—"clips," to the uninitiated—and assorted other weaponry. She wasn't looking for anything fancy, just your basic disposable small-caliber pistol accessorized with the right ammo and sound suppressor.

Before handling any of the items, she slipped on a pair of gloves from her purse. She'd loaded the mags while wearing gloves also, so there would be no fingerprints on the shell casings. All the firearms had been obtained illegally, of course. Given New Jersey's draconian gun laws, her stash was enough to put her away for life. She wasn't entirely satisfied with the hiding place she'd come up with—any halfway competent crime scene investigator would check the ductwork—but so far she hadn't had any better ideas.

The pistol she chose was a Glock 9mm subcompact. It was a ghost gun—untraceable, because it had never carried a serial number. Officially it didn't exist. Ghost guns were made piecemeal; part of the weapon was factory-manufactured, but the pieces needed to make it a working firearm were added later, shaped with power tools or created on a 3D printer. She'd purchased this one from her usual supplier, a lady named Mama Blessing who lived in subsidized housing in Maritime, paid no income taxes, and had a higher net worth than God.

The Glock had a threaded barrel that would accommodate a suppressor—a silencer, in the vernacular. The popular term was misleading. You couldn't really silence a gunshot. The whisper-quiet pistols of Hollywood bad guys were a total fiction. A suppressor dampened a gun's report and might spare you the need for ear protection, but that was as far as it went.

She left the suppressor unattached for now; screwed onto the barrel, it would make the Glock more difficult to conceal in her purse. Plenty of time to secure it after she gained access to Phipps's home.

Henry Phipps. Eyes shut, she visualized his photo.

Like anybody else, Bonnie had built up a mental picture of the Man in the Moon. He would be a man, because almost all serial killers were male; Caucasian, because most serial killers were white, and because a white guy would be less likely to draw attention in the locales where this guy worked. In his thirties, she'd guessed, because most of these psychos went full batshit crazy sometime around that age. With a history of mental illness or criminal charges. Low income, no job or menial labor. Maybe even homeless, sleeping in his car.

Whatever she'd pictured, it hadn't been Henry friggin' Phipps, fifty-eight years old, middle-class, no record, living only a few blocks from her own place. So damn *ordinary*. He looked like someone whose greatest passion was solving the crossword puzzle in the *Harbor Light*, the weekly local newspaper Bonnie never bothered to read, because it was all about town council meetings and borough ordinances. Henry would read it, though. He might even write a sternly worded letter to the editor on the subject of potholes.

If Henry Phipps could be a serial killer, anyone could. Even old Saint Nick himself—who was, after all, a known housebreaker operating under an alias, with a secret hideout in the North Pole.

Even so, it was possible. No one had seen the killer. He'd left no clues. He had no known motive. There was no consistent victim profile. The crimes had a distinctive MO—a single .22 round to the back of the skull at close range—but no signature. As Bonnie understood this profiling stuff, a signature was a superfluous touch that served as a killer's exclamation mark on the crime, like writing *whore* on a dead woman. Stabbing was Jack the Ripper's MO; dissecting the corpse was his signature.

The Man in the Moon left his work unsigned. He took the shot and walked away. He wasn't interested in advertising.

The murders spanned several towns, running the

length of Millstone County. State police and the FBI were involved. There wasn't a lot of media in this part of Jersey, but the few local papers and the sole local TV news outlet were all over it, and the New York and Philly media had gotten in on the action, too.

Could a stoop-shouldered, balding, harmless-looking dweeb like Henry really be responsible for all that mayhem? Had he walked up boldly behind one stranger after another—late at night, or early in the morning, in isolated spots along the Crab River Inlet or in the pine woods out by Iron Town—and executed his victim with a single well-placed shot from behind? Could he have started a panic that now stretched across the whole county, and beyond?

Because people were panicking, of course. Never mind that you were still way more likely to get killed in a car crash on Route 35 than by a mystery man packing a .22. Logic didn't enter into a thing like this. Children were no longer allowed to play outside; joggers and bikers had absented themselves from streets and boardwalks; people complained bitterly about the incompetence of the police, who were presumed to be sitting on their asses.

They were not sitting on their asses. Bonnie knew that much from Brad, who filled her in on the daily updates, task force briefings, BOLOs and person-of-interest alerts.

They were after the Man in the Moon, all right. They just hadn't found him. But Armin Petrossian had. Or so he said.

She shook her head. She had no definite reason to doubt Petrossian or his anonymous source, but she still wasn't sure. And she couldn't shoot Henry without being sure. Like Santa, she had to check her list before deciding if Henry Phipps had been naughty or nice.

She heeled a six-round magazine into the Glock and slipped the gun into her purse along with the suppressor and the gloves. She was reaching for Sammy with the intention of muting him, a necessary precaution when doing wet work—she could hardly have him belting out "Jingle Bells" in the middle of a B&E job—when the damnable ringtone started up again.

It had to be Brad. She couldn't put him off any longer. She lifted the phone to her ear.

"Hey, boyfriend," she said, hoping the word still applied.

There was a moment of silence on the other end, just long enough for her to realize that the caller wasn't Brad, after all. Brad's silence had a different quality. It was friendlier, or something.

"I'm not your boyfriend, Parker," Dan Maguire said.

"Aw, shit. It's you."

"Contain your enthusiasm. I'm not feeling too friendly toward you, either. I'm sure you know why."

"The usual reason, I'm guessing. Roid rage."

"I don't use steroids."

"I was thinking hemorrhoids."

"That's funny. Really. You know what else is funny? I've decided that my department will no longer require the services of Officer Bradley Walsh."

The news was not unexpected, but it was still bad, and it seemed to call for yet another cigarette.

"C'mon, Dan," she said, flicking her lighter, the phone wedged under her chin. "Aren't you overreacting? Where's your Christmas spirit?"

"I should have terminated him the first time I found out he was involved with you. But I thought he'd ended it."

"He did end it. For a while. But, well—I'm a hard habit to break. How'd he react when you told him your decision?"

"He doesn't know yet."

"Letting him twist in the wind?"

"Not exactly. I wanted you to know first, because I'm giving you an option."

"This oughta be good."

"Officer Walsh can keep his job—if you're out of the picture."

"You want me to break up with him for good this time? That's your condition?"

"You're not hearing me, Parker. When I say out of the picture, I mean all the way out. Out of Brighton Cove, out of my jurisdiction, out of my life."

"Oh."

"Let me make myself clear. I'm not just talking about relocating to Miramar or Maritime. I mean you are gone, clean out of Millstone County, and you never come back. You never set foot in my town again."

"So it's *your* town now?"

"It's always been my town. Look, I know your instinct will be to refuse. You're the stubborn type. You hang on like a goddamn deer tick."

"You missed your calling, Dan. You should've written Hallmark cards."

"But in this case," he continued, "you may wish to reconsider. *If* you care about Walsh, which I doubt, because I don't believe you care about anyone but yourself."

"Because I'm a certified sociopath."

"Exactly."

"Yeah, you've told me so. Like, a million times."

"Well, here's your chance to prove me wrong. Get lost for good, and I'll keep Walsh on the payroll. Stay put, and he's over and done, with no letter of recommendation and the absolute guarantee I'll badmouth him to any potential employer. He'll never work in law enforcement again. Maybe he can get a job as a security guard at the Millstone County Mall."

"Brad wasn't trying to disrespect you, you know."

"I don't care about his state of mind. I only know he disobeyed me and lied about it."

"It's his personal life."

"Fraternizing with a known criminal goes beyond

having a personal life."

She wouldn't have used the term *fraternizing* to describe what she'd done with Brad, but now was not the time to argue fine points of vocabulary. "Fair enough," she said.

"So—are you moving on?"

"I'll think about it."

"Think fast. This is a limited-time offer. Walsh has tomorrow off, so I'll give you until first thing Tuesday morning. That way you can enjoy your last Christmas in Brighton Cove."

He ended the call before she could think of a comeback.

She muted the phone, tossed it into the purse, and exhaled a long tendril of smoke. Things had all gone to shit very quickly. Well, life was funny like that. It liked to set you up one way, then give you a quick kick in the brisket when you weren't looking. And she supposed it should have been predictable. The two of them had been naïve to imagine they could get away with it forever. They'd believed they were being clever, but it was hard to keep secrets in a small town.

Sometime after their breakup, Brad had started seeing her again. Naturally they'd kept it on the down-low, meeting at her office downtown, after hours, when the building was dark and empty. He used the back stairs. She shut the blinds. Even if someone noticed his car parked on the side street, there would be nothing to connect him to her.

As a love affair, it was probably pretty tawdry. No romantic dinners, no holidays together, not even a walk on the beach. They would meet and talk and have sex on the sofa. Sometimes there was liquor involved. Once or twice he'd brought pizza. Mostly it was about the sex. Probably not the firmest foundation for a long-term relationship, but she wasn't accustomed to thinking long-term. He was a couple of years younger than she was, too young, maybe, to be thinking very far ahead himself.

Even for Christmas Eve, they hadn't planned anything special. She'd specifically requested no presents. Her excuse was that they couldn't risk buying any trinkets that might get people talking. The truth was that she had no idea what to get him, and the embarrassing reason was that she really didn't know him well enough.

Nevertheless, he'd yielded to temptation and purchased her a case for her phone. Navy blue, the color that blended best with night shadows. A good color for someone who spent her time skulking in darkness. She hadn't dressed Sammy in it yet. She hadn't had the chance.

She'd been thanking him for it with a surprised kiss when the office door drifted open, and Chief Dan Maguire was there.

The room was dimly lit, and she couldn't see his face. But she knew it was Dan from his outline, the wide, aggressive stance and chubby fists. She was sure he was smiling.

"Hope I'm not interrupting. I've heard of an office romance, but this is just kind of sad."

The line sounded rehearsed. She wondered how many times he'd practiced it.

"Hey, Dan." She managed to sound unruffled. "Don't you have anyplace better to be on Christmas Eve?"

"I am exactly where I want to be."

"I don't suppose you'd believe me if I said we were just getting together for old times' sake, you know, as a one-time thing."

"I would not."

"Just checking."

He strode into the office like a man taking ownership of the premises. "So this has been going on the whole time?"

Brad started to speak, but thought better of it. Explanations and details wouldn't help his case. Nothing would help.

"Of course it has," Dan went on, answering his own question. "And you've been laughing about it, haven't you? Having big fun at my expense? You think I'm some kind of idiot, don't you?"

"I know I do," Bonnie said. "Not sure about Brad."

"How did you find out?" Brad asked. His voice was low and strangely hoarse, a smoker's voice, though he'd never smoked a cigarette in his life.

"You can blame Jensen. He told me he tried to fix you up with his sister, and you turned him down. He thought that was weird. His sister's plenty hot."

"Why would he even mention that to you?"

"I don't know. He likes to talk. But it got me thinking. Why would a young guy like you have no personal life? I mean, you never talk about it. Never go out. Unless ... you've been going out on the sly."

"You're real crafty, Dan," Bonnie said. "You're like one of those cops who solve crimes on TV."

He ignored her. "I knew there were only two places where the two of you could meet. Your apartment was out; you knew your neighbor ratted you out the last time. That left Parker's crappy little duplex or her crappy little office."

She thought about objecting to those descriptions, but decided they were, on balance, accurate.

"I staked out the duplex first. When that produced no results, I tried this address tonight. I saw you"—he hooked a finger at Brad—"sneak up the back stairs. You looked awfully damn guilty, Walsh."

"Outside door's locked," Bonnie said. "How'd you get in?"

"He has a key," Brad answered.

"Master key." Dan swirled the key set. It tingled like Christmas bells. "One of the perks of being police chief."

"Gotta say, Dan," Bonnie said, "I would think a grown man has better things to do than spend his nights spying on an employee."

"Yeah, I need to take a long, hard look at myself. But first, I'll be taking a look at this entire situation and its consequences." He moved for the door, pausing to look back. "And there will be consequences, Walsh. Believe me."

He disappeared down the hall, leaving the door open. She heard him take the front stairs, leaving via the main door, which banged shut behind him with an echoing slam.

"Well, piss," Bonnie said, summing up her feelings as economically as possible.

She waited for Brad to say something, but he was disconcertingly silent. After a moment, he got up from the sofa and began pulling on his overcoat.

"Aren't we going to talk about this?" she asked.

He shook his head. She wasn't necessarily a pro when it came to reading people's emotions, but she understood that he was too upset to talk.

She couldn't blame him. Maguire couldn't touch her. He knew the truth about her moonlighting activities, but he'd never been able to prove it in any way that would stand up. But he could do plenty to Brad. The kid had been playing a dangerous game, and Dan wasn't the forgiving sort.

Brad walked out without a word, again taking the back stairs–she heard his retreating footsteps–even though there was no more need for secrecy. After a few minutes, she closed up the office and left. She got in her Jeep and just sat there, not knowing what to do. She had to go somewhere. Couldn't just hang out at home.

There was Frank. She'd been meaning to visit him all day. It was Christmas Eve, after all. And it still wasn't too late.

She aimed the Jeep north, needing to have her talk

with Frank Kershaw. Not that Frank could tell her what to do. But sometimes just saying the words was helpful.

She'd been crossing the bridge into Miramar when Sammy sang out his holiday tune. Certain it was Brad, she'd answered—and received a summons from Armin Petrossian.

Yeah, her night had gone just great. And it wasn't over yet. She had a date with a guy who just might be a killer, a famous one, with a nickname and everything.

He hadn't chosen the nickname. It had been bestowed on him by the press, in a quote from an Algonquin detective stirred to an unexpected flight of poetry.

He's like the Man in the Moon, the cop had said. *He's made of shadows.*

6

THIS WAS WHAT mattered, what life was about. This was the bone-raw truth of things.

In the back of the van, on the orange shag carpet, Jonah Stroud had hold of his woman and was taking her rough and hard. No dignity, no social graces, just two wild animals tearing at each other, ugly and sweaty and coarse.

Jonah's body was lean and ropy, splotchy with scar tissue from old fights and etched with tattoos—some professional, some administered in prison during a three-year slide for assault. He was tall and strong and still young at thirty-six, though going prematurely gray at the temples. His cock was a ramrod, eight inches of poured steel, and he knew how to use it and how to withhold his final release until the girl was begging for it, fuckin' begging, the way Sofia was begging now.

He liked Sofia. Didn't love her. Didn't love anybody. Thought love was bullshit. But he was happy with her, because she was young—a decade younger than himself—and slim and pale and compliant. She never complained about his boozing, though he drank just about all the time, and she never talked about settling down and living a normal life. She floated through a drugged-out haze of smiling bliss, a butterfly wafted on a tepid breeze. She could never be faithful to him, but so what? It saved him the trouble of being faithful to her.

They wrestled on the floor, flexing and groaning together, her long curved nails—raptor talons, painted the deep scarlet of a bruise—grooving his arms as he thrust himself into her, and her small breasts pillowing in his face, tasting salty with sweat, and her bony arms, scored with needle marks, hugging him in a skeletal embrace. She was sweat and pussy and bones, she was everything raw and elemental in the world, life and death together, and he liked being with her, he liked becoming entangled with her body.

When he finally seeded her, the feeling that racked him was more pain than pleasure, and he liked it that way. They both did.

Slowly he drew himself up and buttoned his pants. "We better get going," he said. "We done had enough Christmas cheer."

She rose half upright, clumsy as a cult. Her thin body swayed. "This is a sucky Christmas. No presents."

"You just wait. Santa'll come through yet."

He climbed into the front and slid behind the wheel. When he cranked the engine, the dashboard stereo came on, turned up high. The band was Slipknot, and the song was "The Devil in I," his personal anthem. He sang along, growling the angry, crazy lyrics, as Sofia maneuvered into the passenger seat and the scenery slid by.

The van was hers, but he had made alterations. He'd painted over the hippie-dippy decals on the side panels, replacing the rainbows and sunflowers with a smooth whitewash. He'd installed a secret compartment behind the glove box where he could hide his merchandise. And because you could never be too fuckin' careful, he'd fitted a spring-mounted Luger 9mm under the driver's seat.

The Luger wouldn't be needed tonight. Some of the folks he dealt with were sketchy, but not this one. This one posed no threat.

He swung off the bridge on Route 35 and dropped down onto Seascape Island, then cut his speed, cruising slowly through a maze of streets with jaunty nautical names. The island, a minuscule portion of Maritime overlooking Crab River and its inlet, was more upscale than the rest of the borough, dense with three-story condos shingled in Nantucket gray.

"What's this guy's name again?" Sofia asked over the grinding clash of guitar chords.

"Peter Forrest."

"Forrest. That's a stupid name." She let her torrent of blonde hair fall back against the headrest and pitched her voice in a singsong baritone. "Life is just a box o' choc-o-lates."

Jonah chuckled. "Yeah, he's a dick." This was his opinion of human beings in general.

"What do you need him for?"

He'd told her already, but she never remembered anything. Dumber than a box of hammers, this girl, especially when she was juiced on her meds, which was always.

"He runs a compounding pharmacy," he said, dialing down the volume on the stereo. "Deals specialty shit on the side, made to order in his lab."

"Since when do you need specialty shit?"

"Now and then."

Jonah used Forrest only rarely. He got his Percocet, his Vicodin, his OxyContin from other sources. But occasionally he had a client who wanted something impossible to obtain through the usual channels.

Sofia gazed with childlike interest at a twinkling display of Christmas lights as it glided past. "You sure he won't mind me being with you?"

"He won't say nothing, even if he does mind. He knows better than to be disagreeable with me." Most people did. They took one look at Jonah Stroud and decided friendliness and cooperation were in their best interest.

"This client of yours must be super special if you're going to all this trouble."

"You're right about that, Mommy." Jonah nodded. "He is special, for sure."

He lifted the whiskey bottle and took another swig, enjoying the raw burn. Bottle was nearly empty, which was a tragedy, but there would be more in Forrest's place. Maybe not Jack Daniel's, maybe not even whiskey, but liquor of some kind. He wasn't particular.

It was a shame he had to be dealing with this shit tonight. Christmas Eve was usually his night for robbing houses. Best time for it. The presents were already wrapped, the people out at parties. He broke in and swiped the stuff, the Grinch who stole Christmas. The haul was always good. Plus, there was the pure malicious pleasure of imagining the kiddies waking up in the morning to find nothing under the tree. Served them right, spoiled assholes who had every fuckin' thing handed to them. Sometimes, before leaving, he would take a dump right on the damn carpet, his own personal way of saying *fuck you* to the rich bastards who had more than he did and thought they were better than him.

Way he saw it, nobody was better than anybody else. Everybody was the same, just meat and bone, so why should anybody have more than the rest? He had explained it to Sofia once. *The way it should be is, everybody has the same. Same income, same house, same car. No differences. All equal. You, me, and the nine-to-five office drone, and Donald fuckin' Trump, and a bum in the gutter—all the same.*

He wasn't sure how this would work in practice, but it seemed fair to him. And he really wouldn't mind having the same as anyone else. What made him angry—made him crazy, sometimes—was knowing that somebody, somewhere, had more.

Jonah pulled up outside 32 Spinnaker Way, killed the stereo and the motor, and slipped out of the van. He shut the door softly, making sure Sofia did likewise. No point in advertising their presence at Forrest's home at this late hour. Low profile was the way to go, always. It was why he'd insisted on covering over the airbrushed designs on the van, despite Sofia's indignation at the desecration of art.

He rang the doorbell, waited a half second, and rang again, laying his thumb on the buzzer forever. The night was cold, the wind off the water chilly and damp, and he was pissed off about being outside.

The door opened on a fortyish guy with a salt-and-pepper beard and a weak-ass pussy-tickler mustache.

"Come in, come in," Peter Forrest said irritably. "This couldn't have waited? It's Christmas mother-fucking Eve."

Jonah entered, Sofia trailing him. Forrest glanced briefly at her, correctly judged her to be no one of importance, and looked away.

It might be Christmas motherfucking Eve, but their friendly neighborhood pharmacist hadn't been celebrating. His condo was empty. The only activity was the flicker of a muted TV tuned to an adult movie. Jonah glimpsed some whore's strawberry blonde head buried in another slut's thighs.

"I don't keep the stuff here, you know," Forrest was saying. "Had to drive to the shop to get it. All the way to Broad Bank and back." He stopped just short of complaining. He was smart enough to know better.

Jonah shrugged. "You know I'll make it worth your while."

"Why the sudden hurry? When you placed the order, you said there was no rush."

"Something came up. Hey, Doc, you got anything to drink?"

"Um, sure. Liquor cabinet's over there."

Liquor cabinet. Fancy.

Jonah swaggered over and opened it up. His practiced eye picked out a mostly full bottle of brandy. He unscrewed the top and tipped it to his mouth, guzzling thirstily, excess liquor striping his chin and neck. He set down the bottle with a clunk.

"Good shit," he said, wiping his lips with his sleeve.

"Thanks," Forrest said. He looked mildly scandalized, though Jonah didn't see why. Nothing wrong with a man having a friendly drink with his buddy on Christmas Eve. "Anyway, just be glad I'd already whipped up a batch. You told me you wanted something potent. More potent than China White."

"That I did. I need it potent as hell." His careful enunciation broke the unfamiliar term into two words, *poh tent*.

Sofia slid up behind Forrest and started kneading the muscles at the nape of his neck. Forrest glanced back, reddening.

"Don't be flattered," Jonah said. "She likes men, is all. And women. She got a lot of nympho in her. Right now she's flying high, so she's up for whatever. When she gets like that, she'll fuck anything that moves."

"Okay ..." Forrest said dubiously as the massage went on. "Well, what you're getting is a fentanyl analog, similar to carfentanil. Do you have any idea how dangerous a product like this can be?"

Jonah nodded. He did, in fact, have a very good idea.

"I mean, seriously," Forrest went on. "They use carfentanil to sedate zoo animals. Two milligrams will put down a bull elephant. For a human being, even micrograms can be lethal. Ordinarily I would never deal in something like this."

"Yeah, yeah."

He tuned out the doc's noise and took a leisurely stroll around the apartment, brandy bottle in hand, making mental notes on the stuff that might be worth stealing on a return visit when the owner wasn't home. He didn't see much, though. Most of Forrest's possessions consisted of books, shelves of the damn things, more than anybody could ever want. It was like being in a library or a school, not that Jonah had spent much time in either place. He picked up one of the larger hardbacks, hoping to find its insides hollowed out to hold a stash, but no such luck. The guy really did read the fuckin' things, it appeared.

He himself had never read a damn book in his life, except for picture books. Sure, he could read—more or less—but he didn't see much point to it. He could write, too. Could sign his name, anyway. He had to do it one letter at a time, lifting his pencil after each trembling effort.

When he looked at Forrest again, he saw that Sofia had taken to nuzzling his neck like a playful kitten. He took another long swallow of brandy.

"So," Jonah said, "where's the shit?"

"Right there." Forrest pointed to a Ziploc bag on a coffee table flanked by a leather sectional.

Jonah approached the bag and took a long look. Four pills, round, blue.

"As you can see," Forrest said, "the tablets are pressed with the markings for Percocet, and they're the same color, or as close as I could get. Whatever you do, don't get them mixed up with real Percocets."

"I won't." He picked up the bag and eyeballed the contents up close.

"I have to tell you, this is a one-time-only thing. I really don't feel comfortable synthesizing something this risky."

That was what Jonah hated about the guy. Always talking, saying shit like *synthesizing* and *micrograms*. Like he was a big deal just 'cause he knew a lot of damn words.

He waved the bag. "This shit seriously scares you, don't it, Doc?"

"Damn right it does. The potency is through the roof compared with regular oxy or vike. This is for serious, long-time users with an extraordinarily high threshold.

For anyone else, what you've got here are four bite-size pieces of concentrated death."

"Concentrated death," Sofia repeated. She forgot the pharmacist's neck and stared, mesmerized, at the plastic bag.

Forrest was still talking. "Your client can't just swallow it. And he definitely can't chew it, crunch it—anything like that. Best way is to let the tablet dissolve sublingually. You know, under the tongue. It can take up to twenty minutes."

Sofia's gaze had never left the bag. Her knuckles were in her mouth, her eyes huge. Jonah knew she was getting off on it, which was okay, because Forrest's big-screen TV was throbbing with close-ups of wet pussy, and Jonah was getting kind of hot, himself.

"Understood," he said, uninterested in more lectures. "How much I owe you for?"

"One hundred-twenty-five per pill. I know it's steep—"

"No problem. You came through real good."

He pulled out a wad of crumpled bills and peeled off five of them. He slapped the cash down on the coffee table and stuffed the little bag of death into his pocket.

"Let's get a move on, Mommy," he said, slapping Sofia's butt. "Need to drop off this Christmas present."

He headed for the door, taking the half-finished bottle with him, not asking permission. Out the door he glanced back at the pharmacist.

"Sorry to send you to the office on Christmas Eve, bro."

Forrest shrugged, acknowledging the obvious. "It didn't really matter. Christmas is just another day for me."

"Yeah. We live in a secular fuckin' age. Gotta find meaning somewhere, though." He patted the pocket containing the bag of pills.

"Just be sure your client doesn't find too much

meaning," Forrest said as they went out the door. "People OD on fentanyl and its analogs. It happens all the time."

Jonah knew this.

It was exactly what he was counting on.

7

HENRY PHIPPS, WHO might or might not be made of shadows, lived in a one-story bungalow on a narrow street lined with sycamore trees. The street backed up against the railroad tracks, making it one of the least desirable addresses in Brighton Cove.

Most of his neighbors had decorated their homes—tacky inflatable snowmen and plastic Rudolphs abounded—but his house was bare. That didn't make him a serial killer, of course. Bonnie's place was equally stark, and though she'd done her share of killing, she didn't put herself in the same category as the Man in the Moon.

She ditched the Jeep two blocks from Henry Phipps's place, on a side street with a busted streetlight, where the vehicle was less likely to be spotted. The local gendarmes knew her ride by sight, which was one of the disadvantages of doing a job on her home turf. But Brighton Cove usually ran only two patrols at a time, and the cops spent most of their time hanging out at the Donut Hutch, reinforcing the most obvious clichés about themselves. With any luck, no prowl cars would come by in the next half hour. She didn't expect her work to take any longer than that. She would be in and out like Seal Team Six. And what was so great about Team Six, anyway? You never heard anything about Team Five, and they were probably just as good.

No lights were on when she approached the house. By now it was after midnight. The Man in the Moon killed in early morning or shortly after dark, never in the middle of the night, so even if Henry was her man, she didn't think he would be out trolling for victims. He was probably asleep.

Before leaving her house, she'd changed her outfit. Her boots had been replaced by sneakers, navy blue, with the laces dyed to match. She'd thrown on a dark blue pullover and a matching hoodie. With the hoodie pulled up and her purse concealed in the crook of her arm, she was as anonymous as possible. If any night owls looked out the window, they'd see only a dark figure of uncertain gender, age, and race.

The near side of the house was screened from the neighbors by a high hedge, making it a likely point of entry. She moved along the wall to a window halfway down. Her keychain flashlight revealed no wires or sensors in the window itself, no sign of an alarm system. The room framed in the glass looked like a study—sofa, desk and chair, file cabinet, bookcase. Okay. She was after hard evidence to convict Phipps of his crimes, and this might be just the place to find it.

She pulled on her gloves, removed a straightedge and a razor from her purse, and inscribed a small square in the windowpane, pulling it free with a suction cup. The opening was just large enough for her hand. She undid the latch and raised the window from the outside. Hauling herself up onto the sill took more effort than it should have.

How long was it since she'd been to the gym? Dating Brad, a younger guy in good shape, had once made her more conscious of maintaining her own condition, but lately she'd been slacking off. Too few pull-ups, too many slices of Milano's sausage-and-pepperoni pizza. And way too much tobacco and booze.

She dropped lightly to the carpeted floor. The house was small, and Henry Phipps's bedroom was probably only one or two doors away. She hoped he was a sound sleeper.

She pulled the window shut to minimize the intrusion of cold air, though some would get through the hole she'd cut. The hoodie came down, and the purse was slung over her shoulder.

Her first stop was the bookcase. A man's choice of reading material ought to tell something about him. Henry had accumulated a lot of beat-up hardcovers and coverless paperbacks, library-sale items, mostly mysteries with British settings. The murder of Lord Sausagefest in Lady Snapbeaver's parlor, that kind of crap. The titles did nothing to peg Henry Phipps as the Man in the Moon.

Next, the desk. She opened the drawers, exploring their contents in the flashlight's glow. Checkbooks, stamps, envelopes in one. Paperclips, scotch tape, rubber bands in another. Pencils and pens, keys and coins in a third.

In short, nada. So far, old Henry seemed about as dangerous as a labradoodle.

There was still the file cabinet. Two drawers. The top contained bills and other boring household documents neatly arranged in manila folders with brightly colored tabs. The lower drawer was locked.

The lock intrigued her. She made short work of it with a tool from her purse. When she opened the drawer, she found no manila folders, only a pile of newspaper clippings and printouts of news stories.

Yahtzee.

She knew it before she even looked at the first clipping. It concerned the Man in the Moon, of course. So did all the others. She spent some time riffling through them. The first victim, the second, the third. Rosa Martinez was there. Full coverage of the case.

Below the clippings was a mass of handwritten pages, a journal of some sort. She ran the flashlight over the spidery, crabbed script.

The maze turns & turns again & there is no end to its

turning. There must be a way out. I am the way. I am the truth.

I am death, and no one escapes this hell on earth except through me.

A train clattered past, briefly shaking the house in a rush of chugging noise. The whistle sounded, a long, rising and falling Doppler wail. It sounded like the cry of a madman, a cry torn from the pages in her hands.

Henry Phipps's manifesto. He was on a mission, or something. So Petrossian's informant had not led him astray. The man who resided at 626 Lake Avenue was a bona fide nutjob.

And he had definitely been naughty this year.

She pushed the drawer shut, not bothering to relock it, and left the study. She'd spent less than five minutes in the house, and already she'd learned what she needed to know.

Now there was only the small matter of placing a bullet in Henry Phipps's brain.

The hallway was warm, too warm. Henry kept the heat in his house dialed up high. It sucked all the moisture from the air. It seemed to suck the sweat right out of her pores.

She stood motionless, straining to hear any telltale sounds—snoring, the rustle of sheets. After the clamor of the passing train, the silence enveloping the little house was almost eerie. The only noise was the monotonous, hollow ticking of a grandfather clock, counting off seconds in deep-throated clunks.

Her flashlight was off now. The gun was in her hand, the suppressor already screwed onto the barrel. She had no distinct memory of taking these items from her purse or putting them together. By now she'd performed this ritual often enough that such details took care of themselves. She didn't know whether or not to feel good about that.

Soon, another notch in her gun. But not literally. She never used the same firearm twice. She disposed of each one after a hit. The waterways of Millstone County were littered with her castoffs.

With no sounds to guide her, she turned arbitrarily to the right. Unlike the study, the hallway was uncarpeted. Wary of loose floorboards, she stayed close to the wall. Experience had taught her that the worst creaks were found in the middle of any aisle.

The first doorway on her right framed a bathroom aglow with a low-wattage night-light. Toilet and sink, clawfoot bathtub with a mildewed shower curtain. The floor was ancient linoleum, the strips curling at the edges. The tub's spigot dripped.

Next came a closed door, probably opening on a closet. She didn't bother looking inside. She was more interested in the last door in the hall, which hung open on a decent-sized room, larger than the study.

No night-light in here. No light of any kind, except a glimmer of mercury-vapor haze from the railroad tracks.

In the purplish mist she made out a bed piled high with rumpled sheets and covers, concealing a vaguely human form.

A queen-size bed. A large bed for a single man.

The moon man was nestled all snug in his bed,
While visions of sugarplums danced in his head.

Doubtful. She had a feeling this guy's dreams had precious little to do with sugarplums.

Stealth seemed almost unnecessary. If Henry Phipps could sleep through the locomotive's racket, he wouldn't be roused by floorboard squeaks. Even so, she proceeded carefully, feeling her way with her left hand, training the gun on the bed with her right.

There was a certain poetic justice in what she was about to do. The Man in the Moon shot his victims at close range. They never knew what hit them. Now he would get the same treatment.

She moved closer. She could hear him now. He wasn't entirely silent, after all. The low burr of his snoring was faintly audible. The heap of bedclothes shifted slightly, rhythmically, in time with each breath.

He had very few breaths left. She would be at point-blank range in another two steps.

The white mass of an oversized pillow congealed out of the dark. Flattened against it was an untidy head of hair.

A prickle of uneasiness stopped her. She'd seen Henry Phipps. His photo on the driver's license. His egg-shaped, balding head.

This wasn't him.

Wasn't a person at all. It was a big shaggy dog, sprawled on the pillow.

The dog didn't worry her. It was fast asleep.

What worried her was that it was alone in the bed.

So where the hell was—

"Don't move, missy."

Oh.

Behind her.

That's where.

8

THERE WERE A lot of ways for her to play this situation. She could pivot and duck, firing blind, and hope she got him before he got her. With another assailant she might have risked it. But this was the Man in the Moon. He was used to pulling the trigger at close range.

And she knew there was a trigger. She could feel the gun's muzzle against the back of her head, at the precise point where skull met spine. The sweet spot for him.

Under the circumstances, cooperation seemed advisable. He hadn't shot her yet, which probably meant he didn't want to do it here, in this room. If he attempted a change of venue, she might have more options.

"I'm not moving, Henry," she said.

"Toss the gun on the bed." His voice was low and urgent, but not overly excited. A breathy, slightly high-pitched voice, close to her left ear.

"I might hit your pooch."

"You won't wake him. He sleeps like the dead."

"Not much of a guard dog."

Henry surprised her by chuckling. "He's not, is he? Lazarus is blind and deaf and a little bit senile. He keeps me warm on these cold nights. That's all he's good for. Toss the gun."

She flung it onto the bed, where it disappeared amid the mounds of bedcovers. "I didn't think you liked dogs."

"Why do you say that?"

"The guy in Algonquin."

"Oh, him."

"You shot his dog."

"Only because it started yapping. I couldn't have that. The purse, too. Get rid of it."

"Afraid I'll powder-puff you?"

"How should I know what you've got in there? Lose it."

The purse vanished along with the gun.

"How'd you get into my house?" he asked.

"Window in the study."

"I knew you were in there. I saw your light. Put your hands up."

She didn't raise her hands. She wanted to keep him talking. "I thought you'd be asleep."

"Train woke me. Got up to pee. That's when I saw the light. Put them up."

She obeyed halfheartedly, reaching only high enough to raise her wrists to eye level.

"I read some of your mission statement or whatever it is," she said. "Looked like a lot of mumbo-jumbo to me."

"It wasn't meant for you."

"Because I'm not crazy?"

"You *are* crazy. They're all crazy. This world makes everyone mad."

"Except you, huh?"

"I used to be one of them," he said softly. "But I've *seen*."

"What'd you see?"

"Never mind that. Turn slowly to face the door."

She turned, and he turned with her, staying at her back. The gun never shifted its position. It might have been glued to her hair.

"You saw God," she said, "is that it?"

"God." His tongue clucked. "You're a fool. Start walking. Not fast."

She moved toward the door. "What've you got against God?"

"What's God got against us? That's the question you

should be asking."

"I'll bite. What's the answer?"

She passed through the bedroom doorway into the hall. Behind her, she heard the scuff of his slippers on the bare floor. He must be in his pajamas—a man with a full bladder, roused from bed. The gun would be in his right hand. The police had pegged the Man in the Moon as a right-handed shooter.

"Henry? What's the answer?"

He didn't seem to hear her. "I know a man," he whispered, "who was taken up to the third heaven. I know a man who mastered all the powers and principalities of this world."

"Let me guess. You're the man."

Oh, yeah. She was in the hands of an authentic loony-tune. Disarmed, with a gun to her head. Not a great situation. She tasted bile, felt the hard pounding of her pulse in her temples. Her heart rate was jacked up, her breath quick and shallow. Time expanded, every second filling an hour.

"Woe to those who live and breathe. Woe to the children." His voice was a monotonous chant. "Blessed are the dead, for death has set them free."

They were a few yards down the hall now, the circle of steel still stamped hard against the back of her neck.

"We will make this world a desolation and a grave. We will uncreate creation. Stop here."

The last words took her by surprise. They weren't part of his hymn or prayer. She stopped alongside the door she'd passed earlier, the one she'd taken for a closet.

"Open it," Henry said.

"What's in there?"

"Stairs."

"Going?"

"Down. Into the cellar."

"Why are we going into the cellar, Henry?"

"So I can shoot you without waking the damn

neighbors," he said without emotion.

"Have you killed any other people down there?"

"You'll be the first."

"Lucky me. If you're so goddamn spiritual and enlightened, why are you into homicide? Seems like a really un-Buddha thing to do."

"On the contrary. The Buddha saw the truth under the bodhi tree. He knew we must escape the turning wheel. Open the door."

She didn't move. "I was sent here to take you out. If I don't come back, someone else will be after you. You'll only make things worse for yourself."

"That so? Open the door."

"You could cut me a break. Come on, it's Christmas."

"Open the goddamned door."

She gave in, reaching for the knob. "You're a mean one, Mr. Grinch."

"You shouldn't mock. That's stupid. You need to take me seriously."

"I take anybody seriously when he's got a gun to my head."

Her hand turned the knob. The door swung inward on a rectangle of darkness that smelled musty and damp. Cold down there, where the heat didn't reach.

"Light switch is on the right," he said. "Flip it up."

She groped the wall, discovered the switch, but only pantomimed working it. "Nothing's happening."

"Don't play games, you bitch."

"Bulb's dead, Henry, or the circuit's tripped, or something."

"We'll see about that. Start down the stairs. Start down or I'll push you down."

"I'm going, I'm going."

The staircase was narrow, barely wide enough for one person. There was no banister, only brick walls, claustrophobically close.

She extended her foot into the dark, as if dipping a

toe in the water, and found the edge of the landing. Beyond it was the top step. Old wood, bowed with age, slippery with dust. The step creaked as she planted her sneaker on it.

Once Henry came through the doorway, he would try the switch and turn on the cellar light. She couldn't let that happen. She needed darkness. Darkness, and the steep, narrow stairs, the precarious footing, his slippered feet.

"Who sent you?" Henry asked as she lowered herself onto the next step. She'd been wondering when he would get around to that.

"A drug kingpin. Narcosyndicate type. He was a close personal friend of somebody who got a twenty-two round in the head."

Both of her feet were on the next step. He advanced behind her to the edge of the landing. He had to be close to the wall switch.

But it was on his right. And the gun was in his right hand. To flip the switch, he'd have to reach across his body with his left hand.

"How'd he find out about me?" Henry asked.

"He's like Santa Claus. He sees you when you're sleeping, he knows when you're awake."

She heard the rustle of his pj's, a groan of wood, and she knew he was making his move. For this one moment he would be out of position.

She spun on the staircase, reaching up to seize both of his hands in hers, and kept on turning, her momentum throwing him off balance as she forced his arms up, angling the gun away from her body.

He fired. A single shot, explosively loud, burning a purple muzzle flash onto her retinas. A spray of brick particles pelted her back. The slug had gone into the wall.

He struggled to lower the gun and find his target, but she'd already traded places with him on the landing, and she only had to hook her foot under his legs to sweep him off his feet and send him stumbling backward down the stairs.

She released his hands and dived to her belly, making herself small, then snaked through the doorway. Behind her, he was falling, his outraged yell booming up at her, followed by two more explosions as he squeezed off a pair of wild shots into the dark.

She scissor-kicked herself into the hall and rolled clear of the door. Below, he clattered to the bottom of the staircase and was silent.

She didn't know if he was hurt or not, conscious or not, alive or not, and she didn't intend to find out until she had her gun in her hand.

Retreating to the bedroom, she turned on the overhead light and approached the bed, where remarkably Lazarus still lay dozing. The dog really was deaf. And the confined space of the cellar had probably muffled the shots sufficiently to ensure that no neighbor had heard.

She had just reached the bed when she became aware of a strange tingling numbness, a kind of buzzing sensation in her right arm, and a sharper feeling, multiple pinpricks of pain.

High up on the sleeve of the hoodie was a blasted crater, corkscrews of stitching unraveling from it. She touched it, probing the skin under the sleeve, finding a pulpy, ragged hill of flesh where her bicep muscle should be. Her gloved hand came away striped in dark red ooze.

Funny how pain worked. It wasn't there, and then it was. You felt nothing until you knew you were hurt. Then it hit you like a slap.

A hard slap, hard enough to knock her to her knees. She sank down, nearly swooning.

The son of a bitch had shot her. One of the rounds he'd fired when he was falling had caught her in the arm. Shock had neutralized the pain at first, but now the wound had come to life in a wave of heat and slimy wetness and an aching throb that burned like fire.

"Shit," she hissed. This definitely was not what she wanted for Christmas.

She grabbed the arm again, forcing herself to explore the wound despite the pain. It felt deep. No obvious exit point. The round could still be inside her.

The arm didn't seem to be broken. The bullet must have missed the bone. It had done damage, though. She patted down her sleeve and felt the polyester-lined fabric heavy with sticky ooze as far south as her wrist.

She was losing blood. The first priority was to stanch the flow.

She tore off part of a bedsheet and wound it around her arm below the shoulder. The bite of the cloth delivered a shockwave of pain that was almost enough to put her down for the count. Fear kept her in the game. She was intensely aware that at this moment she was totally vulnerable. If he hadn't been hurt in the fall—if he was already coming up—she would be defenseless against him.

Teeth gritted, she looped the tourniquet tighter, knotting it in place. The layers of cloth were instantly soaked through.

She wasn't sure she'd done enough to control the bleeding, but there was no time to do more. She had to confirm that Henry Phipps was dead, or finish him off if he was only unconscious, then get the hell out of here while she was still ambulatory.

Searching the bed, she found her purse and slung it over her shoulder—the left shoulder, the one attached to an undamaged arm. Her hands hunted in the sheets for the pistol. She found it near Lazarus, who had reluctantly awoken and was looking at her with unseeing, cataract-cloudy eyes. His nose twitched, scenting blood.

As she retrieved the gun, the dog bent his head and licked her hand, emitting a low sympathetic mewl.

"Good doggie," she whispered.

She left the room, dousing the light so it wouldn't silhouette her in the hall. She held the gun in her left hand, its weight unfamiliar there. Occasionally she practiced shooting as a lefty, but she wasn't much good. Using her weak hand, she couldn't hit a target from more than a few feet away.

Quickly she retraced her route down the hallway, worried by the strange rubbery feeling in her legs, the unusual disconnect between her feet and the floor. At the stairs, she turned on the cellar light, ducked behind the doorframe, then risked a cautious look below, taking care not to expose herself to the fire-lane.

The subterranean space was tiny, no more than a fruit cellar, three square feet of brick flooring under a bare lightbulb on a swinging chain. There seemed to be no place for Henry Phipps to hide in that space, yet somehow he wasn't there.

She was reasonably sure he hadn't made it up the stairs. Which meant ...

"It's no good, Henry," she called. "I know where you're hiding."

Under the stairs, of course. Ready to fire straight up, through the wooden treads, if she was reckless enough to descend.

"There's nothing you can do." It was a strain to hold her voice steady. "You're out of options. Toss your gun and show yourself."

"So you can shoot me?" he yelled from below.

No point in denying it. "That's the general idea."

She heard him hawk up something from his throat and spit it out. "Hell, I should've taken the shot in the bedroom."

"You really should."

"It wasn't really the neighbors that worried me. It was my sheets. Bloodstains are so hard to get out."

She guessed he wouldn't be too happy about the

condition of his sheets now.

The pain was getting worse. It was as if somebody had set off an M-80 in her arm. Though the bone probably wasn't broken, it might have been nicked. Hairline fracture, maybe.

Or maybe she was only scaring herself, starting to panic.

Panic was bad. It made her heart work harder, her breath come faster. It accelerated the leakage oozing through the tourniquet.

The gun in her hand was shaking. Actually, her whole body was shaking. She felt feverish and queasy.

If she passed out now, he would come upstairs and deliver the coup de grace before she ever woke up. She had to hang on. That was the one imperative in her life, her guiding principle: Always hang on.

What she needed right now was to reduce the blood loss. She snugged the gun in her waistband and tucked her left hand under her right armpit, applying direct pressure to the brachial artery that ran up the inner arm.

She'd never had to do this before. Amazingly, in her entire life, she'd never taken a bullet. She'd suffered other injuries—she still bore a burn mark on her abdomen where a cigarette had scorched her skin, and random scars from sharp objects, and she'd never been able to take a bath after what Pascal had done to her in that motel room—but although people had taken their share of shots at her, nobody had scored a hit.

Until now.

Well, shit. Her luck was bound to run out eventually. And the wound was survivable. At least, it would be, if she could take care of it in time.

A voice came from below. "I know who you are."

The serial killer in the basement. Funny. She'd almost forgotten about him. Her thinking wasn't as clear as it needed to be. She could feel her concentration slip, and snap back, and slip again. There was a weird kind of rhythm to it, as her lucidity wavered from high to low, sharpened by adrenaline, dulled by falling blood pressure.

Eventually, blood pressure would win. Adrenaline could carry her only so far.

"Yeah?" she answered, just to keep the conversation going. "Who am I?"

"You're the one everybody talks about. The little girl who plays at being a private eye."

"Yeah, when I'm not hosting tea parties with my dollies. You coming out or what?"

"Come get me, missy."

"I'm offering you an easy exit. Otherwise I'll have to call my boss, and he'll send his guys. They'll make it a lot harder on you."

"Don't sling that bull. If he wanted his goons to have at me, he wouldn't have sent you in the first place. I'm guessing you need to handle this job all on your own for some reason. Well, do it, then. Handle it."

He was smarter than she'd hoped. He couldn't expose himself without getting blasted. But she couldn't go downstairs without taking fire from below. Sort of a Mexican standoff. Which seemed wrong. Cultural appropriation and all.

She was starting to feel cold, a bad sign. Her throat was dry. Her eyes were blinking too much. It took an effort to stay vertical, even with the doorframe supporting her.

God damn it, don't quit on me, she told her body.

She'd survived worse situations. She'd gone up against more formidable characters than the Man in the Moon. If narcoterrorists and gangbangers hadn't done her in, she was damned if a screwy little dweeb like Henry Phipps would do the honors.

"There's your dog," she said.

"What about my dog?"

"Come out now and I'll let him live."

"Go ahead and put him down. You'll be doing him a favor."

"Because he's old?"

"Because he's trapped."

"Where?"

"In what you call reality."

Okay, no leverage there. It had been a poor bluff anyway. She hadn't actually intended to shoot the dog. "I think you're pretty fucked up, Henry."

"And I think you're bleeding, missy. I think one of my shots did some damage, and you're bleeding out."

Damn. How'd he know that? "You wish," she said stoically.

"I can hear it in your voice. The pain. Like you're talking through clenched teeth."

"I always talk like that. I'm a basically hostile person."

"Nope, I winged you, or worse. Time's on my side. The longer you wait, the weaker you get. Better amscray while you're still able."

It seemed unsporting to continue her deception. It also seemed like a lot of work, and she was rapidly losing her strength.

"I think you may have a point there, Henry," she acknowledged.

"Sounds to me like you've waited too long already."

She wondered if he was right about that, too. Her legs had gone all wobbly, and her eyesight was breaking up in bursts of static. But she couldn't let him know it. She had to keep him at bay until she was safely out of the house.

"I'm hurting," she said, "but I'm nowhere near done. I don't die that easy. If you want to test that proposition, just come at me. See what happens."

He didn't answer.

She pulled the Glock out of her waistband, again holding it in her left hand. Unsteadily she pushed herself away from the doorway. There was no hope of exiting through the window in the study. She could never hoist herself over the sill. But this house had a front door somewhere. She needed to find it while her legs could still carry her, and before Henry Phipps risked emerging from his spider hole.

Fortunately, it was a small house with a simple layout. She'd already explored one end of the hall. The other end, past the study, opened onto a cozy little kitchen with an ancient refrigerator that cooed and gurgled like a fussy infant. A calendar was tacked to the wall, stuck on October, as if time in this house had stood still.

Beyond the kitchen was a dining room, dusty and unused, and a small living room. Old furniture, not antiques, cheap stuff purchased in the '70s, in places like Two Guys and Bamberger's, stores that didn't even exist anymore. A sofa with a plastic slipcover. A TV, the old-fashioned boxy kind. Potted plants withering in neglect. Stupid porcelain knickknacks. Framed photos of a woman who must have been Henry's wife. She thought of the large bed, a bed for two. He was a widower, she realized. Was it losing his wife that had set him off?

The door was in sight. The way out. Sometimes it was two doors when her vision doubled. She staggered toward it. Her feet tangled in a throw rug until she kicked it aside. She got to the door—or doors—and struggled uselessly with the knob, finally understanding that the deadbolt was in place. Her fingers pried at the thumbturn. She couldn't get a grip on the thing.

Behind her, a noise. It might have been the creak of a stair or a floorboard. Henry, on the move. Coming up—or up already, and closing in.

With a last effort she retracted the bolt and threw the door open. Winter air blasted her, shockingly cold after the dry heat of the house. She flipped the hood over her head as she went outside, leaving the door open at her back.

Down three brick steps, stumbling on each one, only the wrought-iron handrail saving her from a fall. Across the yard to the sidewalk, tripping again on a root-canted slab of concrete, but keeping her balance.

Running seemed impossible, her legs wouldn't do it, her body had forgotten how, but she ran anyway, sure that he was coming up behind her, the Man in the Moon, ready to jam the muzzle of his .22 against the occipital bone of her skull.

At the corner, panting, sick to her stomach, she looked back. No one was after her. The street was empty.

She covered the rest of the distance to her Jeep at a fast trot, lurching drunkenly, feeling an unnatural lightness that threatened to carry her away like a leaf in the wind.

God, what a mess. What a fucking disaster.

She got the Jeep open and fell into the driver's seat, dumping the gun beside her, then started the engine and skidded away from the curb, driving badly, nearly clipping a parked car. Three blocks farther, she came to a stop, slant-parked in front of somebody's driveway where a cardboard Saint Nick leered at her in a red floodlight.

Her duplex was only another few blocks from here, but she couldn't make it. She had nearly passed out twice. She could feel liquid pooling in the armpit of her pullover. The tourniquet wasn't getting the job done. She was bleeding out.

Maybe that was why Henry hadn't followed. Maybe he'd known she couldn't get far before the wound caught up with her.

Well, fuck him. She would get through this. Then she would hunt down the bughouse crazy asshole and take him out.

She stripped off the gloves, then snatched at the bedsheet, layered with blood, the thin cotton thickened to the texture of burlap, and found the knotted end, where there was a foot or so of loose fabric to play with. In the glow of the ceiling light she made a second knot, forcing her fingers through the complicated series of moves, fastening the cloth around her gun's barrel with its long silencer. When the barrel was in place, she began to turn the gun, winding it like a spring, tightening the tourniquet with each turn. She kept on tightening until the pressure and the screaming pain were almost more than she could stand. Then she tightened it some more.

When she was done, with the gun wedged under the tourniquet to prevent the ribboned cloth from unraveling, she had stanched the flow. And the flush of angry pain, the hot-poker stabs tormenting her arm from shoulder to elbow, had the salutary effect of reviving her. For the moment she was wide awake, adrenaline again running the show.

She pushed the Jeep into gear and got it home. She didn't attempt to park in the garage; the walk from there to her door would be impossible. She left the Jeep at the curb, struggling out, her damaged arm pinned to her side. Tapping in the six-digit security code at the front door was an exercise in sheer willpower.

Then she was in. She took two steps into her living room and fell forward, motionless on the floor.

9

DAN MAGUIRE ARRIVED at the scene at 1:17, wearing yesterday's clothes, which he'd fished out of the laundry hamper after receiving the call.

Ordinarily he would have been severely displeased at being pulled out of bed on Christmas Eve—or technically Christmas morning—but from what Phil Gaines had told him, it was worth getting up for.

He parked his Buick Regal outside 626 Lake Avenue, alongside two squad cars and Phil's personal car. The flicker of dome lights competed with the garish twinkling of a holiday display two doors down.

Henry Phipps's house was undecorated, but it wasn't dark. It looked as if every interior light had been turned on. "Why the light show?" he asked Jensen and Quinera at the front door.

"That's how we found it," Quinera said. "And the front door wide open. Garage door, too. As you can see, his vehicle is gone."

Dan had noticed that. "What's he drive?"

"Subaru Impreza sedan, gray, 2008."

"You put out an APB?"

"Yes, sir."

"What prompted you initially to call in Detective Gaines? The blood on the door?" He knew blood spots had been seen on the dead bolt's thumbturn.

"Not just the blood." This was Jensen. "There was a file cabinet left open—"

"I'll walk the chief through it," Phil Gaines interrupted. He was framed in the doorway, his hands already sheathed in latex gloves.

Dan stepped into the house and followed Phil through the living room.

"Phipps lit out of here like a bat out of hell," Phil was saying. "Skid marks in the gravel. Scattered the garbage cans." He clapped his hands in time with a spittle-flecked approximation of a cymbal crash. A born entertainer, was Phil.

"Is that what prompted the nine-one-one call?" Dan asked. "The commotion he made when he left?"

"No, that came later. It was the curious incident of the dog in the night." Like many of the things Phil said, this required further explanation. "Phipps's dog. The poor pooch was howling like crazy. Woke the neighbors."

"Where's the dog now?"

"Good Samaritan down the street took him in. Here's those files they were telling you about."

Phil led him into a study, where the bottom drawer of a metal file cabinet hung ajar, crowded with newspaper clippings and printouts.

"All of it is coverage of the Man in the Moon," Phil said.

Dan blew on his hands to chase away the chill. "Quite a collection. You know, it's not illegal to show an unhealthy interest in local crimes."

"But a tad peculiar, don't you think?"

"I do." He blew harder. "There's a cold draft in here, like a window's open."

"Window's shut, but a rectangular hole was incised in the glass." Phil tapped the windowpane with a gloved finger, indicating the cutout. "Freshly made. We found the missing piece in the dirt outside. And footprints. Size nine, they look like."

Dan digested this as he followed Phil down the hall into the bedroom, where Eddie Myers was taking photos. Click, flash, click, flash.

Phil stopped by the bed, pointing out the confusion of sheets. Bloodstains were plainly visible, as they were throughout the house.

"The dog was in here, on the bed," Phil said. "Yowling up a storm."

"Injured?"

"Not a mark on him. Just upset at being left behind, I guess. And smelling the blood."

"Yeah. The blood. Phipps must've been bleeding pretty bad."

"We think he may have tied off the wound with part of this sheet. See how it's torn? But that's not the most interesting thing. This is."

He pointed at the open drawer of the nightstand beside the bed. Dan peered in.

"Mapbook of Millstone County," Phil said unnecessarily. "No one's touched it, but it's open to the location of his last kill. The exact spot is recorded." A bull's-eye had been neatly drawn with a red felt marker. "I'm betting the other five kills are recorded as well."

"Even so, he could have gotten that information from the media. It was public knowledge."

"Are you seriously skeptical that this is the guy?"

"No. Just playing devil's advocate. Trying to look at it from all angles. The case is too big to go jumping to conclusions."

"Too big for us to screw up, you mean."

"That's exactly what I mean." Dan moved away from the night table, looking down at the bloodied bed. "So we're saying someone broke in and came after Phipps? Wounded him, and Phipps got away?"

"Looks like it."

"A hitter, maybe. A professional."

Phil gave him a shrewd look. "I suppose you have someone in mind for that job."

"I might," Dan said, chewing his thumbnail.

Everybody knew about his private obsession. It

wasn't exactly a secret. He'd been after Bonnie Parker for years, telling anyone who would listen that she was bad news. Though he couldn't say everything he knew, thanks to a gag order imposed after the Streinikov case blew up in his face, he was not averse to dropping hints about her sideline and the growing body count.

He was aware that people thought he was suffering from a paranoid fixation. His own wife had long since given up complaining about his nightly monologues on his bête noire, as she called it. Bernice thought he was overreacting. They all did. He saw the way they rolled their eyes and exchanged side glances whenever he brought up the subject. And then there was Bradley Walsh, one of his own officers, blatantly disobeying his instructions never to be seen with Parker again. Sneaking around with her on the sly.

Nobody understood. Nobody could see her for what she was.

It was coming, though—the day of reckoning. He had never lost his faith in that outcome.

"Detective?" Patrolman Guilfoyle stuck his head into the room. "Oh, hey, Chief. Didn't know you were here."

"Just showed up. You have something?"

"Yes, sir, I do." He held up a plastic bag containing several soiled pieces of paper covered in a minute spidery scrawl. "Found these in the wastebasket under the kitchen sink."

"What are they?" Phil asked, accepting the bag.

"Stuff he wrote."

Dan craned his neck over Phil's shoulder and made out enough of the top page to get an idea of what it was about. "Some kind of manifesto," he said.

"Religious nuttiness." Phil nodded. "Something about an imposter god who created the world to make us suffer. Warmed-over Nag Hammadi."

"Warmed-over what?"

"Nag Hammadi. It's a site in Egypt where a library of

ancient documents turned up. Early Gnostic writings. You know about the Gnostics?"

Dan was pretty sure he'd never heard that word before in his life. "Not a clue."

"They believed the major religions worshipped a false god. An evil god or a crazy one, or possibly just inept. Anyway, one who wasn't worth bowing down to. He'd made a mess of the world, either intentionally or by sheer incompetence. The real God was on a higher plane. Once you knew all this, you'd attained *gnosis*—understanding."

"It's Greek to me," Dan said.

Phil laughed. "That's clever." His smile faded as he realized Dan hadn't been making a witticism. "Anyway," he went on, "our friend Phipps seems to be channeling the Gnostics."

"He some kind of authority on ancient religions, you think?"

"I doubt it. I didn't see any scholarly books in his study. Certainly nothing about Gnosticism."

"Then how'd he glom on to this idea?"

"I suppose it's not so hard to come up with. If life treats you badly enough, you've got to blame it on someone. Why not God?"

Dan grunted. It seemed crazy to him. Then again, this Phipps obviously was crazy, so he supposed Phil was right.

"Hey, Chief," Guilfoyle said from the doorway. "I think Wallace found something in the cellar."

Phil and Dan accompanied Guilfoyle back down the hall to the open cellar door. Wallace, on the stairs, was inspecting the walls.

"Slugs in the bricks," he said. "One here—one there."

"Caliber?" Dan asked.

"Small. Could be twenty-twos. They deformed on impact."

The Man in the Moon, of course, used a .22 revolver. Probably a Colt, a detail gleaned from the counterclockwise rifling twists detected on recovered rounds. Most firearms had right-handed barrels that produced clockwise twists; Colts were the most prominent exception.

"Shots fired in the cellar," Dan said slowly. "Maybe from his gun. That's why the hitter didn't finish him off. Henry put up a fight. Chased the intruder away."

"We can't be sure of that," Phil said.

"I think we can." Dan was thinking hard, working it out. "Because of the lights. The first officers said all the lights were on when they arrived. Why would Phipps go around switching on every light? He thought the intruder was still in the house, hiding. He had to clear the building. So he went room to room until he was sure the intruder was gone. Then he booked. And he left in a hurry, because if the assailant got away, he could be coming back."

"He," Phil said knowingly, "or she."

"That's right, Phil." Dan nodded, unsmiling. "Or she."

10

JONAH LAY ON the air mattress on the floor, his woman beside him in the dark. She'd taken another hit and dozed off, stoned and blissed out, a goofy smile riding her lips, eyelids fluttering with happy dreams.

She had no reason to lie awake, as he did. As far as she knew, the deal he'd done after leaving Peter Forrest's place was just another transaction. She had no way of knowing that with the sale of four blue pills to a special client, he had set things in motion—big things. Things that would keep a man up at night, even when he needed his rest.

People said you ought to count sheep when you were trying to nod off. He didn't much care for sheep. He tried counting pigs.

One little piggy ...

Two little piggies ...

That didn't help. It only got him more worked up. Christmas morning was only hours away, and he was as restless as a kid waiting to see what Santa would bring.

If counting didn't work, maybe memories would. Eyes closed, he thought about his life, the road he'd taken, a road that coiled like a snake—like that ninety-six-inch diamondback Cliff Gantry had killed once, but only after it gave him a bite that would've finished him if Jackson Harris hadn't sucked the venom from the wound. His life was as long as that snake, and as nasty; it slithered and looped in a twisting line from New Jersey to Georgia, to the town of Mandalay, a sprawl of trailer parks and Section 8 housing amid a wasteland of onion fields and powdery red clay. A nothing town, a patch of blight on the southern end of Toombs County. "Bloody Toombs," it was called—the badlands, the no-go zone, where human life was not held in high regard.

His mom LuEvelyn was a reedy hysterical female who got slapped around on a regular basis by his dad. Cody Stroud worked odd jobs some of the time and collected disability the rest of the time, though the exact nature of his disability was not entirely clear. He seemed healthy enough when he took his belt to his kids, which he did whenever he got tired of slugging his wife.

Jonah was the middle child of five. His two sisters were in trouble from the time they started bleeding between the legs—one knocked up at fourteen, the other in and out of the hospital for a string of half-assed suicide attempts. His brothers were no better, both of them mean and stupid, apt to pound on him for the hell of it, or to pound on anybody they pleased.

DFCS caseworkers were always breathing down their necks, yapping about an unstable home environment and inadequate parenting and at-risk kids. A couple of times they pulled Jonah out of the house and dumped him into foster care, but he always made himself so disagreeable that the foster parents gave up and he was sent back home.

He was in the fifth grade when he took to sneaking out of class and making his way to the blackwater swamp at the edge of the Altamaha. There, among the flickering spook lights and the croaking bullfrogs, he fell in with a different breed of people. Outlaws who cooked meth in secret shacks, and men who'd gone off the grid for reasons they didn't care to explain, and the crazy ones who talked to spirits and molded devil dolls out of river mud. He liked hanging with the swampers, dodging cottonmouths and gators, chewing Skoal and hawking gobs of spit into the dark waters, hearing stories of the

Seminole Indians and Chief Billy Bowlegs who'd fought white settlers in the Okefenokee.

He didn't much care about some of their other talk, all that jabber about the blacks and the Jews and the foreigners. None of that stuff mattered to him. The way he saw it, people were really all the same, by which he meant they were all liars, cheats, killers, and scum. Or would be, if given the opportunity. He believed in the absolute equality of mankind, with the provision that said equality was grounded in the utter shittiness of the species.

Over time he went from playing hooky to skipping school altogether. The DFCS people made him submit to a psychological evaluation, but though he was labeled antisocial this and borderline that, they couldn't hold him. At one point or another, they had him on Ritalin and Tofranil and Xanax, but none of it made a damn bit of difference. He was eleven when he started drinking, twelve when he started stealing, thirteen when he fucked his first woman, and fourteen when he killed his first man.

It was a matter of honor, as the best and cleanest killings always were. Deep in the swamp one evening he was taking a whiz behind a tangled mess of muscatine when old Buck Fargo, who hunted gators and ate their meat and sold their hides, caught him with his pecker hanging out. Up till then he'd figured he had an ordinary sized man-muscle, and no female had ever dared say otherwise, but Buck Fargo was of a contrary opinion. He found Jonah's equipment decidedly substandard, a point he made vividly clear in a series of ribald jokes and hurtful comparisons that continued for the next two weeks, whenever he was in the company of friends. Jonah put up with the ribbing long enough to let it die down, and when the matter had been forgotten by everyone but him, he crept up on Buck Fargo, asleep in his bedroll, and picked up Buck's rifle and shot him dead. He wrapped the body in the bedroll, weighted it down with stones and with the rifle—a fine gun, but too easily identifiable—and ferried the whole business to deep water in a pontoon boat. The hungry mud sucked down Buck's remains with an audible slurp.

The gator hunter was never missed by any man, nor by the gators, either. And Jonah got twenty-two dollars out of the deal, cash money, the entire contents of Buck Fargo's billfold.

To commemorate the kill, he incised a tattoo on his left bicep, painstakingly forming the outline of a swastika. That was a Nazi thing. He didn't know much about the Nazis, except that they'd laid down the law someplace overseas a few years back, and they were genuine badasses. Some of the guys in the swamp had told him the Nazis would make a comeback soon, right here in America, and bring back slavery so the goddamn blacks would be put in their place.

Jonah didn't know about that, and he didn't much care about the blacks or the Jews or the foreigners or any of the shit the others were always going on about; but he liked symbols of power, and the crazy slanted cross felt powerful to him.

His first murder had come easy, so naturally there were more. The next two he did for money, hiring himself out to locals too fainthearted to take care of business on their own. One such undertaking involved a fellow who'd won too much money at Texas Hold'em, inspiring rumors that he was a cheat. Whether or not the rumors were true was immaterial to sixteen-year-old Jonah Stroud, who lured the gambler into the swamp with the promise of 190 proof moonshine whiskey, then cut him up piece by piece—finger by finger, then ears, nose, and lips—feeding each separate body part to a brood of gators. The man was alive through all this, and still alive when Jonah gave the rest of him to the nest. He screamed real good even without his lips, and thrashed like fury, the black water boiling with blood.

By now Jonah Stroud was an outcast from his own family, seldom exchanging more than two words with them when he came home at all. He was a pariah in town, too. He knew what folks said about him. He'd heard Graf Driggler, proprietor of the local smoke shop, whisper to a customer that the Stroud clan was a litter of snakes and Jonah was the worst of them all, pure swamper trash, pig-ignorant, mean as a junkyard dog, crazy as a shithouse rat. Jonah let the insults lie for six whole months before defending his honor. One January evening, in the parking lot behind the store, he ambushed Graf Driggler with a crowbar and split his skull. Driggler lived, but only in what they called a vegetative state. Even so, Jonah was disappointed that he hadn't earned another swastika.

It was his second job as a hired killer that nearly got him in the soup. He made Jimbo Cucks disappear all right, just like he was paid to do, but it turned out Jimbo had a relative in the state capital who put heat on law enforcement. Sheriff Tipper started snooping around, and even the Georgia Bureau of Investigation got into the act. Fat old Tipper with his bloodshot eyes and veined nose didn't worry him much, but those GBI boys were pretty slick. Jonah figured it was only a matter of time until Jeff Barrow, the car dealer who'd hired him, was tricked or trapped into a confession. He precluded that eventuality by pouring Jeff Barrow a glass of bourbon laced with the ground-up roots of water hemlock, plentiful in the swamp. Convulsions and death followed. Jonah had hoped it would look like death by natural causes, but it didn't, and when two GBI men came sniffing at his family's doorstep, he decided it was time to light out. He was tired of Georgia anyway, weary of scraping clay off his shoes and being eaten alive by yellow flies.

He was nineteen when he blew out of town, hitching

rides until he was across the state line. By that stage of life, he'd scored four swastikas on his arm. His fifth came courtesy of a driver who picked him up at a rest stop in Virginia. The fellow—"Call me Gonzo, all my friends do"—drove a nice new Miata sports car. Jonah had a hankering for the car, so he took it for himself and left Gonzo on the roadside with a bloody gash where his throat had been. He arrived in New York City, ditching the Miata in a bad neighborhood where it was certain to be stolen again.

New York had been his ultimate destination all along. Bright lights, big city, you know? But it proved a disappointment. He was unaccustomed to crowds and closed-in spaces, and the people there were too sharp to fall for his usual scams. He tried some small-time dealing, but competition was fierce. He nearly got himself sliced open by a Mexican gang when he made the mistake of operating on their turf.

After six months of diminishing returns, he headed out of town in another stolen car, thinking vaguely of California. The car, an old beater he'd lifted because it had no alarm system or special locks on the doors, died on him in central Jersey, leaving him stranded in McKendree Park. This turned out to be a stroke of good fortune. McKendree Park was the right size and appropriately run-down and bedraggled; it had a lake and the ocean and proximity to wealthier towns whose residents would go slumming to purchase recreational drugs. There was competition, but nothing he couldn't handle. In sum, the burned-out beach town was about as close to Mandalay, Georgia, as he was likely to get.

So he stayed. That was fifteen years ago. He was thirty-six now but looked older, graying at the temples, his narrow face with its permanent stubble and squinty eyes giving him the appearance of a man who'd done hard time—as indeed he had, just shy of three years cooped up in a cage like a calf marked out for veal.

In the years before he'd served his stretch, he'd done two more killings, strictly for business reasons. It was never any big thing. For him, killing a human being was as easy as killing a cockroach or a dog. Funny thing, though; it had been only men so far. He had never yet killed himself a woman. He would get around to it one of these days. It was on his bucket list, you might say. Maybe Sofia. Sure, she was his lady, but love didn't last forever.

His left arm was all used up by now, the line of seven swastikas marching from bicep to wrist. He'd have to start on the right arm, which would mean using his left hand to ink the tats. Tricky, but doable. He didn't trust anyone else with the work.

It was a safe bet he'd already earned another one tonight, with two more to come soon. He was smiling over this prospect, drifting into dreams, when his cell phone came alive with "The Devil in I," his ringtone.

He fumbled for the phone and answered with a growly "Yeah?"

"Jonah. I'm on the run."

Then he was bolt upright, blinking into the dark. Beside him, Sofia didn't stir. "What'd you say, Preacher?"

"Someone's after me. A detective, a woman. She broke into my house."

Jonah had no idea what this garbled bullshit was about. A girl detective? Like in a damn comic book? "Sounds like we'd better meet up," he said.

"Yes. Exactly. As soon as possible. It's an emergency."

"All right, all right. Keep your britches on."

Jonah filled a flask with dark rum and a little something extra. He left Sofia asleep. Taking the van, he headed for the spot where he and Preacher always met, the holy church of Domani in downtown McKendree Park.

Things were in motion. Yes, indeed.

11

"BONNIE. HEY, BONNIE."

She came to and found Brad leaning over her, on his knees. It took her a moment to understand that she was flat on her belly on the floor.

"What happened to you?" he asked. "I was about to call nine-one-one."

"Don't do that." She pushed herself half upright, ignoring the shout of pain from her arm. "I'm okay."

He stood. "You don't look okay. You're bleeding all over the damn rug."

She had to smile. Brad hardly ever cursed. *Damn* was his idea of a swearword. Finding her like this had clearly knocked him sideways. He looked haggard and strung out, his wide eyes underscored by dark hollows. He couldn't stop staring at her bloodied sleeve.

"I got shot," she said, struggling to her feet. "But I can deal with it."

"You need to go to the hospital."

"No, I don't. A gunshot wound brings up a lot of questions I don't want to answer. Anyway, I know enough about field surgery to handle it on my own."

"Field surgery? Are you kidding me?"

"Assassin, heal thyself." She headed down the hall, working hard to maintain her equilibrium. "How'd you happen to find me?"

"I was just driving around. You know—just driving." He was in civilian clothes, off-duty tonight. Off-duty forever, probably. "I came by your place, and I saw the

Jeep out front and your front door standing open."

"Guess I forgot to close it."

"You didn't forget. You blacked out."

"Same difference."

"Who shot you?"

"Not important. The less you know, the better."

"As usual."

"I'm a woman of mystery. You knew that when you signed on."

Halfway down the hall, she detoured into her only bathroom. She needed to irrigate the wound, then wrap it in fresh bandages. She was pretty sure she could remain upright for the duration.

"Dan called me," she said as she turned on the bathroom sink, running the water lukewarm.

"What did he say?"

"Nothing much. Generalized threats and put-downs."

"Did he say I'm out of a job?"

"Didn't mention it," she lied. No point in bringing it up until she'd decided what to do about Dan's ultimatum.

Brad dropped his gaze. "It doesn't matter. Of course I'm fired. It couldn't be any other way."

She tested the water with her finger. It was warm enough. She began to work herself loose from the hoodie, taking her time because it wasn't easy.

"How long ago did this happen?" he asked.

"The phone call or the gunshot?"

"Gunshot."

"I dunno. What time is it?"

"One thirty."

"Then about an hour ago."

"So I guess you could have taken my calls. Why didn't you?"

"I was already involved in this whole other thing."

"Too involved to talk to me?"

"I can only deal with one shitstorm at a time."

"I think you can deal with whatever you want to deal with."

"Can we have this conversation later? We're playing doctor now."

She succeeded in freeing herself from the hoodie. Her fingers fumbled at the knots in the tourniquet, making little headway. Brad took over and cut the knots with a penknife. Naturally he carried one. He was such a Boy Scout.

The tourniquet came away, exposing the wound in all its gory glory.

"Good God," Brad muttered.

"Didn't break the bone," she said. "Chewed up some muscle, that's all."

"Through-and-through?"

"Don't think so. Can't find an exit hole."

"Sometimes they're not where you'd think. A bullet can travel."

She almost asked him how he would know. He'd never been shot. But that wasn't fair. She'd never been shot, either, before now.

"Help me get my top off. But don't get any ideas."

"Right now you're not exactly turning me on." His eyes were fixed on the dark goo leaking like molasses from her puckered bicep. "You sure you want to stick with this sideline of yours?"

"Just help me outta this."

He assisted her in drawing the pullover above her head. Together they checked her body for damage.

"No exit wound," he said.

"Yeah, that's what I figured. The round's still in me. It's a twenty-two. Didn't travel far."

"How do you know it's a twenty-two?"

"Woman's intuition."

"I didn't even know you were working a case like this."

"It came up kinda sudden. Sort of a rush job."

"Who was—" He stopped himself.

"The target?" she finished for him.

"Never mind." It was the kind of thing he normally didn't want to know. "So ... we have to take out the bullet, right?"

"Nope. It stays right where it is."

"Is that safe?"

"Safer than rooting around for it, yeah."

She'd seen a million movies and TV shows where the heroic cop or the ruthless gangster dug out a bullet between grimaces and swigs of hard liquor. It was a Hollywood thing, and like most Hollywood things, it was bullshit. In real life, extracting an embedded round would do more harm than good.

"I guess you know best," Brad said dubiously.

"Always do. There's plenty of people walking around with shrapnel in their bodies. Anyhow, sooner or later the bullet will probably nose its way to the surface and come out on its own."

"Unless you get lead poisoning first."

"I plan to die of something else long before that. Hold my hand while I irrigate the wound."

He entwined her fingers with his, and she dipped her bare arm under the stream of water from the tap. It hurt. It really, seriously *hurt*, with deep head-spinning pain.

"Shouldn't you use disinfectant or something?" Brad asked. "Like, hydrogen peroxide?"

Her hand must be shaking pretty hard, because she could feel his clasped hand shaking in sympathy.

"Water's just as good." She did her best to hold her voice steady. "Better, in fact. It doesn't do as much damage to the soft tissue."

"What about germs?"

"A hot round is pretty much self-sterilizing. Some threads from my clothes might've got in there. But you can never clean out all the germs. The best bet is to wash the wound clean of obvious debris, dress it, and pop some antibiotics."

"You have antibiotics?"

"Yeah, amoxicillin." Obtained illegally, of course. "And painkillers."

"Oh, yeah?" His head tilted. "OxyContin? Percocet?"

"Don't sweat it, Walsh. I may be a hot mess, but I'm not hooked on hillbilly heroin. I'll use Tylenol."

He frowned. "That won't be enough."

"Sure it will. I have a high threshold. It's how I can live with myself even though I'm a total pain in the ass."

By now she'd spent enough time with her arm under the faucet. Gratefully she removed it, then hunted in the clutter of her medicine cabinet for bandages. In the mirror, Brad's reflection, looking even more frazzled then before, wiped back the sweaty mess of his hair.

"I really think you should see a doctor," the reflection told her.

"Bad idea. A doctor would want to know how I got shot."

"Exactly how *did* you get shot?"

"You really want me to tell you?"

Brad considered it seriously. "Yes," he said with decision. "I do."

She turned to face him. "I found out the identity of the Man in the Moon. I went to his house. He got the jump on me, and things turned ugly."

He did a slow take as the information registered. "The Man in the ...? Oh. Oh, jeez ..."

"Kind of an interesting twist, huh?"

"Jeez," he said again. He shut his eyes. "So that's how you know it's a twenty-two."

"Bingo."

"How the heck did you learn who he is?"

"That's privileged info."

"Have you been investigating on your own or something?"

"I can't go into it, Walsh. Sorry."

He shook his head with the woeful expression of a

patient who'd just received a bad prognosis. "You went after a serial killer? And ... he shot you?"

"He got lucky, that's all."

"You could have been another statistic."

"Yeah, number six."

"Number seven."

"Seven, right." She shrugged, instantly regretting it because it hurt her arm. "Hey, we're all statistics in the end."

The bandages weren't in the medicine cabinet. She searched for them in the storage space under the sink.

"Who ... who is he?" Brad asked.

"Henry Phipps. Lives right here in town. Know him?"

"I—I don't think so. Did he survive the encounter?"

"Unfortunately, yeah."

"Then you need to tell somebody in authority before he makes a break for it," Brad said.

"I think it's too late for that. I have a feeling he cleared out after I made my exit."

"Yeah. Yeah, I guess he would."

"Anyway, it's not exactly in my interest for the cops to find him."

"Are you saying you want him to remain at large?"

"Well, I kinda want *me* to remain at large, and that could be problematic if he's captured alive. He has no reason not to give me up."

"He got a look at you? He knows you?"

"Yes, and yes." Henry hadn't remembered her name, but he'd known her as a local PI. If he fingered her—and he would—it would be easy-peasy to match her blood to the samples left in the house.

There was also the little matter of having disappointed Armin Petrossian, a man who probably didn't handle disappointment well. The one point he'd insisted on was that Henry Phipps could not be arrested. If the police picked him up, Petrossian would be unhappy.

Yes, things were definitely not going her way.

She found the box of bandages at the rear of the compartment, behind bleach and ammonia and other cleaning supplies she never used. She opened it up and handed him the spool. "Wind off about two feet of that, okay?"

He unspooled the bandage and tore it free. With his help, she secured it to her arm, closing the wound.

"If that's the way it is," Brad said slowly, "you've got to find Phipps first. Before law enforcement does."

"Easier said than done."

"Well, what *are* you going to do?"

"I'll figure something out."

"You don't have any leads?"

"I have squat, Walsh. Satisfied?"

"Sure, Bonnie. Sure, I'm real satisfied."

He was peeved. She couldn't blame him. She'd been treating him curtly, almost like a child. It was something she had a tendency to do, because, to be honest, she did think of him as an innocent, a boy unschooled in the ways of the world.

"Look, Walsh"—she tried to find some better words—"I appreciate your concern and all, but I'm a big girl, and I always find a way out. I'll do it again. Okay?"

"Okay," he said reluctantly.

"Now could you look in the fridge and find me a beer?"

"A beer?"

"Yeah. Or look in the cabinet and get me some scotch. Which would be better."

"I'll get you a beer," he said, as she knew he would.

12

JONAH STROUD TRAMPED through the tall grasses under the hooked moon, slouching toward Domani. He wondered if Henry would bring the dog. He hoped not. He fuckin' hated dogs.

Around him lay desolate emptiness, cold and still in the post-midnight dark. McKendree Park had been a busy resort until the summer of 1970, when it burned. Riots. Blacks or hippies or something—Jonah wasn't sure. It was long before his time. He knew only that somebody's hot sweltering rage had ignited in a whoosh of flame, the Victorian hotels and rental cottages serving as so much tinder, leaving McKendree Park as dead as any ghost town in the desert, but without the tumbleweeds.

Over the years, some neighborhoods had been rebuilt, but the heart of the town, just two blocks from the beach, was still a scorched-earth ruin of shuttered buildings, razed ground, and the four-story skeleton of Domani, looming over the weeds like a steel dinosaur.

Domani was planned as a luxury hotel and commercial center, the first step in a hoped-for revival of the town's fortunes. The girders went up ten years ago. Then the money disappeared; construction was halted, the girders left to rust in the salt air. *Domani*, a billboard outside the property declared in faded letters, *is Italian for tomorrow*. But in McKendree Park, tomorrow never came.

The lots around Domani were a blank expanse of crabgrass and dandelions. The land, untended, had returned to nature. Rabbits scampered among shriveled husks of shrubs. Field mice rustled, living their secret lives.

Here and there were other forms of life, unseen but suggested by signs and portents. Shape-shifting flickers in a hand-dug firepit, a glimmer of moonlight on a shiny black tarpaulin stretched into a makeshift tent, the sweetish waft of marijuana smoke.

Jonah didn't know how many lost people made their homes here, in the abandoned lots, emerging in daylight to cadge dollar bills, returning at dusk, cowering in their hidey-holes when police beamed spotlights through the tattered hurricane fencing that kept no one out.

Dozens, probably. He had spotted only a few. Most were as skilled at taking cover as the rabbits and the mice.

Domani pressed closer, crowding out the stars. Damp earth gave way to a concrete slab as he stepped up to the great steel pile. He passed between girders into the interior, unpartitioned, wide and airy, soaring like a cathedral, the crosshatched beams making a mirrored infinity of crucifixes. His footsteps echoed.

He scanned the darkness. Under a blue quilt of shadows huddled a solitary squatter, curled against the cold.

Irritated, he kicked the sleeper awake.

"Fuck off," Jonah ordered, his voice a mean dog's growl. "Outta here."

There was no arguing with that voice. It was the voice of a man who had killed and who would kill again. The squatter fled, nodding submissively, hugging his blanket to his waist. Jonah watched him shrink into a pixel of darkness.

He bided his time, alone. Well, alone in this part of Domani, anyway. Another part lay below his feet, a vast unfinished basement meant to be a parking garage. There were always people down there, permanent dwellers in the depths. Mole people, he called them. Their belowground world was like the slimy interior of a garbage disposal; the mole people, chunks of refuse too stubborn to be chewed up and flushed away. Scabrous, toothless, pallid, crazy, stinking of filth, bleeding from open sores, copulating in corners, sleeping in their own shit.

Jonah knew that world. He ventured down there occasionally. Slumming, he liked to think of it. It was where he'd met Henry, who came here to preach to those lost souls. He hollered his tirades at the denizens of the dark, working himself up into fits of passion. He didn't seem to mind their lack of response. He just wanted an audience, any audience.

Jonah had responded, though. He and Sofia were the only two among the faithful who were really, you know, faithful. In their own way.

Not that Sofia knew anything. She was a cunt. He didn't mean that in any pejorative sense. It was just, well—that's all she was to him. A convenient place to put his pecker. He never could go without sex for long. Even in prison he couldn't do without it. He'd been a buttfucker, purely by necessity, not because he liked it. Always a giver, never a receiver. Playing the catcher's position was for women and fags. Nobody ever gave him a goddamn rectal exam.

Except for that one time, when he couldn't save himself. One time when he took it up the rear, two men holding him down while the third punched his way inside, spearing him all the way to the navel. And everybody laughing.

Laughing.

He shut his eyes against the memory of his humiliation. He didn't even blame the other cons. They were just doing what came naturally. He himself had done the same to weaker men. But the ones who'd put him there, put him in a cage—them, he did blame.

And yeah, Jonah Stroud was the sort of man to hold a grudge.

He wished he had more of Peter Forrest's brandy. The bottle he'd finished was already wearing off. The flask in his back pocket was a temptation. But it was for Henry.

Speak of the devil. In the distance, a slim silhouette appeared. Jonah recognized the stoop-shouldered stance and hurrying gait.

No dog. Preacher had come alone.

He waited, stone silent, in a deep corner of Domani, erased by shadow, until Henry appeared on the threshold, his gaze blindly panning the blackness.

"I'm here, bro." Jonah's whisper echoed among the steel pillars.

Henry nodded. "Of course you are. In the very belly of the whale."

Quickly he closed the distance between them. He wore a loose winter coat thrown on over an untucked shirt, and big boots like clown shoes.

"It's gone bad," Henry said. "Someone's after me."

"The law?"

"No. I told you on the phone."

"You wasn't making no sense on the phone. Hey, you didn't call from your house, did you?"

"No, I used a payphone in Miramar."

"That's good. Real good."

Jonah's cell was a burner, a throwaway. Calls made to that number couldn't be connected to him, but they could perhaps tell the authorities the approximate location of his phone. Cell-tower triangulation and all that crap. It was safer for Henry to place his calls from a phone that would never be traced.

He drew the flask from his pocket and unscrewed the cap. He handed it to Henry. "Here. Take some."

"What is it?"

"Dark rum. Quality stuff."

"I don't need alcohol."

"I think right now you do."

Reluctantly, Henry took a cautious sip, then another. Jonah watched him, pleased. He enjoyed the drink vicariously, imagined the slow burn like a hot wire down his throat, then the spreading heat in his belly.

"Now tell it to me," Jonah said when Henry returned the flask. "And tell it slow."

"A private detective found me. A woman. She was hired by a mobster, she said. A drug kingpin, supposedly."

"Why?"

"To avenge one of the dead, it seems."

"Some drug guy hired a lady PI to bring you in?"

"No. He hired her to shoot me."

Jonah whistled. "No shit. She a hitter, this girl?"

"I guess so. She must be. But I heard her coming. Things got ... complicated. Anyway, I shot her. I found blood in the bedroom, the hallway—blood all over. I got her, all right. I got her good."

Jonah heard cold satisfaction in the words. "She dead?"

"I don't know. She escaped from the house. What became of her after that ..."

"If she's dead, you got nothing to run from."

"Her employer will send others after me. She told me so, and I don't think she was lying."

Jonah studied Henry's face in a stripe of moonlight. The man looked older than he had three months ago. The work had aged him. "How'd this mob guy know it was you, anyway?"

"Who can say? Someone must have figured it out, as you did. But this was someone who didn't understand. Who just wanted his blood money. His thirty pieces of silver." He choked out a dry chuckle. "Ironic, isn't it?"

"So what's the plan, Preacher?"

He knew Henry didn't like that name. But it suited him so much better than the Man in the Moon.

"This is where it ends for me," Henry said. "I'm a hunted man. I was fortunate to escape, but my luck can't hold. Still, I can go out the right way, and I can count on you to continue the work."

"You got the testimony?"

Henry unbuttoned his overcoat and extracted a bulging manila envelope from an inside pocket. "It's not finished. But I've done what I could."

Jonah took the envelope and wedged it under his belt at the small of his back.

"It will need to be typed up," Henry said.

"Sofia can type." It was one of her few skills.

"And it must be put online, however you do that."

"It's easy. I'll do it through a proxy so it can't be traced. Then the whole world will read it."

Henry nodded, savoring the thought. "That's what we need. To wake up the world. Blow the cover off the whole goddamned thing. That's what it's all about. What it's always been about."

Jonah hesitated. "When you say you're going out the right way ..."

"A final act of violence. A church on Christmas morning. I'll kill as many as I can. That will get their attention, won't it? And the symbolism—one of *his* houses of worship, don't you see? It will be like spitting in his stupid face. The perfect way to stamp an exclamation mark on our message."

A slow minute ticked by. Jonah handed over the flask again. "Take some more."

"I don't need it," Henry said, but he seemed less grudging about it than before.

"We all need it sometimes."

Henry tipped the flask to his mouth and took a good-sized swallow. "So ... what do you think of my exit strategy?"

"It's fucked up, Preacher. It's fuckin' bogus."

Without the hits off the flask, Henry might have taken this criticism badly. He was unaccustomed to being questioned by his followers. As it was, he only blinked. "What are you talking about?"

"Look, I get it, okay? You got the divine light in you, and I don't. Granted. But I know people. And people ain't gonna go for no Christmas massacre. It's a big turnoff."

"I've been taking lives for months," he said petulantly.

"One at a time. Nice and orderly, a man on a mission. People can respect that. It scares 'em, makes 'em shit their pants, but they respect it. You're a lone killer going one-on-one with his prey—that's Hannibal Lecter shit right there, and he got his own TV show. America loves a killer like that."

"No one loves me, Jonah."

"You are wrong, sir," Jonah said with slow precision. "You are very wrong. People talk about you, they see the body count piling up, and they are impressed. You're a shark, a silent killer, sleek and fast. Open fire in a church, and it all goes south."

"Why? I see no difference."

"All the difference in the world, bro. All of a sudden you ain't Son of Sam no more. You're one of them school shooters, or fuckin' Jihad Joe driving his pickup into a crowd, or some dipshit who lets loose with an AK in a shopping mall. Losers. Nobody respects 'em. Nobody remembers their damn names."

"I don't care if they remember my name."

"But you *do* care about having a receptive audience, so the testimony don't fall on deaf ears. Right now you're in the catbird seat, my man. This church thing—it'll fuck everything up. Turn 'em all against you, so they won't even read your words. You'll have no fuckin' credibility." He stretched out the last word into five distinct syllables.

"You honestly think so?"

"Scout's honor, Preach. You do this thing, and you are throwing it all away." He leaned closer, lowering his voice. "Where do you think you got the notion, anyhow?"

"I—I don't know. It just came to me. It seemed right."

"I'll tell you where. You got it from *him*." He jerked a thumb skyward. "The faker upstairs. The phony-ass pretend god who's starting to sweat because you're turning up the heat. You think it's a coincidence, you almost getting popped on Christmas? Fuckin' *Christmas*, of all days? He wanted you to go on the run tonight and make your last stand in the morning. He's playing with you, Preach."

"His ways are subtle," Henry whispered, staring past Jonah into the void.

"And you almost fell for it. Good thing you called me."

"But then—what do I do? I can't go on. I'll be caught."

"You'll hitch a ride with me, is what you'll do. I got a place where you can hole up. You, me, and Sofia. It's safe—totally off the grid. No one'll find you. Guaran-damn-teed."

"Am I supposed to just run and hide?"

"Call it a tactical retreat. So you can fight again another day."

"There will be no other days. I'm done." Henry exhaled a heavy sigh. "It is finished."

"Wrong again, Preacher. Dead wrong." Jonah draped an arm over the older man's shoulder, leading him forward into the night. "Come along now, sir. There's still more work for you to do."

13

BONNIE DRANK THE beer—okay, chugged it—and popped antibiotics and Tylenol, neither of which was supposed to be taken with alcohol. But hell, beer hardly counted.

She got rid of Brad with the excuse that she needed to rest. This was true in the sense that she really did need to rest. It was also a lie in the sense that she had no intention of doing so. Not yet.

She'd already pulled on a clean blouse, and now she donned the coat she'd worn during her visit to Petrossian's house. Not ideal for skulking, but at least it wasn't all bloody and torn up. She had to struggle to get the damn thing on over her arm, which was already going stiff, but with a good deal of creative cursing she managed it.

The hit kit went back inside her purse. She snugged the fedora on her head, left the duplex, and climbed into the Jeep, still parked at the curb.

Next stop, Henry Phipps's house.

Yeah, she was going back. By now Henry had probably cleared out, but there was a chance he was still there. Maybe it hadn't been a footstep she'd heard when she was leaving. Maybe he was trapped in the cellar with a broken leg. Maybe he'd even shot himself, knowing his game was up. Anything was possible. She had to know.

Even if he was gone, at least she might be able to clean up the blood before anyone knew he'd gone on the run. The blood was one of her biggest problems right now. She'd never bled all over a crime scene before. It was the kind of thing that could put her in the hoosegow real easy.

She was pulling away from the curb when headlights expanded behind her. A Buick Regal slid to a stop about a foot from the Jeep's rear bumper. She knew that car. Dan Maguire's personal ride.

A moment later, the door opened, and the man himself stepped out from behind the wheel.

Damn. This was turning into her worst Christmas ever, beating out the one she'd spent as a teenage runaway sleeping on a bench in Grand Central Station.

She put the Jeep into park and waited as Dan approached. When he got close, she cranked down the side window, leaning out.

"Hey, Dan. How's it hanging?" She held up a hand. "Rhetorical question."

He squinted at her, puffing clouds of frozen breath. He was in civilian clothes, and his hair stood up in the funny way that spoke of interrupted sleep.

"Merry Christmas, Parker. Going somewhere?"

"You know me, always on the move."

"We need to have a talk. I don't suppose you'll invite me into your home."

"Already got enough cockroaches. Don't need one more."

"Then how about joining me in my car?"

"I dunno, Dan. My mother taught me never to accept rides from strange men."

"Your mother was a petty criminal, like your father. I doubt either one of them taught you anything at all."

"There's that Christmas spirit."

"We're not going for a ride. We just need a place to sit that's out of the cold." He stalked off without waiting for reply.

Dan was only blowing smoke about her parents, of course. He suspected, but didn't know for sure, that she was the daughter of Tom and Rebecca Parker, who'd been shot to death in a Pennsylvania motel. She'd never confirmed it to him. She wasn't going to talk about her past with Dan. Hell, she didn't even like talking to him about the weather.

She took a moment to remove the gun and silencer from her purse, stashing them under the seat. Not the most ingenious hiding place, but if by any chance Dan decided to take her in, she didn't want one of Mama Blessing's black-market firearms on her person.

Her arm seemed stiffer than before as she walked to the idling Regal. The car was a few years old now. She remembered how, when it was brand-new, she'd dumped a whole mess of dogshit into the interior. Good times.

"Smells funny in here," she said as she slipped into the passenger seat, shutting the door. "You get a dog recently?"

Dan only smiled. "Where were you heading off to?"

"Donut run."

"At this hour?"

"Come on, Dan. You're a cop. You know there's never a bad time for a donut."

"Sounds implausible."

"Okay, truth is, I've been moonlighting as a lap dancer at the Tuxedo Club."

"That club closes at two."

"Got me there, Dan. I just can't put one over on you."

He chuckled like an indulgent parent. "You keep trying to push my buttons, but it's not working. I have the upper hand, and we both know it."

"So you dropped by to gloat?"

"I guess maybe I did."

"Terrific. I'm lighting a cigarette now. If you don't like it, you can arrest me."

"Go ahead, light up."

She was mildly surprised by Dan's hospitality, and more than mildly suspicious of it. "I want to quit," she said as she flicked her lighter. "Even tried nicotine gum for a while."

"How long a while?"

"Two, three hours."

"You should kick the habit. It's bad for your health."

Solicitude for her well-being? This was getting weird. "Yeah, well, I don't foresee a long life for me."

"Then why try to quit?"

"Brad doesn't like it."

"Oh. I see."

She drew smoke into her lungs and expelled it in a feathery swirl. "It's not just a fling, you know. We're serious about each other. If that matters."

"Of course it matters." He let a beat of time pass. "It makes it worse."

"How so?"

"A fling might be almost excusable. He's tasting the forbidden fruit. But if he's serious, then it means he has no moral or ethical qualms about being with someone like you."

"What's the difference between moral and ethical, anyway? I've never been clear on that."

"Me neither. Let's just say an officer of the law shouldn't be sleeping with the enemy."

"Is that what I am? The enemy?"

Dan nodded. "The enemy of due process, law and order—civilization, in a word."

"I never knew I was important enough to pose a threat to civilization."

"You personally? Maybe not. What you represent—yes."

"The whole vigilante thing, is that it?"

"That's right, Parker. The vigilante thing."

She sucked down more smoke. "In a perfect world, you'd be right. In the real world, sometimes a person has to go outside the law."

"Does Brad believe that?"

"No. I'm sure he doesn't."

"But he's keeping company with you, anyway."

Keeping company. That sounded like something her grandmother might have said, though she couldn't be sure, because she'd never known her grandmother. "You can be in a relationship with someone without seeing eye to eye on everything."

"True. But you have to see eye to eye on the big things. And when you're a duly appointed peace officer, upholding the law is a big thing."

Bonnie couldn't argue. The son of a bitch had a point. "Is that why you're here? To talk about me and Brad?"

"Partly. How did he take it when you told him about our conversation?"

"He left my office right after you did. I haven't talked to him since."

"That's probably a lie."

"Yeah, probably. I mean, given that I said it, there's a good chance."

"Have you made up your mind about my ultimatum?"

"You gave me till the day after Christmas."

"So I did." He paused, studying her, that smug smile fixed on his dumb face. "If things work out the way I think they might, you won't be leaving, anyway."

Now they were getting down to it. The real reason for his visit. She took another drag before answering. "Is that right? Which things are those?"

"Recent developments."

"Wow, you're being so mysterious. I'd almost think I was in trouble, if I didn't know you're a total asshole."

"I'm a total asshole who's got your number." His smile slipped momentarily. That hadn't come out the way he'd hoped.

"Well, you're half right." Bonnie put her hand on the door. "We done here?"

"No." The word came out too sharply. Despite what he'd said, she could tell she was pissing him off. "We haven't even started."

"Well, get to it, buddy. You're using a lot of words, but you're not saying anything."

He took a breath. "I just came from a crime scene at 626 Lake Avenue."

So the police had gotten there. Henry was either dead or in custody. Dead would be good. In custody—not good. And it looked like her chance of cleaning up the DNA evidence was kaput.

"Is that supposed to mean something to me?" she asked.

"I'm thinking it might."

"You're thinking wrong. If there's an active scene, shouldn't you be there at least pretending to do your job?"

"The state police have taken over. It's their scene now."

"Way to pass the buck."

"It's standard procedure in a case like this."

"What kind of case is that?"

"A big one, Parker." He leaned back in his seat, looking much too comfortable. "I may as well give you the details. It'll be all over the news, anyway. The Trenton office leaks like a sieve."

"I'm listening."

"A local man named Henry Phipps has gone missing."

Missing. Okay, then. He hadn't been caught, which meant he couldn't tell the authorities about the blonde woman who'd been hired to kill him. So far, so good.

"He appears to have been wounded," Dan added. "There's blood all over his house."

"Maybe he cut himself shaving."

He ignored that. "Someone gained access to the house through a window. At least two shots were fired. Phipps fled the scene shortly after."

"Sounds like some pretty heavy shit for Brighton Cove."

"Definitely. And it made me think of you."

"I'm always on your mind, huh?"

"When there's violence going down, your name does tend to occur to me."

"So what's your theory? Wait, let me guess. I tried to whack this Phipps guy and botched the job."

"I like how you cut to the chase."

"And just why would I be going after some schmo I've never heard of?"

"Phipps isn't just some schmo. Items found in the house link him to the Man in the Moon killings."

She gave her best imitation of surprise. "You found the moon man?"

"That's how it looks." His head swiveled to face her. "The kind of person that somebody might have wanted put out of the way without all the fuss of a trial."

"In other words, you're saying I was hired to clip him."

"Why not? You're a hired gun, aren't you? A paid assassin?"

"That's the kind of question my attorney always advises me not to answer."

"You don't have to answer it. We both know what you are. If you hadn't wriggled out of that Streinikov situation, you'd be doing hard time right now."

"If wishes were horses ..." She'd forgotten how it went. "I dunno, there'd be a lot more horses, I guess."

"Stick to the point. This situation has you written all over it."

"Like hell it does. Sounds like whoever went after Phipps messed up bad. I don't mess up." As lies went, this was a pretty good one, she thought.

"Everybody makes mistakes," Dan said placidly. "Even you."

She tried a different tack. "A professional hitter wouldn't just wound the target and leave. That's not how it's done."

"You would know."

"Anybody who's seen a Quentin Tarantino movie would know."

"You might leave if the target was shooting back. The slugs recovered from the scene look like twenty-twos. I'm betting the state guys will match them with the rounds used in Henry's known kills. That means he was the one who fired those shots. You winged him but didn't finish him off. He took cover in the cellar—maybe that's where he kept his gun—and started firing back. You couldn't get to him, so you left, hoping he would bleed out. He didn't. At least, not in the house."

"Sounds like I had a busy night. I must be exhausted."

Leave it to Dan to put the pieces together just a little bit wrong. He was pretty close to the truth, though.

She wrapped her lips around the cig again, sucking on it like a pacifier.

"You know what I think, Parker? I think that when I arrived, you were about to head back to Henry Phipps's house."

"Why would I do that?"

"Sometimes criminals return to the scene."

"Did you read that in *The Big Book of Police Investigating*?"

"If Phipps was your target, you'd need to confirm the kill. You'd want to go back in and see if he'd bled out by now."

"You have a morbid imagination."

"Of course, there's another possibility altogether."

"This ought to be good."

"It's occurred to me that maybe Phipps wasn't the bleeder. Maybe the intruder took a bullet."

Suddenly his impromptu visit made sense. "And you swung by to see if I was ambulatory?"

"Something like that."

"Sorry to disappoint you, but I'm A-okay."

"I can't really be sure of that without a visual inspection."

"You're looking right at me."

"I mean an inspection of what's under that coat."

"Whoa, baby. You want me to strip for you? I think you've been hitting the eggnog a little too hard."

"I can have a female officer conduct the search."

"Not without a warrant, Danno."

"I thought you'd say that. You know, we'll probably be able to access Phipps's medical records later today. His blood type may rule him out as the source of the stains."

"That still doesn't do fuck-all to tie me to the scene."

"True. But there could be a way. It's funny how many night owls are looking out their windows. And there are houses with security cameras aimed at the street. They get things on tape—or on disk, or whatever it is. Needless to say, my people are canvassing the neighborhood now."

"Santa's little helpers."

She wasn't too worried. Someone might have seen her leaving the house via the front door, but the hoodie would have made her unrecognizable.

"Then there's Phipps himself," Dan went on. "He can't run for long. Once he's in custody, he can tell us who went after him tonight."

"Because nocturnal assassins always introduce themselves. That's just common courtesy."

"I'm not saying he'll know your name. A description will suffice. There aren't that many females in your line of work."

"Yeah, that glass ceiling is tough to crack."

"So you see, I have options. It may take a few days. But I'll find a way to link you to Henry Phipps. Then I'll get a warrant. And I'll serve it personally."

"Thanks for the heads-up. Now I have plenty of time to dispose of incriminating evidence."

"I don't think you can make a gunshot wound disappear."

"If I'd been shot, don't you think I'd be in a hospital by now?"

"Not if you thought you could handle it on your own. And that's what you always think. But in this case, you're wrong. Why not cut a deal? I'll go easier on you if you cooperate."

"I'd rather cooperate with a friendly clown who lives in the sewer."

"Play it your way. I just hope you heal fast."

"You're setting yourself up for a big disappointment. But I guess you're used to that."

"I don't think so. I think I've really got you this time. I already exposed your tawdry little affair with Walsh. That was good. But this is much better. If things work out, I'll have taken two homicidal sociopaths off the street. The Man in the Moon—and you."

She stared at him, amazed. "You don't really put me in the same class with Henry Phipps?"

"On the contrary. That's exactly how I classify you."

"You can't seriously think I'd go after innocent people."

"Why not? You're a born killer. You have zero respect for human life. You and Phipps could be twins. Except you're worse. He, at least, seems to think he's doing God's work, or something. You're just in it for money and thrills."

She kept looking for some sign that he was playing with her, messing with her head. "Look, Dan, we both know I've been involved in some dicey business. But whatever I may or may not have done, I have standards. I'm not anything like the Man in the freakin' Moon. I don't blow random nobodies away for kicks."

"How many people died at Streinikov's estate?"

"They were mobsters, for Christ's sake. Made men in a criminal syndicate. And they tried to kill me. Shit, they wanted to prune my lady parts."

"So you say."

"Are you telling me Streinikov wasn't dirty?"

"I'm saying *you're* dirty, Parker. Dirtier than anyone

knows, except me."

She crushed out her cigarette with an angry stab. "Seriously, you need help. You need to get yourself into a nice warm straitjacket."

"I'm not the one who's crazy, Parker. And I don't buy this idea that you have moral standards. Maybe you did once, but murder gets easier the more you do it. After a while you get a lot less choosy. Eventually you don't have to think twice about it. You just pull the trigger. Like the Zodiac Killer or the Son of Sam. Or the Man in the Moon."

"Fuck you, Dan." She reached for the door. "I don't have to listen to this fucking bullshit."

"You seem upset."

She was. He'd rattled her. And all of a sudden her arm was hurting like a bastard. "Unless you're going to arrest me, this conversation's over."

"I will arrest you, but not tonight. Soon."

"Yeah, good luck with that." She popped the door, letting in a blast of winter air. "You know what? I hope Santa leaves a big steaming pile of dogshit right under your Christmas tree."

"Don't count on it, Parker. I have a feeling I'm going to get exactly what I want this year."

14

THE SLAM OF the Buick's door echoed after her as she marched back to the Jeep. Seated behind the wheel, she waited until Dan's car glided away from the curb, his gaze fixed on her as he drifted by.

When he was gone, she backed up the Jeep and nosed it into the garage. It appeared she wouldn't be visiting Henry Phipps's house, after all. He was long gone, and the place was crowded with cops.

She killed the engine, crammed the hit kit back into her purse, and returned to the duplex. She dumped the purse on a random table and her coat on the floor, then flopped down on the couch, staring at the ceiling, suddenly worn out. It had all been too much—Dan walking into her office, the meeting with Petrossian, getting shot, being interrogated.

And yet that wasn't it. It was what Dan had said to her at the end, the stuff about her and Phipps. Two homicidal sociopaths.

It wasn't the first time he'd called her a sociopath, but until now she'd thought it was mostly bluster. She'd never even been sure he knew what the word meant. Tonight he'd left no doubt. He saw her as no different from the Man in the Moon, an out-and-out psycho who killed for no rational reason at all.

Okay, but so what? Why should she give a rat's ass about his stupid opinion? She didn't. Obviously.

Eyes shut, she thought of the talk she'd had with Frank Kershaw on Thanksgiving. She'd visited him at

Green Arbor, a rest home in Pilgrim Grove. She remembered noticing for the first time how old he'd gotten. He was too skinny, and he had trouble walking, and he never remembered to trim his nose hairs. They'd grown thick and bristly. It was like he was hiding a couple of porcupines in his nostrils.

He was still sharp, though. And no one understood her better. He knew her secrets, and she knew his—or some of them, anyway. She knew that he had been Frank Hatch in an earlier life, that he'd specialized in forging documentation for people who needed a change of identity, and that he'd committed murder once.

"You're not going to get out, are you?" he asked after they'd finished a depressing meal of dry turkey and canned cranberry sauce.

"Don't think so, Frank."

For years he'd been advising her to quit while she was ahead. She'd beaten the odds too often; her luck couldn't hold forever. He was right, too. But she couldn't. Not because she had some hero complex, some noble desire to save widows and orphans. It was just that she didn't have anything else to do. She had to make money somehow, and she couldn't see herself in the typing pool, if only because she couldn't type. And did they even have typing pools anymore?

"I know you won't," he said, licking his lips. That was something he'd taken to doing a lot, a side effect of some meds they were feeding him. "But if this is the life you're stuck with, you need to keep one thing in mind."

That was when he'd warned her about crossing lines. Some you could cross, but with others, there was no way back.

Taking a job from Armin Petrossian had meant crossing a line. Even though she hadn't accepted any money. Even though getting rid of a serial killer would be a public service. Yeah, even given all that, she had still agreed to do his bidding. She'd let him get his hooks into her. And maybe she wouldn't be able to get free.

She slid lower on the couch, her head humming.

And then there was the Man in the Moon. Dan said she was just like him. His twin. And maybe Dan was right. More right even than he knew.

Step up to the victim, squeeze the trigger, walk away ...

Henry Phipps had done that. And so had she. And it had been easy.

Easier every time. Take tonight. She'd treated the job as an errand to be dispatched as quickly as possible. Like picking up a carton of milk from 7-Eleven. In and out like Seal Team Six, right? How very efficient.

Maybe it shouldn't be so goddamned easy to take a life, any life, even the life of the Man in the Moon. Maybe it shouldn't be treated so casually. She had named her detective agency Last Resort, only partly as a joke. But these days, doing a hit didn't seem like a last resort anymore. Sometimes it was the first resort, her go-to move, the all-purpose solution to every problem. No muss, no fuss, no consequences, not even a sleepless night.

Maybe she'd crossed so many lines, she really had lost the chance to come back. That might have been what Frank was trying to say.

She still hadn't seen him. She had to make time, even for a short visit. In the morning. First thing.

Right now, she needed to pull off her clothes, crawl into bed, get some sleep.

In just another minute. Or two ...

She yawned, a small yawn that grew into a big one, and the hum in her head grew louder.

"I'm sorry, Frank," she murmured. "Think I screwed up this time. Really ... seriously ... screwed up ..."

There was more, but she didn't hear it. She was gone.

15

HENRY PHIPPS CAME awake by degrees, climbing out of dreams. They had been good dreams, dreams of Armageddon. He'd seen it so vividly—the great piles of mushroom clouds sprouting like toadstools, the wild winds blowing death everywhere in a killing rain. Barren landscapes, strewn corpses, endless silence.

Reluctantly he returned to the world that was, blinking his vision into focus.

His head hurt. The backs of his eyes. His muscles, stiff. Looking down, he dimly made out a bed. Not his own. Small, a cot. Messy. Smelled dirty. Sheets unlaundered. The room cold. Winter air intruding through a boarded-up window.

Dark. But not entirely. Dim light threaded the gap between the closed door and its frame. Door to where? What was this place?

He thought back. Remembered the woman in his house, the cellar stairs. He hadn't liked the way she'd talked to him. Not just as if he were crazy—he could deal with that. But as if he were ... absurd. Laughable. This was unacceptable. He would not be mocked.

He'd hurt her, though. Made her pay for her insolence. He had found blood spattered in the bedroom and smeared on the cellar doorframe, and more red drippings on the carpet by the wide-open front door.

After that, he'd fled the house, called Jonah, gone to Domani. And now he was here. Somewhere. Nowhere.

Here.

He tried rising from the cot. Sank down, groaning. Felt tired. Old.

The door opened, letting in a blast of daylight. Haloed in the glare, Sofia drifted in on sandaled feet. She wore a white cotton gown, too lightweight for winter. Blonde hair, uncombed, fell across her shoulders in a gossamer splash. Her delicate mouth rounded itself in an O of gratified surprise.

"You're awake. About time, lazybones."

Jonah had told him she was twenty-five. She seemed younger. Her body was thin, waifish. Needle tracks decorated her slender arms, bluish-purple blotches marring her white skin, skin like talcum powder.

"Where is Jonah?" he asked.

"Around," she said vaguely. Everything about her was vague—her tremulous fluttery gestures, her vapid blinking eyes, her blank face, her dreamy tone.

"Where, exactly?" he pressed, knowing the question was useless. Sofia had no conception of space or time.

"In the house, I guess. Where else?"

"Get him for me."

"You should rest. Jonah says it's what you need."

"I want to talk to him."

"Jonah says—"

He raised his voice. "I don't give a damn what Jonah says. Get him for me."

With a sigh she left him, floating down the hall, a girl on a cloud. The door remained open. He thought about shouting for Jonah. But that would be stupid. The last thing he wanted was to call attention to himself. He was on the run, wanted by the female detective and her criminal associates.

For the first time he asked himself if calling Jonah last night had been the right thing to do. He was not altogether certain he could trust the man. Yet he'd had no other option. Jonah and Sofia were the only converts he'd made.

The letter had come after the second killing. It was not sent through the postal system; it bore no stamp, no postmark, no return address. It had simply been slipped into his mailbox by an unseen hand.

We know about you, it said.

The words were written in a flowing cursive hand. A woman's hand, he thought at the time. The meaning was simultaneously obvious and obscure. They—whoever they might be—knew he was responsible for at least one murder, but there was no indication of what they intended to do about it.

His guess was blackmail. Well, they wouldn't get much. He had nothing to give.

When his phone rang that evening, he was by no means surprised.

"Yes," he said evenly.

"Is this Henry?"

A female voice. The letter writer, he assumed. He waited for the threat, the demand, the next move in the game.

"They're calling you the Man in the Moon," the woman said.

He didn't answer, didn't commit to anything. The call was probably being recorded. He would not incriminate himself.

"I don't know why," she added. "It's a silly name."

"I have no idea what you're talking about," Henry declared for the benefit of any recording apparatus. The statement sounded stiff and hollow. He disliked uttering it. He had no wish to disavow his calling. It felt like a betrayal.

The woman tittered, an airy, breathy sound. He wondered if she was drunk.

"*Su-u-ure* you don't," she said, the first word elongating itself like a kitten languorously stretching on a carpet. "We want to meet you."

"Why?"

"To talk."

"I don't want to talk to you. I have nothing to say."

"Henry ..." A tut-tut sound. "Don't be an old meanie. We're your friends. We're not out to get you. We think you're"—she drew a long, wet breath—"really cool."

Really cool?

She told him they would "get together"—she made it sound like a picnic—at Domani. "We know you like it there."

"What makes you say so?"

"We've seen you. We've heard you preach."

Had they now? He began to be intrigued.

Two hours later he was at Domani, entering at night for the first time. He did not descend into the basement as on previous occasions. They were waiting for him above ground, in that vast cage of moonlit girders and crosshatched shadows. Two of them, a woman and a man.

The time for equivocation was over. "How did you know who I was?" Henry asked without preamble.

"You slipped up, bro," the man said. "Last Saturday, when you preached your sermon down below, you talked about the Brae Head lighthouse. Remember? How it would be a light to the world, or something. You was real fuckin' eloquent. And then, what do you know—few hours later, somebody finds the latest victim. Right there in the dunes by the lighthouse. Body'd been there all day, the news said. Been there even before you preached on it. So we knew it was you that did the deed."

"That doesn't explain how you learned my identity, my address."

"Oh, that? Next time you preached, we followed you home. No big deal. Got your name off the crap in your mailbox. Your phone number's listed. Easy-peasy."

"And what is it you want? Cash? I don't have much."

"Nah, bro. We don't want cash. We want to hear more of what you got to say. And maybe help you, if we can."

Had they been anyone else, they would have

blackmailed him or reported him to the police. That it hadn't worked out that way had been deeply encouraging to him. He'd taken it as a sign, a kind of thumbs-up from whatever nebulous cosmic forces might be on his side.

And so they became his converts, his two apostles, the rock on which he would build his church. That night's rendezvous in Domani had been only the first of many. Domani became their church, Noah's half-built ark awaiting the end of all flesh.

It was soon apparent that Sofia lacked the intellect to comprehend his message. She nodded and cooed approval, but her reactions were no more meaningful than the purr of a cat. For Jonah, he had higher hopes.

Jonah Stroud was an unkempt, rangy scarecrow of a man who had come out of the south somewhere, his lean sunburnt face perpetually stubbled, his stringy hair sometimes loose on his shoulders, sometimes knotted in a ponytail. He was older than Sofia, grouchy and grizzled. His eyes were hooded, secretive.

He was no intellectual, but he possessed a certain innate shrewdness, an animal cunning, and a willingness to listen and learn. He received Henry's gospel and nodded his amens. And when Henry spoke of his manifesto, Jonah promised that when the time was right, he would post it on the Internet, where it would "go viral"—apparently a good thing.

Henry was not quite sure he liked either one of them, but he did need them. Their cooperation was necessary to ensure his legacy. In time there would be others, but he would not live to see them. Did he regret this? No. He had done all a man could do. Now the work must be left to his disciples, who would persevere and prevail. The enemy was powerful, but not all-powerful, and against the truth he was helpless. This was Henry Phipps's great gift to humanity—the truth, which would set men free.

Footsteps in the hall. He recognized that slow,

slouching tread even before he made out Jonah's silhouette against the morning light.

"Yo, Preacher. Heard you was among the living again."

Yes, Henry thought. Lucky me. "Where am I?" he asked.

"Pilgrim Grove. Don't you remember?" Jonah sat on the edge of the cot, ignoring the complaint of rusty springs. "I drove you straight here from McKendree Park."

The two towns were right next to each other. The drive must have been short, but Henry couldn't recall even a minute of it. "I don't think I took it in. I seem to be drawing a blank."

"You was kinda out of it, my man. By the time we got here, you was really dragging. Past your bedtime, I guess."

"It's not that. It must have been a delayed reaction to"—shock, he thought—"to everything that happened."

"Well, that's why we let you rest. A little shut-eye's just what the doctor ordered. Does a body good, don't it?"

Henry was quite sure that nothing in this world could do him any good. "What exactly is this place you've brought me to?"

"It started out as an inn, back in the day. Lately it was one of them halfway houses. I stayed here after I got out of prison. Bosom of fuckin' Abraham, believe it or not, Communal Living Center. This was my room. Nice, ain't it?"

"I suppose so," Henry said without enthusiasm. He looked around at the faded wallpaper with its honeysuckle design. "Why is the window boarded up?"

"Well, you know, we can't exactly advertise our presence here. The facility closed down under tragic circumstances—the owner, poor old Mrs. Bailey, passed away real sudden—and everybody had to clear out. But me, I came back. With Sofia. We was tired of living outta her van, and it seemed like a shame to let a perfectly good piece of property go to waste."

"Nobody knows you're here?"

"That's it in a nutshell. We boarded up some of the windows so nobody'll see no lights or nothing. We come and go by the back door. We're squatting, see. Lots of squatters in this town, in old buildings like this."

"So it's ... safe?"

"Yeah, totally. Off the grid, like I told you last night. You can just chill." He stood. "Want some breakfast?"

"I would, thank you. If it's not too much trouble."

"No trouble at all." He took a step, then paused. "In case you're wondering, the cops are taking care of your dog."

Henry didn't understand at first. "The police?"

"They showed up at your place sometime after you amscrayed. They know you're the Man in the Moon, too, though they're being kinda coy about saying so."

"Why ... Why would the police get involved so soon?"

"Dog was making a racket, they say. Some neighbor called. It's all over the news."

Henry shut his eyes. He should have known the old dog might panic if left alone at night.

"Stupid of me," he murmured. "To leave him like that."

"Woulda been mighty inconvenient to take him with you."

"I should have dispatched him. Should have taken him down into the cellar and ... It's funny. I never hesitated to shoot a human being. But Lazarus ... I just couldn't. Stupid," he said again.

"Don't beat yourself up about it. They was bound to get on to you eventually. So how do you like your eggs?"

"However Sofia makes them."

"Her? Damn girl can't even boil water. I'm the chef in this hostelry. How's scrambled work for you?"

Henry nodded. He didn't care. But he did have one more question. "Do you know where I left my gun?"

Jonah, almost at the door, turned back. "Oh, that? I left it in the van, hid real good. Don't worry none, Preacher." He grinned. "I'm taking care of everything."

Henry watched the younger man's narrow back retreating down the hall. That grin lingered in his memory. He hadn't liked it. It was not a friendly grin.

It was, he thought, the fleshless grin of a skull.

16

BONNIE PUT OFF calling Petrossian as long as possible. She woke at seven and spent some time drawing and dry-firing with her left hand. She was not a lefty, and her timing was poor, her aim uncertain. She tried the right arm, but pain defeated her.

She checked the wound, changed the bandages. Her arm was still a mess, and it hurt like a mother, but she saw no sign of infection. To keep it dry, she skipped a shower and rinsed her hair with the pullout sprayer in the kitchen sink. She put on new jeans, a corduroy shirt, and boots, selecting a black faux fur Cossack hat for when she went out. The hat seemed appropriate for the winter season. It made her think of balalaikas, or of the word balalaika, anyway, since she didn't actually know what a balalaika was.

Usually she didn't bother with breakfast, but today she found some eggs in her fridge that weren't too far past their expiration date and scrambled them in a saucepan that was clean if you didn't examine it too closely. She drank coffee, fixing it strong, taking it black. She ate standing up at the kitchen counter, conveniently close to the paper towel dispenser, or as she knew it, the napkin holder. The TV was on, tuned to News 12, the local channel, which was all over the Phipps story. It had broken big. Happily for her, if not for anyone else, he was still on the loose.

By 8 AM she'd washed down more amoxicillin and Tylenol. Her four hours' sleep and morning meal had left her feeling almost like herself, except for the unnatural stiffness of her arm. There were no further excuses for procrastination. She had to call Petrossian. Not just to spin her failure in as positive a way as possible, but because she needed his help. She had to find Henry Phipps before the police did. And her new pal Armin just might have a lead.

She unplugged Sammy from his charger and carried him into the living room. Her plan was to call the number that Petrossian's guy had used last night and, through him, get connected to the big man himself. It would not be a pleasant conversation.

She was looking up the number in her call log when Sammy startled her with a fresh chorus of "Jingle Bells." God damn it, she had to change that ringtone.

The caller was unidentified, but she knew who it had to be.

"Parker," she answered, standing in the middle of the living room and feeling a little too much like a deer in the path of a car.

"I'm disappointed in you, Bonnie."

Petrossian. Of course. "You watched the news, huh?"

"I didn't need to watch the news. I have contacts in the state police. I knew as early as three o'clock that Henry Phipps is on the run and is a person of interest in the Man in the Moon slayings. Person of interest." Petrossian grunted. "You Americans call no one a suspect anymore."

"Okay, Armin. It went sideways. I admit it. But the situation is salvageable. I've got an idea, but I need some information from you. I need—"

"No detailed discussion, please. Not over the phone."

"Time for another face-to-face?"

"Precisely."

"Okay, I'll hump it over to your place pronto."

"There's no need. I've sent men to escort you. They're waiting outside your residence."

She stepped to the window and drew back the curtain. Parked at the curb was a Mercedes sedan, the CLS model, abnormally long. And black, naturally. Bad guys always went for black.

Two men occupied the car. Strangers to her. They looked bored. They'd been sitting there for a little while, apparently.

"What makes you think I need an escort?" she asked.

"I thought you might be reluctant to see me after having failed in your assignment."

"I'm not a runner, if that's what you're saying. And I can drive myself. Just tell me where."

"It is not that I distrust you, Bonnie. But life has made me, shall we say, cynical. There are reasons you might choose not to keep the appointment."

"Why? You gonna bump me off?"

"Nothing so crude as that, surely."

"Then what should I be worried about?" And don't call me Shirley, she added silently.

"Perhaps you won't take my word as a sufficient guarantee of your safety. You, too, are cynical, I think. You couldn't have survived this long otherwise."

"Just give it to me straight, Armin. What am I walking into?"

"A discussion, that's all. You say there's a way to salvage the situation. I'm willing to hear you out."

She looked dubiously at the men in the car. "And you won't let me drive myself?"

"Let's say, I prefer to do it this way. It's no great hardship for you. You'll ride in style. A stretch limousine from my personal fleet. The amenities are most luxurious. There's even a bar cabinet, fully stocked."

"A little early for drinking." She wasn't entirely sure this was true.

"Then there's also a Keurig machine. Make coffee. Play music. I recommend the Spa channel on Sirius XM. It's most relaxing."

"You missed your calling, Armin. You should've been a concierge."

"Then you'll humor my little whim?"

It could be a death sentence. She knew that. But she also knew refusal was not an option, unless she wanted to hole up in her apartment or come out shooting. Neither seemed like a viable plan.

"Okay," she said. "Give me a couple minutes. I, um, I'm not decent. But you already knew that, right?"

She wasn't sure if he got the joke or not. Or if it even was a joke. Anyway, the call was already over.

In the bedroom she removed the vent cover, retrieved the sack of weapons, and found the smallest firearm she currently owned, a LifeCard .22 pocket pistol, a foldable gun no bigger than a deck of cards. It carried one round in the chamber and stored four more in the grip. A single-shot weapon wasn't ideal when potentially going up against two opponents, but it was better than nothing. She didn't have an ankle holster, so she decided to snug it inside her boot—her right boot? No. Not with her right arm barely functional. Left boot then, for a left-handed draw. She wished she'd caught the bullet in her other arm. Well, actually, she wished she hadn't caught the bullet at all.

Anything else? Yeah, something sharp. She selected a stainless-steel dive knife with a serrated edge, which she strapped to her right forearm under her shirt sleeve. She could free it with her left hand and slice or stab.

There were other trick plays in her playbook, but she was running out of time. By now the men in the limo would know their boss had made contact. They'd be suspicious if she took too long to open the door.

In confirmation, the doorbell chimed. She replaced the bag in the vent and screwed the vent cover in place. She retrieved last night's coat from the floor and shrugged it on, then dumped Sammy into her purse, where the hit kit was still stashed. Never having used it, she'd had no reason to dispose of it.

The bell rang again. Fuck, these goons were impatient.

"I'm coming, I'm coming," she groused as she unlocked the door. "Calm your tits, comrades."

The two guys from the car stood there, either one wide enough to fill the doorway on his own. They weren't wearing overcoats, only suit jackets, as if impervious to the cold. Dancer and Prancer, she dubbed them.

She didn't like the look of these two. They were big and young and scowling. She would've preferred older men. The older ones were less likely to do something impulsive and stupid.

"Merry Christmas," she said with a nod.

They didn't answer.

"Happy Hanukkah?" she tried.

Still nothing. This pair seemed even less amiable than Donner and Blitzen last night.

Wordlessly they entered the living room, crowding her space. Dancer was big and lean, with long, greasy hair tied back in a ponytail. He emitted a disagreeable odor that suggested a considerable time had passed since his last bath. Prancer was stouter but better groomed. His hair was buzz cut, and he emitted no particular smell.

"Sucks to work on a holiday, doesn't it?" She smiled. "Hope you're getting overtime."

Flat stares greeted this remark. Dancer confiscated her purse and pawed through it. He found the hit kit and tossed the gun and suppressor on a chair. She'd expected that much. The ghost gun was a red herring. She just hoped they didn't frisk her, or at least didn't do it well.

She was disappointed. Prancer proved annoyingly thorough as he patted her down. He found the dive knife and removed it, strap and all. He didn't do it gently. The rough twist of her arm made her wound shout out, but she showed no reaction. Never a good idea to reveal weakness to an enemy. Or to anyone, really.

Their scowls had deepened now. They appeared to have taken a distinct dislike to her. She didn't care about that. She only wanted them to miss the ankle gun. Come on, time for a Christmas miracle.

No such luck. Prancer plucked the folded gun from her boot and opened it up with an angry shake of his head. Well, she'd stopped believing in Santa Claus a long time ago.

She was now completely disarmed. "You guys are good," she said in resignation. "I'm gonna recommend you for a Christmas bonus."

Still no response. She took back her purse, now emptied of firepower, and stuck the Cossack hat on her head. Just because she might be walking into a death trap was no excuse not to look her best.

With admirable distrust, Dancer removed the hat and checked the lining for weapons before giving it back.

Together they left the house. The two men flanked her as they accompanied her in leisurely fashion down the driveway. The sun had risen about an hour earlier. The morning was frigid, the air raw, the sky the color of sleet. Was there snow in the forecast? More important, would she live long enough to find out?

Dancer opened a rear door for her. He said something in what had to be Armenian. "*Stanal, tsakhu kin.*"

"Oh, I get it. You guys don't talk English. Is that it? No Americanski?"

Neither man replied. No wonder her conversational gambits kept falling flat.

He repeated the order, jerking his thumb at the car's interior.

There were two leather bench seats positioned to face each other. She slid onto the rear bench, facing forward, and was surprised when Dancer joined her, seating himself directly opposite.

That seemed a little hinky. If he was just an escort, why not sit up front with his buddy?

He pulled the door shut. It made a solid clunk, like the shutting of a bank vault. Or a coffin lid, she couldn't help thinking.

Prancer got behind the wheel. She could see his buzz-cut scalp through the transparent partition of the privacy barrier. He gave her a brief stare in the rearview mirror, his eyes cold, before he keyed the ignition and pulled away from the curb, traveling slowly, like a man who wanted to avoid attention.

The engine came on, and with it the sound system. Over the quadraphonic speakers, Andy Williams assured her that this was the most wonderful time of the year. Not the Spa channel, despite Petrossian's recommendation.

The limo's rear compartment was as upscale as he'd promised. And yeah, there was a bar. Her companion pointed it out to her, sliding open a cabinet door to reveal a rack of bottles and glasses. "*Kokteyl, tsakhu kin*?"

She was almost tempted to pour herself a couple fingers of scotch. But she had a feeling she needed to stay sharp. She didn't really think Petrossian would just have her whacked without even waiting for her explanation, but it was just possible she was wrong.

Dancer shut the cabinet. "*Tsakhu kin ch'i uzum kokteyl*," he shouted to the driver through the glass. Prancer laughed. His pal joined him.

Bonnie wasn't real big on laughter when she wasn't in on the gag. Experience had shown that sometimes the joke was on her.

17

THE LITTLE ROOM with the boarded-up window had no clock on the wall, no clock anywhere, and no light by which to see a clock anyway. Henry had no means of judging the time. Intuitively he felt it must be midmorning or later. He had not seen Jonah or Sofia for what seemed like many hours. His last glimpse of either had been when Jonah carried off the breakfast tray, advising him to get more rest.

Henry had indeed tried to rest, but sleep would not come. His stomach was troubled, his nerves tight, his mind a confusion of thoughts and fears.

At length he rose from the cot and approached the door, closed by Jonah upon leaving. As he put his hand on the knob, it occurred to him that he might be locked in. Strange notion. There was no logic to it. Still, he realized he wouldn't be entirely surprised if the door refused to open.

It did open, though. This fact should have been reassuring. Somehow it was not.

He stepped into the unaccustomed brilliance of the sun-streaked hall. The window at the front end was boarded up also, but light from side rooms ribboned the corridor. The side windows of the building were unblocked, apparently. He supposed no one ever went into those rooms, so there was no need for concealment.

He started down the hall, pausing to hitch up his beltless pants. For the first time, he was aware of how ridiculous he must look, in his untucked shirt and baggy trousers, the things he'd thrown on last night in a mad rush to escape the house. At some point he must have removed his overcoat and boots, or Jonah had; his feet were bare except for white woolen socks. The left sock had a hole in it; his big toe poked through.

The hallway was chilly, the hardwood floor cold. He padded down the hall, peering into one room after another. Whatever curtains or shades had covered the windows were gone. Through the bare panes he could see buildings on either side, Victorian piles with rotting shingles and rusting fire escapes. Graffiti defaced a rickety fence. Someone's ancient station wagon sat on blocks in a yard.

Not a good neighborhood. Pilgrim Grove was a patchwork of gentrification and decay. He was in one of the undesirable areas.

From the view, he gathered he was on the third floor. The highest floor, evidently, since the staircase only went down. As he descended, the building warmed up a little. The upper stories had been closed off to save on fuel. However Jonah and Sofia heated the place, they could afford to do only a partial job.

The former halfway house had been gutted, the light fixtures removed, even most of the carpet ripped up, leaving strips of carpet tacks and trains of beetles scuttling along the baseboards. He found no one on the second floor or the first, though he did discover the room his hosts occupied, the largest room he'd seen, its windows safely blocked out, liquor bottles and syringes scattered everywhere. It was on the ground floor near the kitchen, which advertised its presence with the stink of rotten food. Paper plates and Styrofoam cups were piled high in the sink. The walls were spray-painted with psychedelic swirls of fluorescent color. Sofia's contribution, he was sure.

He was beginning to think the two of them had gone out when he heard muffled laughter from beneath his feet. There was a cellar, apparently, accessible via a separate staircase. He found the closed door and eased it open. A strong draft of heat drifted up from below, and with it—voices.

"... an active principle at work, corrupting and, um, corroding everything, making a stink pit of the universe, making life hell."

The voice belonged to Sofia, but the words were his own. Lines from his testimony, recited in singsong fashion.

"And it came to me that in a world like this, there is no worse punishment than to be born and no greater cruelty than the prolongation of life. The dead, at least, are happy."

A burst of shared laughter punctuated the quotation, Jonah's phlegmy guffaws mixing with Sofia's titters.

Fear crawled up Henry's belly, clutching at his heart. That laughter scared him. It threatened to unmake all his hopes.

He started down the stairs. The cellar was lit by an orange fireglow. He heard the dull roar of a furnace.

"Life itself is sickness, but the sickness is not in us, but in the thing that made us. Death is the cure."

More laughter.

He reached the bottom of the stairs and dared to peer around the corner. Jonah lounged cross-legged on a shapeless beanbag chair, his face lit by the flames of an ancient coal-fired furnace, its huge white ducts climbing into the low ceiling like a cluster of tentacles. The feed door was open, red-orange flame dancing against the sooty firebrick.

Before the furnace stood Sofia in the stance of an orator, the pages of the testimony in her hand.

"I know the truth, because I have seen it." Her cheeks were streaked in sweat from the fierce heat. "I was lifted to the mountaintop. I touched the roof of heaven."

"Heaven's got a fuckin' roof!" Jonah barked, chortling. He took a long pull on a bottle. "Leave it to

Preacher to come up with a nutty thing like that."

"My face shone like the sun, and everywhere there was bright light and flames of fire."

"Well," Jonah said, "he got that part right, didn't he, Mommy?"

Sofia grinned. "He sure did." She peeled off that page of the manuscript, crumpled it into a wad, and tossed it casually into the furnace.

It was too much. It was—sacrilege.

"Stop," Henry said, the word scarcely audible, choked off at the back of his throat. "Stop it." With a grinding effort he found his voice. *"Stop it!"*

They turned their faces toward him, Sofia happy and guiltless, Jonah's smile congealing into a frown.

"You're a hard man to keep down, Preacher," Jonah said. "This is the second time you done woke up ahead of schedule."

Henry stepped forward. "What are you talking about?"

He wanted the question to sound bold, challenging, but somehow it didn't come out that way.

Jonah stood up slowly, stretching his long limbs as if waking from a nap. "Remember last night, how I gave you my flask? The rum was spiked with Rohypnol. That's a powerful sedative, bro. It's why you was so woozy and cooperative, and why you blanked on subsequent events. It should've kept you out longer than it did."

"I remember. But"—he struggled to recall the long, cold trudge from Domani to the van—"but I didn't drink it all. I poured out most of it."

"Now, why would you do a foolish thing like that? Waste of good liquor. That's positively sinful." To underline the point, he retrieved the bottle and took another slug.

"I didn't like the taste. I knew you expected me to drink it. I dumped it when you weren't looking."

"Guess that explains it. But the OJ you got with your eggs had some more catnip in it. And you downed the whole glass. It was drained dry when I took it back. So how the fuck are you still vertical?"

"My breakfast didn't agree with me. I—I was sick after you left."

Jonah gulped more liquor. "'Nother mystery solved."

"Nothing is solved. Nothing makes any sense at all." Henry drew his shoulders back, staring down his adversary. "Just what is going on here? Why are you—how can you—how—"

"Cool your jets, Preach." Jonah waved off his outrage with all the passion of a man brushing away a fly. "I been trying to keep you in the dark, 'cause it seemed like the easiest way to handle things. But I guess now you need to hear the truth, huh? Gotta warn you—truth's gonna hurt."

"He can take it," Sofia said. "He's, like, a god or something." She giggled.

Henry ignored her. Studying Jonah, slowly he put it together. "You betrayed me to that criminal, the drug lord or whatever he is. The one who hired the private eye. Didn't you?"

"Indirectly, yeah. I used, you might say, a proxy. Didn't want to get personally involved. I find, as a general practice, it's best to put distance between one's self and these narcoterrorist types. That's just, you know, fuckin' prudent."

"Then it was you who collected the thirty pieces of silver."

"The price was ten thousand dollars American, and no, I didn't collect. Though I got a mind to, before this is all over. But that ain't my principal concern. I got other ambitions."

"If you didn't care about money, why not just tell the police? You could have phoned in an anonymous tip to their hotline."

Jonah resumed his seat on the beanbag chair. "Nah, that ain't the way this needs to work. Police catch you,

you're outta action. No good. What I wanted was for you to be took care of on the sly. I figured Mr. Big's guys would do you in your house, nice and quiet. Then I could sneak in and hide the body before anyone knew about it. Instead, looks like Mr. Big outsourced the job to some silly female who bungled it, as silly females are wont to do."

Sofia chuckled, unoffended. She plopped down beside Jonah, the manuscript -- or what was left of it—still in her hand.

"So I had to improvise," Jonah went on. "Brought you here, where I can keep you as long as you're needed."

"You've been lying to me all along. From the very start. You never intended to publish my testimony."

"Figured that out, did you?"

"You haven't understood a single thing I've taught you."

"I never believed none of your crazy bullshit, that's for sure. Only reason Mommy and me glommed on to you was so we could use you when the time came."

"Use me for what?"

Jonah tipped the bottle to his mouth. Over the rim, his mouth curved into that familiar death's-head grin. "Now, that's the first intelligent question you asked. What's the biggest drawback about playing shoot-'em-up? Getting caught. But what if you can't get caught 'cause no one's looking for you?"

Henry took a step closer. He wished he, too, could sit. His knees were feeling all wobbly. But there were no other chairs.

"What are you trying to say?" he whispered.

"The cops is after you. Long as they don't find you, any more murders will be *your* murders. Even when they ain't."

Jonah set down the bottle and leaned back, elbows on the floor, smiling broadly. Sofia stroked his belly, her hand making slow circles on his hardened abs.

"See if you can follow me, Preach. I got a hit list of my own. The authorities in your little town of Brighton Cove fucked me over real good a couple years ago. So I made myself a promise. Three little piggies, said I." He counted on his fingers. "One ... two ... three. They all go to market, which, if you think about it, ain't such a great place for a piggy to end up. You with me so far?"

Henry nodded slowly.

"Well, I couldn't just go after 'em, 'cause I got a motive, understand? I'm an obvious suspect. Unless I'm not. Because you are. Who better to take the blame than the Man in the Moon? I use your gun and your MO. One shot, back of the head. Who's to say it's not you? No one'll even think of digging deeper."

Henry had no more strength. He slumped against a wall, feeling the furnace's warmth through the bricks.

"When they find you, it'll be case closed. 'Course, you'll be dead—killed by your own hand. That's how it'll look, at least."

"Why not just kill me now?" Henry asked in a lifeless monotone.

"'Cause then I'd have to hide the body. With all the CSI shit they got going on nowadays, them lab monkeys can time your demise down to the split second, and they'd know you died before the last couple targets got bumped off. You might say, why not burn the remains right here in this very furnace? That was, in point of fact, my original idea. But it was always kind of a weak point in my plan. You can see why, can't you?"

Henry didn't answer, couldn't think.

"It's a weak point because things that's hid have got a way of turning up, and things that's burnt don't always burn completely. There'd still be the hardest parts of you—teeth and such—buried in that ash pit. I know that for a fact, Preacher. A solid fact. So it's much better if I let them find you intact. It just means you gotta hang around for the duration."

"As your prisoner."

"Now you're catching on."

"You can't hold me here."

Jonah chuckled. "'Course we can."

"We can do what we want," Sofia added. "We always do."

Jonah took the manuscript from her. Idly he flipped through it, licking his finger as he turned each page.

"I'll shout for help," Henry said. "I'll bring the police. I have no reason to hide from the law if this is all that's left for me."

Jonah shook his head. "Window in the back bedroom's boarded up. That's why we stashed you there."

"If I make enough noise, someone will hear."

"Maybe so. Thing is, the place next door is a nursing home. Them senile old folks get to screamin' sometimes. It's like a fuckin' wolf pack, the way them coots howl when they got a mind to. So go ahead, shout if you want. Knock yourself out. No one'll pay you a lick of attention."

Henry could support himself no longer. His legs simply wouldn't hold him. He slid down the wall, very slowly, as his knees folded under him.

"You're a trickster, Jonah," he breathed. "You're an agent of the impostor god."

"Whatever floats your duck, Preach."

He sat staring at the floor for what seemed like a long time. Then slowly he raised his head to face Jonah, still reclining on the chair a yard away.

"Give me the testimony."

Jonah lifted an eyebrow. "Half of it's burnt, bro. And in all honesty, it ain't no loss. Gotta tell you, you cranked up the crazy to eleven on this fuckin' thing."

"Just give me what's left."

"Why should I?"

"It's mine."

"I never been a great respecter of other people's property."

"It can't be of any value to you. Let me have it. Please."

"Okay, sure. Why not. It's your magnum possum, right? Guess you got a right to it, if anybody does."

"Thank you."

Jonah leaned forward, extending the precious pages in his hand, and then with a jerk of his arm he flung the entire sheaf into the furnace.

"Oops."

The pages went up in a shout of flame. Charred curling wisps drifted amid the smoke.

Sofia emitted a shriek of laughter.

Henry stared at the furnace, then at the pair before him.

"You *garbage*," he whispered. "Damned ignorant *filth.*"

"Whoa, now, Preach." Jonah half shut his eyes, lazing like a cat on the beanbag chair. "No need to get abusive. It ain't our fault you're as crazy as a fuckin' loon."

There was a cry then, a high yodeling yell, and it came out of Henry's mouth as he launched himself off the floor. His hands were fists. He wanted to smash bone.

Jonah was a bigger man, younger, stronger, his rangy body knotted in tight ropes of muscle, but leaning back, resting on his elbows, he was temporarily at a disadvantage as Henry crashed on top of him, beating with his fists.

Sofia, dislodged from the chair, fell sprawling on her side. She was up in a moment, yelling, "Get off him, *get off*!" Her fingers clutched at Henry's face, her nails grooving scratches in his cheeks. He flung out an elbow and caught her in the mouth, and she fell backward, wailing.

The distraction was momentary, but it was enough. Jonah powered himself to a sitting position and grabbed Henry by the chin, pushing him away, straight-arming him to hold him at bay.

"Quit it, old man," he growled. "Just fuckin' quit it."

Henry wouldn't quit. He flailed and twisted, windmilling his arms, kicking wildly, accomplishing nothing, wearing himself out.

Finally he was done. Breathing hard, weak and limp, he slumped, held up only by Jonah's hand.

"He's crazy," Sofia said. "I mean, really, really *crazy*. And he's ... mean."

Jonah glanced at her, and his eyes narrowed. Henry followed his gaze and saw the girl's lower lip swollen and bleeding.

"He do that to you, Mommy?" Jonah asked in a quiet voice.

Sofia didn't seem to have noticed the injury until that moment. She raised a hand to her mouth and winced at her lip's tenderness.

"Hurts," she moaned, and a single teardrop spilled down her cheek.

Jonah released Henry and pushed him backward onto the floor. Slowly he stood, glaring down, the bottle once again in his hand.

"You shouldn't oughta've done that, Preach. That's my woman you messed with."

Henry struggled for breath. "Your woman ... is a crazy slut."

Something hotter than the fireglow flickered on Jonah's face. "You hear that, sweetness? You hear what this fuckin' nutjob called you?"

"He's a bad man," she whimpered.

"He surely is. Think he should get away with that kind of talk?"

She shook her head sullenly.

"Then I guess you know what you gotta do. We got the stuff?"

"It's in my room."

"Go fetch it. I'll detain our blessed lord and savior until your return."

She glided up the stairs, still touching her bloody

mouth. Henry lay on his back, helpless as a turtle, gazing up at the tall man who filled his world.

"Mommy don't like what you done to her." Jonah poured the rest of the bottle down his throat, his larynx jerked thirstily, the residue sluicing over his chin. Finished, he threw it aside with a clink of glass. "And Mommy got a real bad temper when people don't treat her right."

18

THE LIMO RATTLED over the railroad tracks and continued west. Dancer watched her steadily, with a kind of lazy hunger that felt predatory. He was lanky and loose-limbed, and somehow he gave the impression of sprawling in his seat even while sitting upright. His body odor, concentrated in a confined space, was more objectionable than before.

"I know why your boss picked you," Bonnie told him as the car crossed Highway 71. "It's the language barrier. He doesn't want me spilling any details about his main squeeze. With you, I can blab all I want, and you're none the wiser."

"*Sus mna, tsakhu kin,*" he said with a twist of his lip that was both a scowl and a smirk.

It was the fourth time he'd referred to her by that term, *tsakhu kin*. She didn't know what it meant, but she was pretty sure it wasn't complimentary.

She gave him a good looking-over. He wore a rumpled suit jacket, showing the obvious bulge of an armpit holster. Sloppy. These days, with all the high-quality concealment holsters available, there was no excuse for letting your gun print through the fabric.

Highway 35 came up next, but Prancer didn't take it.

"Yeah," she went on, "he's worked it all out. Now either you're taking me to see him, or you're taking me for a ride. I mean, you know, a ride, like in the movies. You like movies, sport?"

Dancer drummed his long fingers on his knees,

looking bored. Or impatient, maybe. The way she always got before doing a hit.

The car was warm, too warm, overheated. She was sweating inside her coat.

She crossed her legs, resting a fur-lined boot on her knee. An epitaph flashed through her mind: *She died with her boots on.*

A cigarette would help. She fished a lighter out of her purse. Dancer smacked it down. Non-smoking car? More likely, he didn't want her handling anything that could be used as a weapon, even a flickable Bic or a lit cigarette.

Which meant he anticipated resistance. A struggle. She didn't like that.

The car passed an on-ramp to the parkway without slowing down. Not going north, then. Straight west. By now it was clear that they weren't going to Petrossian's estate. Of course, he'd never actually said he would be meeting her at the house. But where else would he be at this hour of the morning?

They were past Farmdell now, heading deeper into the countryside. She didn't even know the name of the town they were in, if it was a town. All she saw was pine woods, densely overgrown, the high branches bristling with needles, crowding out the sky.

Visitors from out of state, who saw only the refineries along the turnpike near the airport, would never guess how much rural country was left in New Jersey. The limo was heading into miles of forest, undeveloped, seldom visited in winter, completely deserted on Christmas morning.

A good place to make somebody disappear.

Her stomach clenched. She tasted something sour at the back of her throat.

"I am deep in the suck, aren't I?" she asked her uncommunicative friend. "You've probably got my grave already dug. Or am I supposed to dig it myself?"

That would really piss her off. She hated digging.

A new song played on the radio. A winter sleigh ride, over the river and through the woods, on the way to grandmother's house ... She doubted she'd be seeing her grandma today, unless it was at the end of a tunnel of light.

The car cruised past walls of evergreens, the driver still not hurrying. The last thing he wanted was to be pulled over by a traffic cop.

A cautious speed, but fast enough that jumping from the car wasn't an option. The rear doors were locked, anyway—she'd heard the double click as the car started up—and it was a safe bet they couldn't be unlocked by a passenger.

At a seemingly random intersection, Prancer hooked south. The sun shot orange spears through gaps in the foliage to her left, the sharp side light throwing mosaics of capillaries across her field of vision.

They were on a back road now. The tires turned slowly over rutted ground. She heard small pings of loose gravel against the chassis.

Yeah, this was bad.

She considered her options. They were scant. She was alone and unarmed. Her opponents were two powerfully built men, toting guns and inured to violence.

But she did have Sammy. He'd never failed her yet.

She reached into her purse and took out her cell. Dancer stirred. "*Zanger ch'kan,*" he said with a firm head shake.

She got the drift. No calls. But she wasn't giving up that easily.

Leaning forward, she showed him the call log. She pointed to the latest entry.

"Petrossian," she said, then repeated the name, enunciating it syllable by syllable. "Pet-ros-si-an."

The ponytailed doofus might not speak her language, but he had to know his boss's name.

She watched his face and saw a flicker of comprehension in his eyes. Comprehension, but not necessarily assent. He still might grab the phone away from her at any moment.

She pressed the callback button and let him hear the ringing sound at the other end of the line. He hesitated, uncertain whether to let the call the call go through or stop it. Finally he shrugged.

One hurdle cleared. Now she just had to hope Petrossian would pick up. For all she knew he'd gone back to bed, or he was taking a crap or something. It was weird to think that her continued existence might depend on a middle-aged man's bowel movements.

Three rings. Four. She was beginning to think Plan A was a bust when Petrossian answered. "Hello again, Bonnie."

"I'm not en route to a meeting with you, am I?"

He laughed, a disconcertingly carefree sound. "I'm afraid not."

Up to that moment, she hadn't been a hundred percent certain she was fucked. Call it ninety-nine percent. There had been that one percent of hopeful doubt. Which was now gone.

"Can't help feeling you kinda misled me." She was relieved to hear no tremor in her voice.

"I'm a sociopath, Bonnie. I said as much in our meeting. Lies come easily to me. In this case it was convenient to remove you from a crowded residential area with a minimum of fuss."

"Why are you doing this, Armin?"

"Perhaps, if you'll excuse a slight change of policy, you'll call me Mr. Petrossian."

"We're not on the first-name basis anymore?"

"I'm on a first-name basis with you, Bonnie. It is not reciprocal."

"It's starting to look like nothing about this situation is reciprocal."

"Now you catch on."

She sighed. "This is so disappointing. Just when I thought we were pals."

"You never thought that. You'd be a fool to think so. You could trust me no more than you can trust a scorpion. Your life is inconsequential to me. Your death is equally unimportant. You'll die in the woods, on your knees. Small animals will pick at your bones."

She really didn't need the imagery. She could already visualize it—the car stopping in a secluded glen, a brief tramp through the forest, the dénouement in a clearing well away from the road, where there might or might not be a freshly dug grave.

"Bullet in the head, huh?" Her throat had gone dry.

"I'm afraid so."

"It's not so much me I'm worried about. But this hat is brand new." She licked her lips. "You know, I did my best for you. I went after Phipps. The son of a bitch got the jump on me. I barely survived."

"Is that so?"

"He fucking shot me."

"This is your day for getting shot, it would seem."

"It doesn't have to be like that."

"I'm afraid it does. My men have their orders."

The road changed from gravel to dirt. Plumes of mocha-brown dust trailed in the limo's wake.

From asphalt to gravel to dirt. There couldn't be much farther to go.

"Who are these two chuckleheads, anyway?" she asked.

"Recent arrivals to our shores."

"They keep calling me *tsakhu kin*. What's that about?"

"It means sellable woman. A whore."

She looked across at Dancer. He'd heard her use the Armenian term. He was smiling.

"Seeing as how they don't speak English," she said, "maybe you should've used them to take out Henry in the first place."

"That job required a certain finesse. I'd been told you possessed this quality. Evidently I was misinformed. You let Phipps beat you."

"He didn't beat me. I'm still in the game."

"Wounded, by your own admission. And with no idea where he's gone. I think we're done here."

The car slowed. Ahead, the dirt road was petering out, dead-ending in a grove of leafless oaks.

"We're not done." She tried not to sound desperate. "We can still make this work."

"I see no likelihood of that."

"Henry's on the run. I just have to find him before the police do."

"How will you manage that?"

"I have an idea."

"I'm not interested in your ideas."

He was about to hang up on her. She could tell. And she would never get him back on the line.

"Who's your informer?" she asked.

There was a pause. "What?"

"The one who ratted out Henry. He's the key to this whole thing."

She felt the brakes come on. The limo halted.

This was it. Her stop. End of the line.

"In what way?" Petrossian asked.

"He knows Henry's secret. That means he knows Henry. He'll know where Henry's gone."

"An implausible series of suppositions. And false. He doesn't know Henry Phipps. He was passing on information obtained from someone else. A third party, someone unknown to me."

"Then the third party knows Henry. Knows him really well. Henry wouldn't confess to a stranger. If he told somebody what he was up to, it's got to be one of the few people he trusts."

"Perhaps he didn't confess. Perhaps this third party witnessed one of the shootings, or learned the truth in some other way."

The driver cranked the gearshift into Park but kept the engine idling. Over the speakers, Burl Ives announced that it was a holly jolly Christmas.

She heard the rear doors unlock.

"But we don't know that," she said. "It's at least equally likely that the guy who talked to you can lead me to the one person Henry knows well enough to confide in. The one person he'll turn to now, when the chips are down."

The driver flung open his door and climbed out.

"It is possible," Petrossian said slowly.

She had his interest. Now close the deal. Sell. Sell hard.

"Give me your informer's name, and I'll find Henry before the police do."

"Perhaps I don't want you talking to him. Perhaps I've taken steps to prevent him from knowing my identity."

The rear door swung open on the driver's side. Prancer leaned in, his buzz-cut scalp glowing pink, like a peach, in a shaft of sun. He snapped his fingers, wanting her out of the car. *"Tsakhu kin."*

"Yeah, yeah, *tsakhu kin*," Bonnie agreed, not budging. To Petrossian she said, "I won't tell him who you are. That would only scare him, anyway. I'll only tell him I'm looking for Henry. It's our best chance. Otherwise Henry lives out his life in a cell. He could live a long time."

Prancer thumped his hand on the doorframe. He glared at his partner, who hesitated, reluctant to interrupt her conversation with his employer.

Petrossian clucked his tongue. "You can be persuasive, Bonnie. But I don't offer second chances."

Another thump from the driver.

"And now," Petrossian said, "I'm afraid we really are done."

Dancer bent forward, about to make his move.

"Okay, then." Bonnie took a breath. "I guess it's Plan B."

She dropped the phone and head-butted Dancer in the nose, cracking cartilage, rocking him back in his seat, and her left hand snaked inside his jacket, wrenching his poorly concealed gun out of its holster.

In the doorway Prancer drew his pistol. She pivoted behind Dancer, shielding herself with his body, and fired three times at his partner, blowing the gun out of his hand with the first shot—pure luck, she'd been aiming for his chest—and catching him in the heart and the face with the second and third rounds.

With an outraged roar, Dancer reared up and threw her off. Blood lathered his nose and mouth. His eyes were wild. She was looking into those eyes when she jammed the muzzle under his collarbone and fired twice.

He fell sideways across the seat. His chest heaved, and a bubble of bloody spit ballooned between his lips. The bubble popped, and he was dead.

Then the car was silent except for Burl Ives' dulcet baritone.

Blankly she gazed down at the gun in her left hand. Dancer's gun, a Makarov nine. The gun gave a little twitch, then twitched again. It started quivering like a nervous puppy. It shook.

This was odd. Then she realized she was the one who was shaking—her hand, her arm, her whole damn body.

Posttraumatic shock or something. Not too surprising. This was the second time in eight hours that she'd faced the prospect of being executed. It wasn't her idea of a happy holiday.

She'd survived, though. Which was amazing. She hadn't figured on it working out that way. She'd thought she might get one of them at best. Not both. But sometimes you got lucky.

With exaggerated care she set down the gun on the seat beside her. She looked around her, thinking it might be time to sample some of that scotch in the bar, and saw poor old Sammy lying discarded on the floor.

Still on. The call still in progress.

Petrossian must have heard everything.

First things first. She dug a cigarette out of her purse and lit up. Then she picked up the phone.

"I'm back. Sorry about the interruption."

"They're dead, then?" Petrossian said. "Arshag and Suren?"

"If you mean Dancer and Prancer—stone cold."

"How ever did you manage that?"

"A magician never reveals her secrets. Let's just say the hand was quicker than the eye."

He chuckled. "You're not completely incompetent, it would appear."

"You seem real choked up about your two employees."

"They were expendable. My country breeds violent, stupid men as readily as dung breeds flies. I can obtain more."

She pulled a draft of smoke deep into her lungs. "How long till you send another couple hitters after me?"

"I think you've earned some additional time. Just as I thought you might."

At the point of taking another drag, she paused. "Wait a minute. Was this some kind of dumbass test?"

"It did occur to me that if your talents hadn't been too greatly exaggerated, you might contrive an escape from this situation."

She shook her head, inhaled more smoke, and expelled it with a growl. "You're an asshole."

"And you are a survivor. For the present, that is. I'll give you until nightfall. But there'll be no more reprieves. If Henry Phipps has another night on this earth, you don't."

"That's not a lot of time."

"It's more than you had a minute ago. Goodbye, Bonnie."

"Hold on. Aren't we forgetting one little thing? Your informant?"

"Oh, him." He made another clucking sound. "All right, I'll tell you. As it happens, he's a police officer. A patrolman in your town."

She sat very still, the cigarette smoldering between her fingers.

"Perhaps you know him," Petrossian said. "Officer Bradley Walsh."

19

IT BURNED WHEN it went in, liquid fire. It seared.

Henry felt that burn again, even now, although the ordeal was over and he wasn't in the basement anymore. At some point afterward, while he was unconscious, he'd been returned to his room on the third floor. His mind had come back to him while he lay facedown on the cot, his clothes pasted to his skin with sweat. The door to the hallway was closed, and he was in darkness.

In darkness ... and in hell.

Hell was where he'd gone when Sofia stamped the needle into his arm. Hell was where he remained, and where he was trapped, forever.

Eyes shut, he remembered the slow descent of the plunger as the syringe emptied its contents into his blood.

"This is Lady Salvia," she informed him. "I call her Sally, because she's an old friend. Sally, meet Henry." Turning her head, she gave Jonah a quizzical look. "Wasn't that a movie? *When Henry Met Sally*?"

Jonah disregarded the question. "You sure it's safe to mainline that shit?"

"The way I do it, it is. Trust me." To Henry she said, "Sally's nice when you treat her with respect. But when you bang her like this, it makes her mad. And when Sally's mad, she can be kind of a bitch."

He lay helpless on the cellar floor, Jonah straddling him. He felt the burning flame of the injection. Part of him wanted to cry out, to ask what they were giving him, what it would do. He said nothing. He would not show fear. He was their superior, their master. He knew it, even if they did not.

A shudder skipped through him, a shock of cold following the infusion of heat, and then he was hot and cold together, fire and ice, and something was happening to his body. It was flattening, losing its dimensionality. He watched, fascinated, as his right hand elongated, the fingers unspooling like ribbons, extending to the walls of the cellar and through them to infinity. He was immeasurably large, yet he had no substance, no reality.

Sofia leaned closer, her face giving up its round contours, becoming blocky and flat. She looked like a Lego figure. She was smiling, a wicked smile painted on the square sharp-edged face.

"Twisty-twist," Sofia whispered in his ear. "You're twisting, Henry. Feel yourself turning inside out."

It was true. He *was* twisting. He saw it, somehow, with his skin. Saw himself twisting in on himself. Folding like origami, and folding and refolding until he folded one last time and was gone, disappearing into his own emptiness, winking out.

After that, the logical sequence of cause-and-effect was confused, reduced to disordered impressions, flashes of perception bursting like fireworks.

At some point he was falling and falling, an endless plummet through a darkness sticky with pulsating gelatinous screams. At another point he was mired in sulfurous foulness and things crawled on him, pale slimy things that played strange atonal chords on his body, things with rodent claws and human faces. He thrashed and flailed, trying to beat away the crawling things, but iron bands held him down.

Sometime earlier or later, he slid down the slippery wall of a well, and at the bottom was a grinning idiot face with metal jaws that opened with a grinding of gears, and he knew it was the face of this world's god, his enemy, opening his immense mouth to swallow him up. He scrabbled at the mossy bricks, fighting for a handhold, but he kept slipping lower, the giant mouth widening in hungry all-devouring expectation.

He remembered shouting for help. Begging Sofia to save him. But Sofia was gone, and in her place was something insectile, a creature of bulbous eyes and clicking mandibles and armored tiers of legs. It laughed at him, obscene chittering laughter, and the sound was taken up by other creatures, unseen, a vast horde of them hiding in darkness, like his sad congregation in the depths of Domani.

And a voice. Her voice? Or was it the spitting hiss of the cockroach thing? "You don't exist, Henry. You never did."

This, too, was true. He was in the dark, bodiless, adrift. Where was the world?

It had gone away. Everything was gone. His environment had resolved into a tiled mosaic, a screen of pixels, and the pixels had dropped off in clusters, erasing time and space, color and light, leaving infinite emptiness, an eternal void.

All was clear to him then. Everything he'd thought to be real had been only a trick of the mind, and not even of his own mind, but the minds of others, operating slyly behind the scenes, the cockroach creatures and the trickster god.

Grief overcame him. He heard his disembodied sobbing—gulping, gasping sobs that pleaded: *Is this it? Is this all there is? This nothingness? Is this what it was all about?*

"You're alone, Henry," the spitting hiss told him, its taste more bitter than smoke, "and lost, and nobody will find you or even look. Those you loved weren't real, either. None of them."

Then Katie, too ... Even Katie ...

It was too much. He rebelled against this final insult. His wife, at least, had lived. Had *been*. He couldn't be wrong about that. He couldn't let them take her from him, not like this. Not by making it so she had never existed at all. It was too pointless, too cruel, even for the imposter god he hated.

Henry tried to scream in protest, but there was no Henry and there never had been. The thing called Henry had been only a made-up character in a book no one would read.

His first clear memory of being himself again, or almost himself, was of waking on the cot. He'd held tight to the metal frame, anchoring himself to the world. That had been many minutes ago. He held on still.

His head hurt. Tears burned his eyes. His throat was tight, choked with grief.

He had been wrong about this universe. Hell it was, but not the lowest pit of hell. Torture could be endured. But that timeless, spaceless, friendless emptiness ...

No one could tolerate that.

And if that was the true nature of things, there was no way out. No way to beat the system. The dungeon of reality was escape-proof. Nothing was beyond it or outside it, and any door that could be opened led only to the void.

He ground his face into the mattress and cried.

After a long time he felt strong enough to rise. His legs were weak and shaky, his steps uncoordinated. In darkness he stumbled to the door and tested the knob. Locked.

They were taking no chances with him this time. He had expected as much.

Peeling back his sleeve, he massaged the bruise on the inside of his elbow where the needle had bitten. The tenderness of the wound cheered him a little. It allowed him to classify his experience as merely a chemical reaction, a bad trip.

He wasn't sure he believed this. What he'd seen and felt had been too persuasively real to be rationalized away. And yet ...

Every jailer told his captives there was no escape. It was part of the prisoner's mental conditioning, the ceaseless efforts to break his will. Could it truly be the case that this world, this hell, was the be-all and end-all, a slaughterhouse with no exit?

Or had his nightmarish journey been only a snare and a delusion? A trap laid by Sofia, who'd dosed him with her witch's potion and whispered evil thoughts in his ear. A disinformation campaign, deliberate misdirection, a black op.

Possibly. It would be just like the god of lies to employ a strategy of deception.

Slowly he nodded.

In his moment of weakness, he'd almost forgotten the revelation he'd been granted. He must hold tight to his truth, even in this hour of testing. The trickster was marshaling every resource against him. He must be strong enough to hold out.

To hold out ... and fight back.

Henry sat on the cot, his thoughts coming into focus.

Of all the acolytes he might have found, how was it that Jonah and Sofia had come to him? It could not have been an accident. No misfortune in this cosmic puzzle palace ever happened by chance.

In the basement he'd called Jonah an agent of the trickster god. The truth, he now saw, was something larger. Something worse.

Jonah was not a mere agent. He *was* the impostor. He was the lying god incarnate.

And Sofia was his consort, the eternal nurturer and enabler, wife-mother-whore.

The two of them, male and female avatars of the evil one, had taken form on this plane in a desperate rearguard effort to intercept and silence him.

Yes.

He should have expected nothing less.

"In the beginning was the Lie," Henry whispered, his voice a chanting monotone, "and the Lie was called God. In him was pain, and pain was the life of all things. And the Lie became flesh and dwelt among us ..."

He raised his head. In the ink-blot blackness glittered a faint residue of the radiance that had suffused him in his epiphany. He saw it. He welcomed it. He felt renewed.

This was the final stage of his mission. His last living purpose. To confront the monster face to face, in human form—and destroy him.

To expunge Jonah and his woman from this earth.

20

BONNIE DROVE THE limo back into Brighton Cove with her two friends on the floor of the backseat. It hadn't been easy getting Prancer inside. She'd thought she was going to bust a gut.

She abandoned the car behind a bowling alley on 71, texting Petrossian on where to pick it up. She knew he could take care of it. She walked home, covering two miles of frozen distance, and retrieved the Jeep from her garage, along with the hit kit in her house. From there, she set off for Brad's apartment in Algonquin.

The whole time, her mind was working hard, stitching together bits and pieces of information—things she should have paid more attention to—things she *would* have paid more attention to if she hadn't been distracted by so much other shit.

The picture was more than half developed by the time she parked outside his building. But there were blank spots, big ones, and only he could fill them in.

It felt strange to venture into his neighborhood. Throughout their relationship they'd practiced stealth. He'd never gone to her duplex, and his apartment had been off-limits since they'd learned that his downstairs neighbor had ratted them out to Dan. Since then, her office had been their meeting place, a safe choice, they'd thought, because no one would notice his personal car if it was parked downtown.

No need for secrecy now. The cat was out of the bag, whatever the hell that meant. What kind of sicko went around putting cats in bags, anyway? Language was so fucked up.

It was after ten thirty when she arrived. Brad's fire-red Mustang wasn't parked on the street, a worrying sign. She climbed the stairs to the second floor and rapped on his door. No answer. She was taking a close look at the keyhole, wondering which of her lock picks would work best, when she remembered that he'd given her a key. Though she hadn't used it in more than a year, luckily her purse was a graveyard of discarded junk, where all useless possessions went to die. Excavating multiple strata of debris, she unearthed the key. It still fit the lock.

She entered, not bothering to call his name. He was gone. She could see it at once. The apartment was a studio—nowhere to hide. There was the narrow kitchenette, the bathroom with a shower stall, the cheap sofa that folded out into an uncomfortable bed. The creaking of the springs must have left little to the imagination of the busybody downstairs.

His place was the same as she remembered it, except emptier. Dusty rectangles marked the spots where a TV and cable box, boombox and vintage turntable, and several model schooners had stood. The kitchenette was similarly depopulated. None of this surprised her.

She checked the medicine cabinet, then all the usual hiding places, but she couldn't find what she was after. In the fridge, however, she found something else—a brick of hundred-dollar bills wrapped in tinfoil, masquerading as a block of cheese. She counted out ten thousand dollars exactly. The full amount Petrossian had paid him. None of it had been spent.

The cash, sans foil, went into her purse. It was better off with her.

"All right," she said to the fridge. "If you were Bradley Walsh, where would you be?"

The fridge was an idiot. It knew nothing. But Sammy

might. Some time ago she'd linked her phone to Brad's, using a locator app. He didn't even know about it. She'd done it on the sly. She was crafty that way.

She pulled up the app. His phone was currently situated in the Central Jersey Medical Center in Maritime.

That didn't sound good. She thought about calling, but decided not to give him a heads-up. Maritime was only twenty minutes away. She could wait that long to find out what was going on.

Besides, she knew most of it already. Petrossian had told her part of it, the apartment had told her more, and a question he'd asked last night had filled in one of the gaps.

She wasn't impressed with herself for figuring it out. Truth was, she should have seen it sooner. Her only defense was that Brad just wasn't that that kind of guy, or so she'd thought. With someone like him, your mind just didn't go there. Not to mention that a relationship built around hurried clandestine meetings after hours in her office didn't necessarily afford a lot of room for emotional intimacy.

None of that was much of an excuse. She was supposed to be streetwise. She liked to think she was smart.

And yet for months now, probably six months or more, her boyfriend had been hooked on OxyContin or Percocet, or both, and she hadn't had a clue.

Sammy was smart—she was pretty sure her phone was smarter than she was—but there were limits even to his wisdom. He could narrow down the location of Brad's cell to a range of about ten yards. After that, she was on her own.

The app placed the target outside the medical building itself, somewhere in the vast, perpetually overcrowded parking lot that sprawled around it. Apparently Brad was parked in the general vicinity of the ER.

She steered the Jeep down the aisles, looking for his Mustang. She found it wedged between a minivan and a sloppily parked Lexus that took up two spaces.

She was a little surprised he'd left his phone in the car, until she drove past and saw a huddled figure behind the wheel. The motor was off, and he was just sitting there. He must have been slumped in the driver's seat for some time. She took a long enough look to see him shift his position, confirming that he was alive.

The only available space was marked *Reserved for Clergy*. Screw it. On Christmas morning most of the clergy probably had other shit going on. She stole the space and killed her engine, waiting while the Jeep coughed smoke from its tailpipe and shuddered on its shocks. Fishing a number out of Sammy's list of contacts, she placed a call, talked for three minutes, and worked everything out, including payment. This accomplished, she left the Jeep and hoofed it back to the Mustang through the stinging cold. The sky was darkening, and a snow shower threatened.

Brad didn't see her until her knuckles rapped the side window. He looked up, his eyes underscored with dark crescents, his face pale and damp with sweat. He didn't seem upset to see her, or pleased. He didn't register any reaction. He just stared.

She tried the door. It was locked. "Open up, Walsh."

She was half-afraid he might start the engine and pull away. The haunted look in his eyes spoke of a man who wanted to run. But after a brief hesitation he waved her around to the passenger side and unlocked the door.

She slid in beside him. "Merry Christmas," she said. "You look like hell."

He ran a hand through his hair, pushing it up in a spiky hedge. "I'm not feeling so great."

"So you decided to hang out by the hospital and see if proximity could effect a cure?"

"I thought I'd go in. But—well, I don't know. Maybe I'm just tired. I, uh, I didn't get much sleep."

"I'm guessing you didn't get any." She'd noticed he was wearing last night's clothes. She'd also noticed that he hadn't asked how she'd found him. It was as if he was past the point of questioning anything that happened to him. "What's really going on, Walsh?"

"Going on? What the hell is *not* going on? Dan knows about us ... you got shot ... the news says Phipps is still at large ..."

"And you're the one who fingered him to Petrossian for the reward."

He sank lower in his seat. For a bad moment she thought he might actually pass out.

"Okay ..." he whispered in a low, toneless voice.

She waited. Patience was not ordinarily among her virtues, but in this case she could fake it.

"How'd you know?" he said after almost a full minute.

"He told me, Walsh. He gave me your name."

"Told you?"

"There's no honor among thieves. Or among millionaire drug dealers, apparently. Who'd have thought?"

"So it was Petrossian? Armin Petrossian, the Armenian guy?"

"Didn't you know?"

"He never identified himself. I don't even know if I talked to him directly or to some flunky."

"It would have been him. He's playing this one close to the vest."

"Yeah. Well, he did have kind of an air of authority, I guess you'd say. I didn't know him, but he knew me. Called me by name. We met behind Alcatraz."

Alcatraz was a bar on the highway. Not a high-class establishment.

"Behind?" She couldn't think of anything in back of the bar.

"In the alley. By the dumpster. With the rats."

He was probably exaggerating about the rats. Then again, maybe not. "Okay."

"It was dark back there. I didn't get a good look at him. Which I'm sure is how he wanted it. I told him what I knew, and he handed me the cash."

"Yeah. I found it in the fridge. Great hiding place. Almost as original as the sock drawer."

"Who knows, maybe I want it to get stolen."

"Why? You earned it. Ten grand is pretty good for a night's work."

He flared up, his eyes widening. "You're gonna say that to me? After the things *you've* done for money? You're working for him right now, you've got to be, and I'll bet it's for a lot more than ten thousand dollars. What's the going rate for a hit these days?"

She held up her hands. "Whoa, Nellie. First of all, my going rate is forty thousand—I raised it a few months ago—and I'm worth every nickel. Second of all, I'm not judging you. I just need to know what happened. You're a Boy Scout, Walsh. You don't *do* stuff like this. I mean, *ever*. You don't break the rules."

"I hooked up with you, didn't I?"

"That's a special case. I'm irresistible." She hoped she would coax a smile out of him, but he only glared at her. "Look, I need to know everything that went down. You might as well talk. You're in no condition to hold out on me."

"Because I'm under the weather?"

"Because you're in withdrawal. How long have you been using?"

His jaw clenched. His gaze jerked sideways. "I didn't say anything about drugs."

"You didn't need to. Your apartment's been cleaned out one item at a time. You're selling your inventory for cash. You're sweaty and pale and you look like you're gonna spew, which, by the way, if you think you are, try to aim the firehose away from me, 'cause these boots are new."

Still no smile. "So you think I'm a heroin addict?"

"Not heroin. Oxycodone or something like it."

"Where'd you come up with that idea?"

"From a question you asked last night, though it didn't register with me at the time. I mentioned painkillers, and your mind went straight to oxy and Percocet."

"Because there's an opiate epidemic. Try reading a goddamn newspaper. Assuming you *can* read, with your third-grade education."

Strong language for him. And personal abuse. He was spiraling down into a dark place really fast.

"I made it through eighth grade," she said calmly, "and I don't need to read any newspapers to know you're hurting, Walsh. You're sitting here shivering in your car. You need help, but you're afraid to go into the ER because if your opiate habit goes on your record, you're shit outta luck for employment in law enforcement, here or anywhere."

"I'm out of luck anyway. I'm finished. I fucked up—I fucked up everything—I fucked up my whole life."

Suddenly the hostility was gone. He deflated, collapsing in on himself, his eyes screwed shut against a rush of tears.

Bonnie wasn't much good at comforting people. A bedside manner wasn't really in her wheelhouse. She was better at tough love, or maybe she was just a bitch.

Even so, she put her arm around his shoulders and guided his head to her chest.

"Everybody fucks up," she said softly. "Me, more than most. But I'm still in there pitching. So are you."

"Sure," he whispered. "Sure I am."

She didn't say anything after that. She let him cry it out, sobbing quietly like the hurt little boy he was.

21

TRUTH BE TOLD, Jonah was just a tad shaken by what his girl had done to the old man. That had been some seriously fucked up shit. At the end, poor Henry had been curled in a fetal pose, drool striping his chin, murmuring *no no no* in a hopeless monotone.

Humping him up to the third floor hadn't been any picnic, either. Not because Henry weighed much of anything, but because he was crying the whole time. Really, for God's sake, crying like a little girl. He wasn't even awake, just blubbering in his sleep. Jonah hadn't liked it. It'd kinda creeped him out.

That had been some time ago, before he'd stoked the furnace and retrieved his Luger from the van. By now he was more or less over it. He washed away any residual unease with a swig from a bottle of cognac he'd lifted from a liquor store last week. Five-finger discount, you know. Nasty stuff, cognac, but it had been the only hard liquor he could filch, and at least it would help get him through the day.

He set down the bottle on the kitchen counter and listened to the transistor radio as he scavenged for edibles among the moldy loaves of bread and stale potato chips. There was plenty of news coverage of the Man in the Moon and scattered stories on other topics, but nothing on a dead cop named Bradley Walsh. This bothered him a little. Walsh ought to be dead by now. But probably he'd died alone, and nobody had found the body. Yeah, that was it.

In a cabinet he scored a jar of peanut butter. He scooped out big chunks with his fingers, licked them clean, then washed down the meal by dropping his head level with the sink and drinking straight from the tap.

He was shaking himself dry, like a big wet dog, when Sofia glided in. "Henry's acting weird," she said.

"What else is new? Hey, you ain't been talking to him or nothing?"

He didn't want her in communication with Preacher. The son of a bitch was way smarter than his girl, not that this was any high bar to clear, and he would wrap her pea-brain around his little finger if she let him.

"Just listening," she said.

"To what?"

"To him. He's up there yelling about the mother of harlots and the scarlet dragon."

"Must be preaching another sermon. Sounds like a real humdinger."

"Yeah, but who's he talking to?"

"Hisself. Nobody." Jonah hoisted himself onto the counter. "I dunno, babe. I think you mighta broke the old man."

"He was broken already."

"Now he's broke worse. You unzipped him pretty good. For a few minutes there, I thought we might lose him altogether."

"That would never happen. The lady is a lover, not a killer."

The lady. Lady Salvia, she meant, or sometimes just plain Sally. Salvia divinorum, an egghead like Peter Forrest would say. A powerful hallucinogen, seriously scary. Jonah had never smoked it or even chewed the leaves. He'd heard too many bad things. And mainlining it the way Henry had, jacking it straight into the bloodstream—well, *damn*. That was a surefire ticket to Mr. Toad's Wild Ride.

Sofia, of course, had tried salvia—she'd tried every

fuckin' thing, one time or another—but never with a needle, and never in such a concentrated dose. And on her trips, she hadn't had a whispery voice in her ear, sweetly coaxing her ever deeper into hell.

"You may be right," he said judiciously. "But he still had me worried. It's okay if he's got a needle mark on him. Nobody's gonna bat an eye if the Man in the Moon was a user. But we sure don't want him stroking out or some damn thing."

"I could give him a hundred trips like that, and he'd still be alive. After what he did to me, he deserves it. I've been thinking ..."

He knew what she'd been thinking. Putting a big hurt on people revved his gal's motor like nobody's business.

Firmly he shook his head. "No way, honeybunch. He can't die before his time."

She pouted, her lower lip jutting out.

"How's your mouth?" he remembered to ask.

"It still hurts. But it's only pain. Pain doesn't have to be part of me unless I let it."

The yards of scar tissue ribboning his body put him in some doubt on that score, but he didn't argue. "Well, that's good, then. Look, I'll be going out for a bit, and I don't want you listening in on him again. I need you to steer clear of his room."

"What for?"

"'Cause I told you so, is what-for. And 'cause I don't trust you not to be asshole enough to unlock the door if Preacher tells you to."

"I wouldn't do that."

"You might do anything, if you're flying high. And even when you're sober, if you ever are, you still ain't no smarter than a stump."

She frowned, taking no offense, merely registering disappointment. "Do you really have to go out? It's Christmas."

Jonah didn't give a rat's ass about Christmas. "Yeah,

I do. Gotta put things in motion. Like we talked about."

"What things?"

"I told you. I told you twenty times."

"I don't remember."

Damn girl had the brainpower of a fruit fly. "The plan," he said, enunciating clearly. "My revenge on them that put me in stir."

"Oh, that."

"Yeah. That." He took another hit off the bottle and belched grandly. "I already got one of 'em."

Her eyes widened. "You did?"

"Yeah. You know my client from last night, the one who bought Doc Forrest's magic beans?" He'd kept quiet about the reason behind that purchase, not wanting her to blurt out something stupid around Forrest. But it didn't matter now. "I sold 'em to a certain Bradley Walsh, who just happens to be a patrol officer in the Brighton Cove Police Department. He thought them pills was just more of his regular supply. He didn't know he was buying—what'd the doc call it?"

"Concentrated death," Sofia said, her tongue tasting the words. "You think he took one already?"

"Shit, yeah. He was jonesin' real bad for a fix." He thought of the radio, the absence of news. He shook off his doubts. "Yeah, that son of a bitch has gotta be good 'n' dead."

"Dead," she whispered, and he heard the flutter of arousal in her voice.

"That's right, Mommy. Can't you just picture him kicking his feet on the floor, his face all splotchy purple?"

She made a small, shuddery sound of pleasure. "How about the others?"

"Them two go out Man-in-the-Moon-style. I'll get one this afternoon, t'other one tonight. Works out real good, see? The Brighton Cove cops raided Preacher's house, so naturally he got a bee in his bonnet about them. That there's a nice touch. Something I didn't even plan for to happen."

"It will work. I'm sure it will."

"'Course it'll work. My daddy didn't raise no fools. Now here's the thing." He plucked the Luger from his waistband. "While I'm away, I need you to carry this. Don't put it down and leave it nowhere. Keep it with you."

"Why?"

"Case anything happens. With Preacher, you know."

"He's locked up."

"Yeah, and I expect he'll stay that way. But you never know. He's a crafty one. Pulled off a six-pack of homicides without getting pinched. He might be able to think his way out of a locked room."

"You're being silly." Sofia pouted again, but she accepted the gun, weighing it doubtfully in her hand.

"Just humor me, okay? Keep him shut up tight, don't go near him, and keep the Luger close."

Her face brightened with a smile. "You're worried about me."

"Could be. Just a little."

She lowered her eyes almost bashfully. "You know, I never did give you your Christmas present."

"Is that so?"

"You want it now?"

"Baby, I always want it."

Kneeling, she unbuttoned his fly. Her gentle hands eased his cock out of his pants. He sat back on the counter, leaning against the cabinets, and let her go to work. And damn, she was good. He might not love this girl, but he sure did love what she could do.

He shut his eyes and thought about Abbott and Costello. It was what he always did to keep himself from coming too soon. For some guys, it was baseball or the times tables. What'd they call it? Multi-pli-cation.

For him it was, *Who's on first. What's on second. Idunno's on third ...*

She worked him harder, drawing him deeper into her moist warmth and loving softness.

Who's on first ...

What's on second ...

He never did get back to third.

22

WHEN HE'D FINALLY cried himself out, Bonnie asked him how it happened. "Tell it from the beginning."

Brad lifted his head, blinking his eyes dry. "Remember a couple years ago, when I had surgery? Torn Achilles'?"

"From a pickup basketball game. Proving once again that white men can't jump."

"They wrote me a prescription for Percocet. I didn't need it, so I ended up stockpiling the pills. Just in case. Then, maybe six months ago ... might have been seven... I think it was May ..."

"Close enough. Go on."

"I'd been feeling stressed. Tension headaches, you know? Muscular tension in general. One night, I think of the pills, and I figure, why not? So I took one. And it worked."

She knew where he was going with this. The story wasn't exactly original.

"No big deal, right?" He chuckled, a sad, hopeless sound. "Except the next week I did it again. And—well, it became a regular thing. Have a headache, pop a pill. Think a headache might be coming on? Pop one just to be safe. Feel kind of down, want to be happy? Take a pill."

"You couldn't have had that many Percocets."

"They ran out within a month. I got more. Guy I knew. Guy I'd busted once."

"In Brighton Cove?"

"He usually operates out of McKendree Park. Less heat on him there."

"And by then you were hooked."

"Maybe not totally hooked. I mean, I probably still could've stopped. But I liked it. That's the thing. I'm not making excuses. I *liked* the high."

He said it with a kind of plaintive honesty that touched her.

"Yeah," she said quietly. "I know the feeling. I can be a little too fond of whiskey sometimes." She considered it. "And rum." She considered further. "And cigarettes."

He nodded, though she didn't think he was listening. "The, um, the dependence, I guess you'd call it, came later. It came on so slowly that I was hardly aware of it. I kept saying I had it under control, and as long as nobody found out ... Even when I started selling off my stuff, I rationalized. How much TV do I watch, anyway? Who needs a microwave when you've got a toaster oven? Who needs a toaster oven when you've got a regular oven?"

"Sounds like you're not making excuses anymore," she said gently.

"No. Not after last night." He looked directly at her. "Not after I found you on the floor and you told me it was the Man in the Moon. I knew right away it had to be because of me. The guy I tipped off hired you to do the job. And you got shot."

"Getting shot is on me, not you. And he didn't exactly hire me. It's not a pay-for-play deal. I'm doing it gratis."

"Why?"

"I'm public-spirited."

He waved away her answer. "Anyhow, I quit. Cold turkey." A ripple of shivers passed through him. He hugged himself.

"When's the last time you got a fix?"

"Two days ago. I ran out of pills. Last night, after I left your office, I called my guy. I was—well, you know. I was in a bad way. Super stressed. I needed a refill, even if it was after hours."

"He come through for you?"

A nod. "I made the buy after midnight. By then I'd calmed down a little, so I didn't take one right away. Wanted to get home first, maybe think about it. Maybe even hold off. I was driving back when I passed your place."

"And just like that, you were scared straight?"

"I flushed my whole stash. Three little blue pills, right down the toilet."

So that was why she hadn't found any. "Okay. Now tell me the rest of the story."

"There's nothing else. I told it all."

"Nope. You left out the most important part. How'd you find out about Phipps?"

"What difference does it make now?"

"My job's not over yet."

"The police are on the case. You can let them handle it."

"Not an option. Petrossian's unhappy with me. I have until tonight to rectify the situation."

"Or?"

"Or he rectifies me."

"Jeez, Bonnie ..." He put his head in his hands. "Jeez."

"Cowboy up, Walsh. I've been in worse jams. Just talk. And do it fast. There's a friend of mine who'll be here any minute."

"What friend?"

"Somebody discreet and trustworthy. Talk."

He talked.

Four years ago, he'd arrested Jonah Stroud, a small-time dealer who'd been visiting a special client in Brighton Cove. By the town's standards it had been a pretty big bust. Stroud was sent away for three years.

"Jonah hails from someplace called Mandalay, Georgia," Brad said. "Hard luck story, or so his lawyer said. He lit out on his own at nineteen and made his way north. Been in and out of trouble ever since."

Six or seven months ago, right around the time he was developing a taste for opiates, Brad spotted Jonah Stroud in McKendree Park. Out of curiosity he followed Stroud long enough to observe him enter the unfinished construction project called Domani, a known hangout for druggies and street people.

He remembered the incident. He found himself loitering near Domani, keeping an eye out for Stroud. Finally he saw him again, leaving the site in the company of a woman.

"What woman?"

"We were never introduced, but I saw her at his trial. His girlfriend, Sofia Windsor."

"Windsor. She sounds classy."

"She's not. Well, she does come from money, but she took a big fall. Her family kicked her loose when she was seventeen. Story is, she got an abortion and her folks didn't like it. She's an obvious user, stoned all the time. She's about twenty-five, ten years younger than him."

"They been together long?"

"Since before his arrest, so yeah, four years at least. Of course, I don't know what she was up to while he was cooling his heels in prison, but she took up with him again as soon as he got out."

Stroud wasn't exactly enthusiastic about doing a deal with his arresting officer. Somehow Brad persuaded him to go along. Maybe Stroud could sense that his desperation wasn't an act.

So they started meeting. They would arrange a rendezvous via text messages, and Brad would exchange cash for pills.

"You use your regular phone or a burner?" she asked.

"Regular one."

"Did you erase his texts, at least?"

"Um ...no."

"Seriously, Walsh?"

"I wasn't thinking."

"Damn straight you weren't. Give it over."

Reluctantly he surrendered the cell. She thumbed the power switch, and the main screen came right up. Not even password-protected. Jeez.

She found the texts and looked them over. It wasn't often she had the chance to feel superior to someone else in terms of education. Today she'd hit the jackpot.

"Not a great speller, is he?" she said, scrolling through the messages.

"He's borderline illiterate."

"Borderline might be giving him the benefit of the doubt." She switched the phone off and dropped it into her purse.

"Hey," Brad said, "I need that."

"No, you don't. When you're clean, you'll get a new one. This one needs to disappear. It's chock-full of what you law enforcement types call incriminating evidence. *Capisce*?"

"Yeah, I guess.

"So where were we? Oh, right. You became Jonah's customer. And ..."

"And last week he told me he had a secret. He knew the identity of the Man in the Moon. He'd gained the guy's confidence, he said. Got him to open up."

"Why'd he tell you?"

"Because I'm a cop."

"And why didn't you tell Dan?"

"You know why. He'd want to know my source, and then everything would come out."

"What made you believe Stroud in the first place?"

"He had a video."

The video—shaky, muffled, and two minutes long—had been shot surreptitiously with a cameraphone. The camera must have been held by the girlfriend and aimed at Stroud and Phipps from under a table.

The recorded conversation was short and to the

point. Stroud asked Phipps when the Man in the Moon killings would stop. Henry said they never would. Even after he was dead, his disciples would continue the job. If Jonah lacked the stomach for it, there would be others.

"He said the testimony, whatever that is, would convert thousands and change the world."

Bonnie knew what the testimony was. The scribbled pages of craziness in Henry's file drawer. Apparently to be made public after his death.

"Okay," she said. "So you had proof. Just email the vid to the police."

"Jonah erased it after he showed it to me. He was on the video, and he didn't want to be involved. That was what he kept saying, over and over. He couldn't be involved."

"Even without proof, you could've called in an anonymous tip to the police hotline. They have to check out every lead."

"There are too many leads. It could be weeks before they followed up."

"Then you could've told me. I'm always up for some vigilante action."

"I was trying to keep you out of it."

"Why? To preserve my girlish innocence?"

"I've learned to be okay with what you do. That doesn't mean I'm going to encourage you to do it."

Maybe this was true. But it was also true that if he'd told her, she would have been just as curious as Dan about his source. "Whatever. So you went to somebody who wouldn't be too particular about proof. Namely Petrossian."

"I didn't know that's who he was. Jonah said he'd heard rumors about a reward offered by some big syndicate guy, name unknown. A bartender could schedule a meet. I went there and made arrangements."

"Stroud could have done that himself. Then he'd have pocketed the reward."

"Like I said, he didn't want to get involved."

Or he was setting you up, Bonnie thought, but she didn't push it. "When did you meet Petrossian?"

"The day before yesterday."

Which gave Petrossian just enough time to gather details on Phipps before calling her last night.

A white Grand Caravan appeared in the rearview mirror like a breaching whale. The words BEACH CAB were stenciled across the side panels.

"Your ride is here," she said.

Brad turned awkwardly in his seat. "Felix Ramirez? You called him?" Panic jumped in his voice, backed up by an encore of his irrational anger.

"Relax, Walsh. He's good people."

"He knows me. He knows I'm a cop."

"Yeah, yeah. He knows a lot of things. But he keeps his mouth shut about all of it."

"He's mixed up in a lot of really questionable stuff."

"So am I." And so are you, she thought.

"Even so, I just can't trust him."

"You trusted Jonah Stroud, a guy you arrested and sent away. You trusted Armin Petrossian, even if you didn't know who he was."

"That was different," he said stubbornly.

She was tired of fighting him. "It's either Felix, or you walk into the ER with me and put it all on the record."

"God damn it."

"You got quite a mouth on you, Walsh."

She saw Felix emerge from his taxi and slide open the side door. He gave her a friendly wave.

"We're getting out now," she said. "You can leave your car here. It's not like it'll be ticketed at a hospital. Come on."

He didn't argue, though he still looked seriously pissed off.

As unobtrusively as possible, she assisted him in the short walk from the Mustang to the SUV. His legs were shaky, and his muscles were losing their coordination.

Felix helped her strap him into the backseat.

"*A la gran chucha,*" he said after a long look at Brad, "you are having a bad day."

Brad turned away, his face red in a mixture of fury and shame.

"You know what you're getting into here?" Bonnie asked Felix when they were out of the vehicle.

"Of course. I am well prepared. I stopped in the drugstore on my way over. You see?"

He handed her a bag from the front seat. She looked over his purchases. Dramamine for nausea. Imodium for the runs. Tylenol for pain. Gatorade to replenish fluids and electrolytes. Good choices.

"What's this stuff?" She pointed to the last package.

"Tai-Kang-Ning. Chinese herb, good for opiate withdrawal."

"How the heck do you know these things?"

Felix shrugged in such a way as to suggest simultaneously that he knew everything that mattered and that he was too modest to admit it.

"You'll keep him hydrated when he starts to spew?"

"Of course."

"Anything that gets ruined—your clothes, sheets, carpet, whatever—just add it to my tab."

"The price may be big before we are done."

"I'll pay it. If I'm still alive."

"Of this I have no worries. I have told you before, *bandida*. You are a survivor. You always come through."

She hoped this was true.

While Felix settled behind the wheel, she slid into the backseat for a last chat with Brad. "Hang in there, slugger. I'll check in when I can."

He turned to face her. "You're going after Stroud, aren't you?"

"It's pretty much my only move. You don't happen to know where I'd find him?"

"No idea. His last known address was a halfway house

in Pilgrim Grove. The place is closed now."

"I could text him," she said. "Pretend to be you. Set up a meet."

"What's your excuse?"

"I need more stuff."

"After I bought four pills just last night? He'd never believe it. He'd know something was up."

"Yeah, probably. I'll figure something out." She was withdrawing from the car when she paused. "Wait a sec. Four pills?"

He nodded, looking uncomfortable.

"You said you flushed three."

He shut his eyes, worked his jaw for a long moment, then extracted a single blue pill from his shirt pocket. He handed it over. "I was sorta holding it in reserve."

She stuck it in the side pocket of her jeans. "This the last one?"

"Yeah." He blew out a shaky breath. "What can I say? The spirit is willing, but the flesh is weak."

She frowned. "Shakespeare?"

"I think it's the Bible."

"Potato, po-tah-to."

Felix started the engine. She climbed out. As she was closing the door, Brad said, "Hey, Bonnie—watch yourself. Jonah Stroud's a really sketchy character."

"My whole life involves really sketchy characters."

"But right now you've got only one good arm. Can you even draw and fire?"

"Left-handed."

"You any good that way?"

"I'm good every way. Get better, Walsh."

She shut the door, then stood there in the cold as the taxi slowly drove off into the darkening day.

23

AT NOON, DAN Maguire was having lunch at the establishment formerly known as the Main Street Diner, which, under new management, had recently been reinvented as an upscale coffee shop called La Vida Mocha. Dan found this to be wrong on many levels, but it was the only eatery in town that was actually serving food on Christmas Day, even if the food consisted of crumb cakes and scones.

He ought to be thinking about Henry Phipps, still at large. Instead his thoughts were occupied, as they so often were, with Bonnie Parker. His nemesis—his bête noire, as Bernice liked to say.

This morning, a pair of patrol officers, going off duty, had mentioned seeing an unfamiliar car outside Parker's address. It was a black Mercedes CLS, stretched, a kind of vehicle that called attention to itself. Cruising past, they'd seen two men inside. When they'd circled back fifteen minutes later, the limo was gone.

A small thing. Probably not important. But somehow he wished he knew more about that car.

He was polishing off his second scone—raspberry vanilla—when Bruce Haynes walked in. Dan lifted a hand in a half wave. Bruce nodded recognition and approached the table. "Hey, Dan. Mind if I join you?"

"Feel free."

"Food here any good?"

"Not as good as TastyCake. And a lot more expensive."

The waitress came by. Bruce ordered a muffin and

coffee. Not cappuccino, cafe mocha, macchiato, or any of the other exotic offerings listed in chalk on the blackboard menu. Just regular coffee. Dan admired him for that.

"You guys finish up at Lake Avenue?" Dan asked.

Bruce was a detective with the state police. Major Crime Bureau, Homicide South. He'd been working the Man in the Moon case from the start. And he was young—annoyingly so, to Dan's way of thinking. Just when did it happen that everyone around him started getting so young?

"Pretty much," Bruce said. "Dug the slugs out of the wall and sent them to Ballistics. I can tell you right now, they'll match."

"Phipps is definitely our guy?"

"Looks like."

"Weird. Milquetoast character like that."

"You know him?"

"Only by sight. He's never had any run-ins with the law. Not in this town, anyway."

"Not anywhere. We checked."

"Any idea where he would hole up?"

"We're going through his receipts and bills, credit card statements, bankbooks, the usual crap. Looking for a motel, a campground, anywhere he might have frequented. Nothing yet."

"His Subaru was found."

"In McKendree Park, yeah. But he wasn't in it. No blood in it, either."

Dan hadn't heard that detail. "Yeah?"

"Apparently he wasn't the one who was bleeding."

"Huh." Then at least one of his suspicions from last night had been confirmed. It was the intruder who'd taken the bullet. He remembered how Bonnie Parker had refused to be strip-searched. How she wouldn't even take off her coat. And was it his imagination, or had she been holding her right arm a little too stiffly at her side?

Clothing conceals a multitude of sins, his mom used to say.

"One funny thing." Bruce's order had arrived, and he was cutting into his muffin with a knife, then spearing the pieces with a fork. Dan lost a smidgen of respect for him. "Phipps kept clippings on his kills. They all do that. Had a mapbook of Millstone County too. He'd marked the locations of his greatest hits."

Phil Gaines had shown him that. "Okay."

"All the hits except one. Rosa Martinez. No mapbook page for her. She was left out of the mix."

Dan paused with his coffee mug in his hand. "Is that so?"

"Makes you think, doesn't it?"

"Was she included in the clippings?"

"Yeah, her murder was covered there. But it looks like Phipps collected every single story that mentioned the Man in the Moon. He might have saved those articles, even if ..." He let the thought dangle, uncompleted.

"Even if," Dan said slowly, "Rosa Martinez was a copycat job."

"That's always been a possibility."

The way Bruce said it, Dan had a feeling there was an added dimension to the story. "Always?"

Bruce shrugged. "I'm sort of talking out of school."

Dan said nothing. He was good at getting people to talk. He knew when to push and when to shut up.

"The thing is," Bruce went on after a moment, "when Rosa was found, the FBI got in touch. Not Behavioral Science. This was the TOC Section."

TOC. Transnational organized crime.

Dan made the faintest possible sound, simply to establish that he was listening. He didn't want to break Bruce's rhythm.

"You know Armin Petrossian? Armenian mob boss in Swan Neck?"

"Know *of* him," Dan said, keeping his answer to a minimum.

"The feds have been monitoring his movements. According to them, he paid a number of visits to Rosa Martinez's home in Algonquin."

Dan lifted an eyebrow.

"Then she turns up dead. Just another random victim of a nut. Or maybe not. Maybe Petrossian got tired of her, or she was threatening to blackmail him or write a book—who knows?"

"And he has her taken out in a way that won't look mob-related," Dan said.

"That was their idea. Just a theory, obviously. But it would explain a few things. Like the fact that the killer waited until Rosa was on the railroad tracks."

"Where she was mangled by the next train."

Bruce shrugged. "Might not mean anything. But with the round crushed and fragmented, it was impossible to do a ballistics match. So we can't be sure it wasn't a copycat thing."

"If we can get Phipps in custody," Dan said, "and make him talk—"

"Right. If he admits to the others but disavows Rosa, we'll have to look deeper into that one. So maybe it's in someone's interest that he isn't taken alive."

Dan put it together. "You're saying Petrossian sent someone after Phipps last night. The intention was to do a straight hit. It went sideways, the shooter got wounded, Phipps panicked and booked."

"It's one way to make sense of things. The shots fired in the house, the blood, the mapbook."

"Anybody looking at Petrossian's known associates to see if one of them checked into an ER?"

"Naturally. Nothing so far. Of course, these guys tend to have their own kind of medical plan. Doctors on call."

"Right."

If it was one of Petrossian's known associates.

But suppose it was someone else. Someone who couldn't be tied to him. Someone who knew Brighton

Cove, because she lived here. Someone who would kill for a price.

"You okay, Dan? You look a little distracted."

Dan plunked down his empty coffee cup. "I'm fine. Just have to get back to work. This is the busiest Christmas our guys have seen in a long time."

He left cash on the table, covering Bruce's meal as well as his own, brushing off an offer of reimbursement. He needed to find out more about that stretch Mercedes his men had seen. And he needed to get in touch with Phil Gaines.

Right now.

24

JONAH PARKED THE van a block away from the target location and took a long pull on the bottle of cognac. He was buzzed pretty good—hell, he was downright loaded—but that was okay. It helped get him up for what he was about to do.

Brighton Cove had its upscale neighborhoods, but this wasn't one of them. Tiny houses, postage stamp lots. Low-end cars in the driveways. Handmade signs tacked up on utility poles advertising garage sales and offering rewards for lost pets. The kind of area that depressed him, because it spoke of wasted time and boring lives—people commuting to stupid jobs they hated, raising bratty kids they didn't love, paying bills they couldn't afford, growing old and losing interest in life, in sex, in each other, even in their own selves. And dying, to be buried under a mat of turf that looked just like the weedy lawns they'd labored over on summer weekends.

He'd never wanted to be one of them. Better to die a million times than to live one day of a life like that.

Replacing the bottle on the passenger seat, he left the van and made his way through unfenced backyards toward the little house at 1235 Gardenia, the home of Detective Philip Gaines, Brighton Cove PD.

He was well acquainted with Detective Gaines. Son of a bitch had testified against him in court. Lot of mumbo-jumbo about latent prints and fibers. He remembered Gaines on the witness stand. His smug smile. The way he'd looked right at Jonah while testifying. Sending him away, delivering him straight into the sweaty embrace of A.T. Wilmington.

They got him on third-degree aggravated assault, with a sentence just shy of three years. He'd caused significant bodily harm while using a deadly weapon. Specifically, he'd sliced off the left index, middle, and ring fingers of Mr. Sheldon Rice.

Rice was a client with a taste for Adderall. He lived in a much nicer part of Brighton Cove than this one, in a roomy house that came just shy of being a mansion, a stair Colonial with a brace of marble greyhounds guarding the front steps. He pulled down a lot of money doing something called arbitrage, which could have been a made-up word as far as Jonah was concerned. Apparently his job required him to maintain high alertness on very little sleep, and the Adderall, at first an occasional luxury, had gradually morphed into a necessity.

Jonah didn't do a lot of business in Brighton Cove, but Rice was a good customer with a steady habit and a penchant for generous tips. On the night in question, however, Rice had also been inebriated. That in itself wouldn't have been a problem, except he was also horny, and as it turned out, what he was horny for was Jonah Stroud. The business transaction was, in fact, a thinly disguised booty call. Only, Jonah wasn't willing to cooperate. There were limits to the customer service he would provide.

Sober, Sheldon Rice would have understood that no meant no, especially when the no was delivered by a man with a line of swastikas marching down his arm. But alcohol made him reckless. When he reached down and gave Jonah's package a friendly squeeze, Jonah took it poorly.

The thing was, Jonah had been drinking, too. And he had his own issues with anger management and impulse control. It was, as you might say, the perfect storm.

Long story short, his knife had done a number on

Rice's digits. Naturally, Rice started screaming—you could hardly blame the guy, what with the cherry red blood spurting from the stumps of his fingers like water from a sprinkler. It was a summer night, and the windows were open, the screams audible throughout the neighborhood—the kind of neighborhood where people called 911.

Jonah left the house and fled in the van, but a witness saw him speed away. A cop car caught sight of him a few blocks south. He tried driving down an alley, an evasive maneuver that played out great in his head, but not so great in reality. He arrived at a brick wall with thc prowl car closing in from behind. His only option was to ditch the van and scale the wall. He was almost over the top when Bradley Walsh grabbed his ankles and hauled him back down.

Yes, sir, Officer Walsh was a genuine hero that night. He'd been riding solo when he heard the radio alert. He'd spotted, pursued, detained, and subdued the suspect. That was how they put it in court. What Jonah remembered was being held on the ground with his face in the muck while Walsh twisted his arms behind his back and snapped on the cuffs.

Didn't read him his rights, though. That didn't happen when you were facedown on the street, no matter what bullshit you saw on TV. It was always done later, after things settled down a bit and the cops could be sure you were listening.

The whole thing was a stupid mess, but Jonah had made one or two smart moves. He'd tossed the baggie of Adderall into a storm drain; the rain later that night must've swept it away before anyone thought of looking there. And he'd used his one phone call to give Sofia a heads-up, so that when the authorities arrived at the apartment they shared, the place was clean.

He had tossed the knife, too, pitching it over the wall when Walsh pulled him down. But the cops recovered it.

Of course he denied ever owning the damn thing, but that was where Detective Gaines came in. He matched the blood to Rice, matched the fingerprints on the handle to Jonah, even found fibers from Jonah's pants pocket glued by dried blood to the blade. He testified to all of the above in the courtroom, looking real prim and prissy and proud of himself.

And now it was time to pay the fuckin' piper.

Jonah approached the whitewashed bungalow from the rear. Ten minutes ago he'd stopped at a pay phone and called Detective Gaines's landline, his home phone. A sleepy voice had answered, proving the guy was at home.

He had expected no less. From his research—yeah, he did research, because he took this shit seriously—he knew that Gaines, though middle-aged, lived alone. Like Sheldon Rice. And probably, like Rice, this guy Gaines was a goddamn homo. He didn't figure the faggot would have any special plans for Christmas, and even if he did, most likely he wouldn't be heading out until later in the day.

Sidling up against the rear of the house, Jonah peered in through one window after another until he caught sight of his quarry, still in pajamas and robe despite the hour. Gaines must have been up late, going over Henry's house. Now he occupied the stool at his kitchen counter, sipping something that looked like a purple milkshake through a plastic straw, the bendy kind, and watching News 12 on TV.

Bendy straw, fruit drink. Definitely a homo.

Jonah pulled on latex gloves, which he used when robbing houses. He'd use the same gloves when he'd broken into this very house a month ago.

Research, bitches. No joke.

The back door was locked, but he had a key. He opened the door without a sound and waltzed in, drawing the pretty little .22 Colt Frontier Scout from his coat pocket. Henry's gun.

The gun was the very fuckin' essence of his plan. The ballistics had to match, so the law would blame it all on Henry. For it to work, he had to make this kill as close to a Xerox photocopy of the other ones as possible. Yeah, it took place indoors and wasn't random, but nobody would question that. They'd figure Henry went after two Brighton Cove cops because they'd been all over his house.

And the door? Just leave it open and let people think Gaines forgot to lock it. Must happen all the time in this one-stoplight town.

He made his way down a hallway paneled in imitation wood. The floor was linoleum, cracked and yellowed. He recalled those details from last time. The house must have been put up around 1970, and it had never been remodeled or updated. It was like a goddamn time capsule.

The kitchen was on his left. The TV droned. He heard a weather forecast. Snow expected, three inches or more. Then back to continuing coverage of the hunt for a serial killer.

That story was about to get an exciting new twist.

He advanced into the kitchen. Like the rest of the house, it smelled old and looked sad. Formica counters, outdated appliances. Tacked to the wall, a cheap calendar, the kind that came in charity mailings. Only a handful of appointments were marked in the squares. Nothing was listed for today.

In front of him sat Detective Phil Gaines, hunched over the counter, his back to the intruder whose presence he didn't even suspect.

It would be easy to kill him now. He had a bald spot, perfectly centered, the bull's-eye on the target.

But Jonah wanted the fucker to know what was happening. To feel the fear, to know the lights were about to go out.

"Hey, Phil," he said in a nice friendly voice, like he was a neighbor dropping by for a chat.

Gaines turned. He didn't whip around, the way you might expect. He swiveled on the stool, nice and slow, showing no surprise. A cool customer. Jonah gave him that.

"'Member me?" Jonah asked, lifting the gun a little higher.

"Stroud," Gaines said with a nod.

"That's me. I'm like a bad penny, I guess. Always turning up."

"How did you get in here?"

"With the key." Jonah smiled. "About a month ago you had a break-in. Some shit got stolen. That was me. I wasn't really after your merch. I just wanted to case the house, make sure you didn't got a dog or nothing. I truly hate dogs."

"I'm allergic," Gaines said.

"Are you now? Well, anyway, while I was here, I took the liberty of borrowing a spare key out of your kitchen drawer."

"I counted my keys after the break-in. There were none missing."

"You so sly, but so'm I. I stuck in an old key of mine to replace the one I pinched. Just in case you didn't think to count."

"Smart."

"Wasn't it, though? I ain't your average ne'er-do-well."

"Even so, if you go through with this"—there was the first hint of a quaver in the man's voice—"you'll be the number one suspect. You have to know that."

"Nuh-uh, mister detective man. The bullet they find in you is gonna match the ones fired by Henry Phipps. This here is his gun."

Gaines took a moment to process this news. He swallowed once, his larynx bobbing like a cork. "How'd you get hold of that?"

"I'm filling in for him, you might say. Continuing his legacy. Okay, that's enough getting reacquainted. Turn your ass around."

"So you can shoot me in the back of the head?"

"That's the idea, dipshit."

Were those tears at the edges of his eyes? Oh, man, this was getting good.

"What if I refuse?" Gaines said with a last stubborn stab at heroism.

Jonah was about to answer, push the conversation a little further, maybe see if he could get this fag to do some serious begging, and then he saw Gaines's hand sneaking into the pocket of his robe. It didn't look like he had a gun in there, but it seemed foolish to take chances, so he reached out with his free hand and spun the stool around, then jammed the Colt against the bald spot and pulled the trigger.

Gaines jerked upright, then went limp and slumped forward, his head thumping the counter. As Jonah watched, he slipped bonelessly off the stool and collapsed on the linoleum floor.

The shot had been fairly loud in the enclosed space. Even a .22 made some noise. But he didn't think anybody had heard. The TV was turned up pretty high, the windows were shut against the cold, and the kitchen was at the back of the house.

He crouched, checking his pulse, purely as a formality. Yep, the detective was dead, all right. Dead as a damn dodo.

"Shouldn't have spoke against me, Phil," Jonah said. "That was a mistake."

In the pocket of the robe he found what Gaines had been reaching for. Not a gun. A cell phone. He'd probably been hoping to switch it on and record their conversation or something. Jonah tossed it aside.

As he walked away, the phone started ringing. The

ring tone was the tick-tock theme from that game show, *Jeopardy*. Not that he ever watched it, but old Mrs. Bailey had, in the halfway house. She used to shout out the answers to prove how fuckin' smart she was. It was just one of many things about her that pissed him off.

Jonah started moving a little faster. Maybe someone had heard the shot, after all, and was calling Gaines to ask about it. No sense sticking around to find out.

He left through the back door, leaving it open, as planned. Inside, the tick-tock theme went on and on. But even though Detective Gaines was at home, it was a sure bet he wasn't going to answer.

25

IT WAS TRUE what they said: Google really was your friend. Bonnie had no trouble finding the address of the only halfway house in Pilgrim Grove that had closed its doors within the past year. The place had operated under the presumably inspirational moniker of the Bosom of Abraham Communal Living Center. Kind of a mouthful.

She took twenty minutes to drive there from the hospital. Right now, Felix was probably moving Brad into his apartment in McKendree Park. He lived in a neat little studio above a paranormal bookstore, where a sign in the window advertised psychic readings.

She had great confidence in Felix. He was a wiry little Guatemalan import, barely five feet tall, who'd survived a war and a reign of narcosyndicalist terror. He'd told her about it—the machete attacks, the severed heads on people's doorsteps, the well in the town square stuffed with dead bodies.

Having seen all this, he genuinely detested drugs. True, he was known to drive dealers back and forth to motels on the highway, where they conducted business at odd hours, but that was just business. He didn't have to like the people who paid him.

Besides, she had once trusted Felix Ramirez with her entire arsenal of weapons when it wasn't safe to hide them at her house. This was equivalent to trusting him with her life. She figured she could trust him with Brad's life too.

In Pilgrim Grove, she cruised past the three-story Victorian pile that had been the Bosom of Abraham. A chicken-wire fence enclosed the unkempt lot. A ragged awning flapped over the porch. Paint peeled away from the siding in long curling strips. The front windows were boarded shut with plywood squares.

Not a place where Jonah Stroud was likely to hole up. Even so, she circled the block for another look. On her second lap, she noticed that the name of the halfway house over the porch was gradually being erased as the paint sloughed off. Another name had been printed below. She made out a few faded letters.

G ... R B ... HO ... E

It was a hotel's name she was seeing, obviously. The name the place had used when it was a smart little inn offering accommodations two blocks from the beach, back when men wore a suit and tie to stroll the boardwalk and women wore bathing suits that looked like leotards. And hats. Everybody wore hats. Good times.

Garbage Hole? Gerbil Home? Too short. Wouldn't fill the blank spaces. The last part was probably House. Garbanzo House? Glitterball House? Maybe. But who would name a hotel after a Mexican bean or a disco ball?

Anyway, the building still looked deserted. That left only Sofia Windsor as a possible lead.

Sammy could do a lot, but the private database she subscribed to wasn't too mobile-friendly. Better to use a real computer when accessing it. She drove into Brighton Cove, parking in the gravel lot beside the two-story building where she rented an office. The building on the other side used to house Oxfords, the upscale shoe store where she'd bought her new boots, but the store had just gone out of business, the front window sadly empty. She'd heard rumors that a realtor was moving in, as if downtown wasn't stupid with realtors already.

Her office building was predictably unoccupied on Christmas. She let herself in through the main door and climbed the stairs. The phone case Brad had bought for her as a Christmas gift was still on her desk. She hadn't thought to take it with her when she'd left. She hadn't been thinking of very much at all. It was like Mike Tyson once said: Everyone has a plan till they get punched in the mouth. Dan Maguire had punched her pretty good last night.

She gulped down some Tylenol pillaged from her desk drawer, then fired up her computer and traced Sofia Windsor, getting tripped up at first because she'd assumed the first name was spelled with a *ph*. Once she got the spelling right, there was only one of the right age—the other two were elderly ladies, and she doubted Jonah was into the *Harold and Maude* scene—and her last known address was an apartment in Maritime, not far from the residence of Mama Blessing, Bonnie's very own black-market arms supplier. Not an A-plus neighborhood, unsurprisingly.

As long as she was online, she ran a trace on Jonah Stroud too, but since his time in the halfway house, he'd become a ghost.

Before leaving her office, she took a long wistful look at the sofa, where she and Brad had done the nasty on countless nights. For the first time she found herself questioning the basic logic of their relationship. Yeah, the sex had been good, once she'd gotten him to loosen up a little and discover all the erogenous zones his prior education had overlooked, but there'd been little more to it than that. No going out, no movies, no restaurants, no dancing, no long, dumb walks on the beach holding hands. No time together in any public space, because of the risk of being seen and reported to his boss.

She hadn't thought it mattered. Now she wasn't sure. She could get by on nookie alone, but Brad was the sensitive type. He felt things in a deeper way. He wanted more of a connection. What he needed was a real partner, someone he could live his life with. Instead he'd handcuffed himself to the town pariah, who had to be visited in secret and pleasured on the couch in her office. That was no kind of life for him. At some level he must have known it.

She remembered his haggard look when he found her unconscious in her house. The first stages of withdrawal, maybe. But she had a feeling he'd worn that look for a while. All the sneaking around, lying, playing games—it just wasn't his style. For her, it was no problem. But then, she was a born outlaw, as Dan liked to remind her.

At one time, her office had featured a framed photo of the historical Bonnie Parker, Clyde's gal, gun moll of the Barrow gang. She was posing for the camera, a stogie in her mouth and a gat in her hand. The picture had been blown to bits by unfriendly machine-gun fire. She hadn't replaced it. Now she wished she had. She would have liked to ask the first Bonnie what it was like to be with someone as crazy and lawless as herself, someone who didn't give a rat's ass about rules and conventions, someone who didn't care what anybody thought.

Clyde Barrow was no prize, of course, but he and his girl had been right for each other. Even after the first Bonnie got crippled in a car accident and had to be carried everywhere like an invalid, Clyde remained devoted. They'd lived their crazy, anarchic, homicidal lives together, and they'd died together in the same ambush.

She envied them. Because it was a pretty safe bet that she would die alone.

26

"BABYLON, MOTHER OF harlots and abominations, the great whore upon the waters. The idolatress astride the scarlet beast ..."

Henry chanted prayers, nourishing his strength. The task he'd set himself was hard. His wrists were hurting, his fingers scraped raw.

The idea had come to him in the dark. Locked in the little room, he'd taken inventory of its contents from memory. There was nothing of possible use to him except the cot—a mattress, some bedding, a flattened pillow, a metal frame.

Four metal legs.

One of those legs, if detached, would make a sturdy weapon. Twelve inches of metal, a steel pipe, a blunt instrument that could crack a spine or split a skull.

He had tested each leg in turn, choosing the one that seemed easiest to remove. But even that one posed a challenge to a man without tools. If he'd had a wrench to grip the nut or a hammer to deliver percussive shocks, he might have done the job in no time. As it was, he had to turn the stubborn nut by hand, his fingers slipping on the edges, the sharp metal biting into his skin. After a while he hit on the idea of wrapping the nut in a strip of torn bedding to improve his purchase. It helped, but not enough.

Still, it was working. The bolt was coming loose one quarter twist at a time. He could feel it.

"Filthy with all vices, heavy with the sins of the world,

doomed with the end of all flesh ..."

End of all flesh. Yes, that was the goal. That was what he was aiming for. His purpose, his faith. Faith could move mountains. Surely it could unscrew a paltry stick of metal from a child-size bed.

He lay on his back, half under the cot, working blind. Jonah or Sofia could come in at any moment. He had to chance it. But actually he suspected that Jonah had left; he thought he'd heard someone depart via the rear door a short time ago. It had been probably Jonah, off to commit his mayhem and secure his revenge.

Clever Jonah. Duplicitous, deceitful Jonah. The rock on which he would have built his church. A false front, a masquerade, an incarnation of the trickster. But Henry could play tricks, too.

If Jonah had left, then only Sofia was at home. She might come visiting, but more likely she would occupy herself with her drugs and potions, her necromancer's apothecary.

They were quite a pair. He should have seen it sooner. But he'd been so eager to make converts. In his naivety he'd accepted wolves into his fold.

"The apostate queen and her bridegroom, drunk on fornication and bloodguilt ..."

Another twist, a half-turn this time. The nut was nearly off. He would have his weapon soon.

Then he would lie in wait, in the doorless closet on the far side of the room, until one of his captors ventured into his den.

Sofia Windsor's last known address turned out to be a two-story brick apartment complex dating from the 1960s, with hunks of dead crabgrass uglifying the brown lawn. Her unit was on the ground floor. If she still lived there, Jonah Stroud might be with her, a consideration that prompted Bonnie to confirm that the Glock was in her handbag before she left the Jeep.

She rang the bell. An exhausted woman, her eyes sunk deep in the pale dough of her face, opened the door.

This was not Jonah Stroud's girlfriend. She couldn't possibly be his type.

"I'm looking for Sofia Windsor," Bonnie said briskly, hoping she sounded sufficiently official to be mistaken for an officer of the law, or at least a less sketchy PI.

"The one who was in here before me?" The woman bared her teeth alarmingly, revealing a wide gap between the upper incisors. "She's gone."

"Did you know her?"

"Never met the bitch."

"If you never met her, how come you know she's a bitch?"

"'Cause of how she left this place. I moved in here with my little boy. He's two, you know."

Bonnie didn't know, but nodded obligingly.

"He's at that age where they wander. They, you know, explore. And it's been a friggin' nightmare."

"Why's that?"

"'Cause of her. She's a damn drug addict. Left needles everyplace. Syringes, you know? I keep finding 'em. Back of a drawer, in a cabinet, under the bed, you name it. That girl left her drug paraphernalia"—she drew out the word with bitter precision—"in every nook and cranny."

"I see."

"I live in fear Godfrey's gonna get himself poked by some needle. Like I say, he's always toddlin' around. What'm I supposed to do?"

She posed the question as if honestly expecting an answer. Bonnie had none. She was still stuck on why anyone would name their kid Godfrey.

"So"—she sidestepped the inquiry—"I guess you don't know where Sofia Windsor went."

"To hell, I hope."

"She moved in with her boyfriend."

Bonnie turned toward the new voice. Another woman, gray-haired and so badly stooped as to be nearly hunchbacked, stood on the lawn, a Grateful Dead T-shirt peeking out incongruously from behind the unbuttoned flaps of her coat.

"Her boyfriend?" Bonnie prompted.

"I was here the day she left. That was a good day. We were all so happy to see her leave. Some of us threw a little pot luck supper later to celebrate. I made macaroni and cheese."

She was a talker. That was okay. "And the boyfriend?"

"Oh, he was with her. Scuzzy-looking dude. Older than her. Mean eyes. They went off together."

The description would fit Jonah Stroud, Bonnie was sure. "Did she say where she was going?"

"All she said was they were gonna play Hansel and Gretel."

"Hansel and Gretel?"

"That's what she said. Then she made this little giggle. Of course, she was always high on something, that one. Half the stuff she said didn't make no sense."

"Right. Well, thanks." Bonnie bobbed her head at the two of them, including both in her gratitude.

"You should stay away from them," the Grateful Dead fan said. "Her man's trouble."

Bonnie nodded and walked away. Trouble didn't scare her. She was trouble, too.

Back in the Jeep, she gave the matter some thought. Jonah and Sofia, playing Hansel and Gretel.

Crazy talk from a burned-out hippie chick? Maybe. But it could be a private joke. Probably not a very complicated joke, because they didn't strike her as very complicated people.

She knew the story of Hansel and Gretel. Everybody did. Two kids who got lost in the woods after birds ate their trail of breadcrumbs. They came across a candy cottage. Spun sugar windows, gingerbread walls ...

G ... RB ... HO ... E.

Gingerbread House?

Maybe it wasn't as deserted as it looked.

◉

Freedom was close now. Tantalizingly close.

Funny to think of it like that, when there could be no freedom in a world that was a dungeon and an abattoir. But all things were relative. After his long confinement in darkness, Henry couldn't help feeling free as he watched carousels of dust motes revolve in slanting beams of late afternoon sun.

He was in the closet of his room, where he'd retreated after finally detaching the cot leg. His plan had been to wait there, but while resting against a corner, he'd made a discovery. One section of the wall was water-damaged, the crumbly plaster soft and yielding. He tore it away with his bare hands, dislodging chunks of the chalky stuff, exposing the studs like an X-ray of the wall.

The studs were spaced at intervals of two feet, just wide enough for him to slip through—if he could defeat the wall on the far side.

That wall, unlike the first, was in decent condition. Reaching between the studs, he ran his hands over smooth plasterboard, finding no weak spots. But plasterboard was flimsy stuff. And he had a tool.

And so he had gone to work. Using the metal leg, he'd begun punching holes in the drywall. With each new hole, a slender beam of daylight pierced his darkness. It was the first light he'd seen in hours. Until then he'd been unsure if it was day or night.

Working slowly, keeping the noise to a minimum, he was methodically clearing out a small section between two studs. Once the gap was just a little larger, he would wriggle into the room adjacent to his own, a room with an unblocked window and an open door. He'd passed it on his way down the hall this morning.

The two tricksters had locked him in, but they hadn't

counted on his resourcefulness. His tenacity. His will.

They had burned his testimony, betrayed his trust. They had laughed at him, mocked him, all but spat in his face.

And now they would pay the price for their apostasy.

27

SNOW WAS BEGINNING to fall in thick white plumes, like feathers shaken loose from a down pillow, when Bonnie parked the Jeep one block over from the Gingerbread House. It was her usual precaution—never park too close to the scene of a break-in. Given the noisy show the vehicle put on whenever the motor was shut off, she also found it prudent to park well out of earshot of her quarry.

The snow hadn't started to stick yet. It melted on the asphalt, leaving the street soaked as if with rain. If it kept falling, there would be high drifts by midnight.

She checked the time on Sammy's welcome screen, a necessity inasmuch as the clock in the Jeep was busted and she didn't wear a watch. It was 3:15. The sun would be gone in about an hour. Already it was sagging low in the west, screened by clouds, a faded orange smear like a half-erased stain.

She slung her purse over her shoulder but left the hat in the Jeep. No need for it indoors, and it was awkward to carry. Quickly she made her way through someone's side yard and around back, where a tumbledown picket fence marked the rear property line. Getting through the fence was easy, but a foot beyond it stood another barrier, a hurricane fence put up more recently, *No Trespassing* signs poking up belligerently at the corners.

If the place was occupied, there ought to be a way in. She prowled along the fence until she found a line of cut links in the wire mesh, then pushed on the fence and made a gap big enough to crawl through.

The rear yard was barely ten feet deep. She crouched in a stand of stunted evergreens and studied the backside of the Gingerbread House, rising before her in the dying light. The rear windows were all boarded up, but from the chimney a thin curl of smoke drifted sluggishly upward. Someone was running the furnace.

Not necessarily a sign of occupancy. The furnace might be stoked on a daily basis simply to keep the pipes from freezing. But there were other clues. In a corner of the yard lay a sloppy mound of big plastic garbage bags. The ones on the bottom had been there a while; the plastic had been ripped open by scavengers, the contents partially scattered. The higher ones were untouched; they'd been dumped recently. Nobody would break into a fenced-off lot just to toss a bag of garbage, but squatters living in the house might dump their trash outside.

Leaving cover, she crossed the backyard to the rear door. With the windows covered by plywood, the door was her only way in. A lock pick and tension wrench from her purse got it open in under a minute.

Before going inside, she took out the ghost gun, holding it awkwardly in her left hand. She had yet to find a use for it—but the day wasn't over yet.

On hands and knees, Henry squirmed through the hole he'd made, into the next room. He lay on the floor, collecting himself after his efforts. An early evening sky, choked with clouds, was framed in the window. Wet snowflakes settled on the windowpane.

Almost night now. His last night on this wretched earth.

He pulled himself to a standing position. He was contemplating his next move when he heard the clip-clops of sandals on the hallway's hardwood floor.

Sofia was coming. And she was alone.

Perfect.

He retreated to the farthest corner of the room, where she wouldn't see him if she happened to glance through the open doorway as she passed by.

She thought he was still locked up, of course. She could have no idea that he was free, and armed, and ready.

Things were about to get really interesting.

◉

Bonnie had already decided how this would have to be played. If Henry was in here, she would shoot him, obviously. That was a given. But she would also have to take care of anyone she found with him—namely Jonah Stroud and his girlfriend.

It probably should have bothered her to know that she might have to end three lives in the next few minutes. A dream came back to her, a dream from last night—Frank Kershaw warning her about the road she was on. Frank, who had become Dan, and when she'd looked in the mirror, she'd seen Henry Phipps, the Man in the Moon, staring back.

She shook her head. Fuck that shit. Now was not the time for therapy. If Henry was in there, she would take care of him. And anyone else, too.

She made a quick sweep of the ground floor. It was mostly unused. The central hallway opened on rooms emptied of their furnishings. The walls were covered in discolored fleur-de-lis wallpaper, dark rectangles marking the spots where paintings and mirrors had hung. They were gone, along with the light fixtures that had lined the hallway at head height. All that remained of them were bristly wires poking out of ragged holes.

The carpet remained, too worthless to salvage, a dark maroon runner littered with bits of plaster and splinters of wood, a fallen smoke detector, empty water bottles, dead bugs, mouse turds, and for some inexplicable reason, a pair of dentures.

She found a door to a cellar and went far enough down the stairs to see a dance of orange light and purple shadow. The furnace was running just hot enough to take the chill off the building. Above ground, the temperature couldn't be more than sixty degrees. She wouldn't have been tempted to take off her coat even if she'd been planning to stay.

On the other side of the hall was a larger space that had been a dining room, with a large circular gap in the ceiling where a chandelier had been suspended over a long-gone rectangular table, its position memorialized by permanent indentations in the mildewed carpet.

Next door was the kitchen. It was different from the other rooms. It was still in use.

In the dim light she saw a plastic table and a folding chair—not the original furniture, just yard-sale junk—and a profusion of liquor bottles. Fast food containers, too, strewn everywhere, crawling with roaches. In a doorless cabinet, cans of soup and chili. She wondered how the residents heated the food. The stove and all other appliances were gone. Maybe they cooked it in the furnace. Maybe they ate it cold.

A battery-operated lantern sat on the table. She switched it on. The room lit up, assaulting her with a rush of color. Somebody had spray-painted every inch of the kitchen in psychedelic smears. Walls, floor, ceiling, even the filthy countertops and warped cabinets had served as a canvas for swirls and loops and whirls. In the wavering electric glow, the haphazard designs were weirdly bright, almost luminous. It was like being inside a disturbed mind.

People were living here, all right. But where the hell were they?

◉

From the corner where he hid, Henry saw Sofia's shadow flit across the wall. She stopped outside the door to the back room.

"Henry? You okay in there?"

He let the seconds inch past.

"Henry? You've been making noises. I heard you."

He stayed quiet, as quiet as the dead.

"It's no good playing possum. I know you can hear me. You answer me right now." She gave the order petulantly, like the spoiled child she was.

He waited while she puzzled out what to do. Jonah clearly wasn't back yet. He had probably cautioned her against going in alone. Still, she was suspicious–and curious, too.

"I'm coming in to check on you," she said with sudden determination. "I've got a gun. Jonah lent it to me. It's a loogey–a, um, a Luger. I know how to use it."

Her voice lilted up on the last word, making the statement into a question.

"If you try anything, I'll shoot you. I won't kill you, though. I'll give you to Sally. Another bad trip. You don't want that."

No, he didn't want that. But she wouldn't be sending him to hell again. Hell was where *she* belonged, she and her consort, the scarlet beast. And hell was where he would send them both.

He heard the rattle of a key in the lock. He emerged from his corner, sidling along the wall opposite the window until he could look out the doorway and see her, a yard away, a blonde woman in a white gossamer gown, her back to him as she pushed open the door.

She hadn't lied about the gun. He saw it in her right hand. He doubted she was any good with it, but at close range she wouldn't have to be.

He wanted her inside the other room. It was darker in there, where less light from the hall could reach. And her attention would be focused in front of her.

"Henry? Where are you?"

She crossed the threshold.

He slipped into the hall, approaching her from behind.

She took another step into the back room. She was looking toward the cot. The gun was gripped tight, her knuckles bloodless with pressure.

He closed the distance between them and drew back the shaft of metal in his hands for a killing blow.

"Henry?"

And he swung out, wielding his weapon like a club, driving it at her skull.

28

BONNIE LOOKED UP.

Above her, distant sounds. A scuffle. A thud. Footfalls.

She stood motionless, tracking the noise. Something was happening on one of the upper floors, and she had a feeling Henry Phipps was involved.

She put the lantern back on the table—carrying a light was a good way to make yourself a target—and left the kitchen. At the front of the house she found the main staircase. She wasn't a big fan of stairs. A stairway was a classic kill zone, an enclosed space that could funnel a person directly into the line of fire.

Her rule of thumb—pertaining to kill zones and life in general—was that if you were going to do something stupid and crazy, at least do it fast.

She charged up the stairs, taking them two at a time. The temperature dropped with each step. She was climbing into a nest of cold.

At the second-story landing she took a quick look to scope out the hallway. It was empty.

Top floor, then.

◉

Henry should have had the girl then and there. But at the last moment, as he'd swung out, some sixth sense had warned her of his presence. She turned just as his makeshift weapon was circling down.

Her reflexes were faster than he'd expected. She spun away, diving to the carpet inside the room, and the pipe swept overhead, missing its target. It slammed into the wall and dropped free.

He had time for a twitch of regret. He'd failed. She could finish him with one shot.

She had the same thought. She flipped onto her side, raising the gun in her hand –

But it wasn't in her hand. She'd lost it when she hit the floor.

Her face collapsed, registering disappointment as plainly as a child whose ice cream cone had slipped from her fingers.

He looked past her and saw the gun a yard away. She grabbed for it. Her first try only sent it skidding. On hands and knees she scrambled after it, chasing it down like a terrier chasing a rat.

She almost had it in her grasp, and then he was on top of her, flinging her onto her back, wrapping his hands around her white throat.

He didn't need the gun. He would strangle the bitch. Choke the life out of her, and watch her eyes go blank with death.

"Whore," he whispered, tightening his grip. "Bride of sin."

A rattling moan shuddered out of her. She flailed, her fingernails scratching ineffectually at his face.

He squeezed harder. Her eyes bulged. She tried to scream, but her mouth was clogged with the thick wet mass of her tongue.

It was different, he thought, to kill this way. More personal. More intense. More pure. Had he known, he would never have used the .22. He would have used only his naked hands.

She was nearly gone. He could see her light fading. Outside, dusk was coming fast, and inside, her life, too, was dimming to darkness. He might have pitied her, had he not known her for what she was.

From down the hall, a woman's shout.

"Henry!"

He looked over his shoulder, through the open doorway. At the far end of the hall stood a female figure, holding a gun on him.

Her face was in shadow. Even so, he knew her.

And he knew he was done.

Bonnie didn't know why she'd shouted. The smart play would have been to let him finish choking the girl, who had to be Sofia Windsor, then take him out before he knew she was there. Sofia would be no loss. But somehow it just didn't feel right to watch the Man in the Moon take another life when she was in a position to stop it.

"Get off her," she said. She had his attention now.

He released the girl, who lay without moving. Slowly he climbed off, squatting on his haunches behind her, in a room with a blacked-out window, a room of shadows.

"Get up."

He didn't.

She advanced down the hallway, keeping the gun trained on him. The sun had dropped behind other buildings, and the light filtering through the side windows was dim and chancy.

"Get up, I said." She didn't like him crouching there, screened by darkness.

He placed his hands on the floor as if bracing himself to stand. Something about the move looked unnatural.

His hands came up, and he was holding something—something he'd plucked off the floor.

She took no time to analyze the situation. Her finger flexed, the Glock bucked, Henry fell backward.

Firing right-handed, she would have scored an easy kill. Her left hand wasn't so accurate. She'd only wounded him. Shoulder, it looked like.

She continued down the hall, not increasing her speed. Impatience was a mistake. Slow and steady won the race.

At the doorway to the room, she paused, letting her

eyesight adjust to the dim light. She saw a damaged cot leaning at an angle, a metal pipe dropped on the floor. The girl lay on her back, so still that she might be dead. The room smelled of sweat and fear.

Henry had crawled into a corner, holding his arm. His right arm. She'd paid him back for her wound. Now she would repay him with interest.

The gun he'd tried to grab lay on the carpet, half under the cot. He'd dropped it when he took the bullet.

"That your twenty-two?" she asked.

He shook his head. "It's a Luger. Jonah has my gun."

"Where's he?"

"Out."

She stepped over the girl and retrieved the Luger, her gaze never leaving Henry Phipps. She dumped it into her purse. As she moved back to the doorway, the girl groaned, coming around. Her neck was ringed with purple bruises. They matched the needle marks decorating her arms.

"Doesn't look like you finished her off," Bonnie said.

Henry leaned against the wall. "It makes no difference. It's over. My race is run."

"Looks to me like you came in last."

"I was defeated by a power greater than myself. Greater than any of us. You don't understand."

"Can't say I want to. You know I've got a job to do?"

"I'm not afraid of dying. It's all I ever wanted, really. To be free. To be released from this charnel house, this garbage dump of a world."

"You could have offed yourself at any time. No need to take other people with you."

"I was doing them a kindness," Henry said with the plain simplicity of genuine madness.

The girl's eyes opened, and she gave a little start, surprised to see another person there.

"You okay?" Bonnie asked, not really caring.

"I ... think so." Her voice was strained and thick. She

touched her throat self-consciously. “Who are you?”

“Never mind. You’re Sofia, I guess.”

“How’d you know that?”

She ignored the question. “Where’s Jonah Stroud?”

“What you want with him? I mean ... I don’t know who you’re talking about.”

“Smooth. Let me guess. You did the redecorating in the kitchen.”

“She’s the universal harlot,” Henry murmured. “Mother of spiders. Dragon seed.”

“Shut up, Henry.” To Sofia, she said, “Get up and stand by the bed.”

“What are you going to do?”

“Just stand the hell up, God damn it.”

Sofia obeyed, rising on unsteady legs. She retreated to a corner of the room, walking backward, never taking her eyes off the stranger and her gun.

The girl was no threat. Bonnie returned her attention to the Man in the Moon. “Looks like it’s my turn to do you a kindness,” she said.

He watched her in the dying light. “We’re not so very different, I think.”

“So I’ve been told.”

“But you don’t believe it.”

“I’m not crazy.”

“This world is an asylum.” He shut his eyes. “We’re all crazy.”

“I can’t argue with that,” she said, and she pulled the trigger and shot him dead.

He fell forward, folding over onto his stomach. Blood leaked from his forehead, puddling in a maroon stain on the carpet. A clean kill, right between the eyes. At this range she could hit the bull’s-eye even with her left hand.

In the corner Sofia made a low whimpering noise.

Bonnie looked at her. The girl seemed to shrink inside herself, her thin body disappearing in the folds of her white gown, now speckled with maroon pinpoints of

Henry's blood. Her eyes were fixed on the Glock.

"Not me," Sofia said in a small, hoarse voice. "Please."

In her line of work there was a simple rule: no witnesses. Sofia Windsor had been harboring a fugitive, a serial killer; she was complicit in his crimes; she was an addict and a loser; she would never be missed.

All perfectly valid reasons to pull the trigger.

But she couldn't do it. Killing Henry Phipps was one thing. Killing this spaced-out street kid was something else.

Bonnie lowered the gun. "You didn't see me here. Right?"

Sofia blinked, not comprehending.

"You're not a witness to anything. That's what I'm saying. Okay?"

"Oh. Yes. Of course. I ... I didn't see a thing."

Not a very convincing performance. The truth was, a girl like this would talk. She couldn't help herself. If she was ever arrested, she'd probably spill everything she knew to the police.

All in all, keeping her alive was a rookie mistake. But shooting her in the heart—well, somehow it just wasn't an option.

Bonnie snugged the gun in her waistband and retrieved Sammy from her purse. She nudged Henry's corpse onto its side with the toe of her boot, then snapped a photo. It was the first time she'd ever needed proof of a kill. She had to have something to show Petrossian, and cutting off her victim's head to take with her seemed like a lot of work.

"I'm going now," she said, stuffing the phone back into her purse. "I'd advise you to clear out real soon."

"Thank you," Sofia whispered. She stepped away from the wall, hugging herself with her thin, needle-tracked arms.

Bonnie thought about telling her to get some help, check into rehab, reconnect with her family, save herself. But she knew that no advice would make any difference. Anyway, she'd already done one intervention today.

So she only nodded and said, "Take care of yourself." Safely meaningless words.

She turned away, toward the deep dusk of the hall. She had just stepped through the doorway when something crashed down from behind, igniting a starburst of colors before her eyes—bright and dazzling and amazingly like the spray-painted designs in the kitchen.

She had time for a last thought before the colors and her awareness winked out.

Oh, fuck.

As an epitaph, it wasn't much, but it just might have to do.

29

DAN NEEDED TO talk to Phil Gaines. For the fourth time that afternoon he called Gaines's cell. Once again, the call hopped to voicemail. He tried the landline. No answer.

Unacceptable. Yes, it was a holiday, but with the Man in the Moon case breaking and with this new development he was chasing down, his detective couldn't just take the day off.

"Screw it." He buzzed the duty sergeant on the intercom. "Are Jensen and Quinera doing anything?"

"They called in ten-ninety-eight a half hour ago." The code meant they were available for calls.

"Send them to Phil Gaines's house. Roust him out of bed or wherever he is. I need that son of a bitch."

"On Christmas? He won't like it."

"I don't care what he likes."

Gaines had to be part of this. Because things were starting to get interesting.

Dan had spent the whole afternoon in his office, rebuffing his wife's pleas to come home for dinner. He had more important things than roast turkey on his plate.

He was chasing a link between Bonnie Parker and Armin Petrossian, and thus possibly a link to the shots fired in Henry Phipps's house last night.

It was the car, the Mercedes limo his guys had seen outside Parker's house. A car that had assumed a new importance in his mind after his impromptu lunch with Bruce Haynes. The anomalies in the Rosa Martinez killing, and the introduction of Petrossian's name, had started him thinking along new and interesting lines.

Suppose Petrossian had done away with Martinez. Suppose he'd outsourced the job to Parker. Suppose he'd then hired Parker to hit Henry Phipps before Phipps could testify that Rosa wasn't one of his victims.

The stretched black Mercedes could be the key. If it could be linked to Petrossian.

Fortunately, the patrolmen had taken the precaution of running the mystery car's plate number. It had come back to an entity called Internex, which was short for "international exports." With no red flags on the vehicle, they hadn't taken it any further.

Dan was taking it further. He'd spent the past two hours calling people who didn't want to be called on Christmas and cajoling them into doing additional research.

His first call was to a CPA who was occasionally hired as a fraud examiner when the department needed to review a suspect's books. The CPA got back to him in a half hour with news that Internex was registered at a Delaware post office box known as a hotspot for shell corporations. Over 200,000 dubious entities shared that same address, and virtually none had any detectable presence online or in the real world. Delaware, Dan learned to his surprise, was every bit as much of a haven for dummy corporations as the Cayman Islands or Russia.

No useful information was provided with the Delaware registration, but searching further, the CPA had found Internex recorded as the company manager of another corporation, NextITX, registered in Nevada. According to him, it wasn't unusual for one dummy corporation to serve as the manager of another dummy corporation. NextITX, in turn, had subsidiaries in Liberia, on the Caribbean island of Nevis, and in Miami. No information on any of these was available, though the Florida entity did have a bare-bones website. For the CPA, that was where the trail ran cold.

The website gave Dan an idea. He called his fourteen-year-old nephew, a whiz at all things digital, and asked for his help. Asking proved insufficient; bribery was necessary. Dan agreed to buy the kid an Xbox, whatever the hell that was. In short order, the boy had performed something called a WHOIS lookup, which yielded the name of the domain owner, a certain Alex Gevorkian.

His last call had been to an FBI man in the Broad Bank resident agency who had an encyclopedic knowledge of local crime syndicates. The guy's wife refused to let him come to the phone until the family repast had been consumed. This was a pain in the ass, but Dan swallowed his annoyance. He waited.

He needed to bounce ideas off someone, though. He needed Phil.

He paced his office, trying to think like a detective, which was hard, because he'd come up on the patrol side. Let's just say Gevorkian could be linked to the Petrossian syndicate. It was possible—the name sounded Armenian, at least. Would that be enough for a warrant on Parker? Probably not. There was no proof she'd even been in the car or spoken with its occupants. Unless someone saw her.

The odds were against it. The Mercedes had been there early, around eight in the morning. Most people would have been asleep or preoccupied with opening the presents under the tree. But you never did know. There were a lot of senior citizens in Brighton Cove, and seniors got up early and sometimes showed a voyeuristic interest in their neighbors.

He buzzed the duty desk again. "Any word from Jensen and Quinera?"

"They just arrived at Gaines's house."

"Guilfoyle and Wallace available?"

"Yeah. You, um, you want them to pick up Phil, too?" He sounded dubious.

"No. I want them to go to the vicinity of 874 Windlass

Court and canvass the area. Ask if anyone saw Bonnie Parker get in or out of a black Mercedes sedan this morning around eight. Or if she had any contact with the individuals who were in it."

"Okay." The word was drawn out in a way that sounded even more dubious.

They all thought he was nuts. Thought he was obsessed with Parker, Ahab and the whale. He'd heard the jokes, seen the rolled eyes and smirks.

But he would have the last laugh. All he had to do was tie Parker to the car and tie the car to Petrossian, and he would have enough for a warrant. It might be tough to find a judge to sign off on Christmas, but he could track somebody down. Then he'd be inside Parker's home and office, and when he caught up with her, he'd search her Jeep and have her strip-searched.

The warrant might or might not turn up evidence of her involvement in the events in Henry Phipps's house, but it was sure to turn up *something*. Illegal firearms, hidden cash, secret bank accounts, suspicious contacts. A gunshot wound from last night, probably. Perhaps the bullet itself, tweezed free and dropped in a wastebasket.

He could put her away for years even if she didn't cop to any actual killings. The firearms violations alone would guarantee her a long lonely stretch in the Edna Mahan Correctional Facility in Clinton.

By this time tomorrow, assuming she didn't manage to run out on him, he could have her safely locked up and looking at a bail bond so high she could never get out.

She'd messed with him and played games and shot up his quiet little town, even corrupted one of his men. Now he was sure, absolutely sure, he would get something on her—enough to charge her, enough to hang her.

If he got the warrant.

The phone rang. It was the agent in Broad Bank, finally calling back. The guy sounded pissed off, which was too damn bad.

“Just one question,” Dan said smoothly. “Alex Gevorkian. Name mean anything to you?”

“Lawyer out of Newark,” the agent said around a mouthful of food. “Dirty.”

“Mobbed up?”

“To the hilt. He’s a fixer for the Petrossian organization.”

“Bingo” was not a thing Dan Maguire said. It was too Hollywood, too cliché. Besides, he’d never played Bingo in his life. But after concluding his call with the federal agent, he was sorely tempted to say it.

He’d linked the car to Petrossian, and the feds had linked Petrossian to Rosa Martinez. He was close. Closer than he’d been in years—since the Streinikov case, which should have gone his way, except she’d outmaneuvered him at the end. This time he wouldn’t be outmaneuvered. But he had to do everything right. And he needed a break, just one lucky break.

The intercom buzzed. Duty sergeant on the phone. It was too early for Guilfoyle and Wallace to have found anything. “Yeah, Sarge?”

“Dan.” The man’s voice was funny. Strained, as if he’d been shouting. “Jensen and Quinera called in.”

“They find Phil?”

“They found him. But it’s bad, Dan. It’s really bad.”

30

HER HEAD HURT. That was the first thing she was aware of. The first sharp thrust of reality after a timeless interval of peace.

With effort Bonnie pieced together her circumstances. Her body was horizontal. She was on the carpet. People stood over her. Two people, male and female—she heard their voices, though her eyes remained shut.

One was the girl in the white dress, the girl in the Gingerbread House. Right. That was where she was, in the back room on the top floor, and Henry Phipps was dead, and the girl was Sofia Windsor, and the man talking with her had to be Jonah Stroud.

She was all caught up now, the recap complete, but her head still throbbed with painful insistence, and falling on the floor hadn't done her wounded arm any good.

"I didn't know what to do," Sofia was saying. "She shot Henry. I couldn't stop her."

"She's that bitch from last night. The one sent by the mob guy. Gotta be."

"Her purse must be around somewhere. Maybe her ID is in it. She dropped it when I hit her, I guess."

"What'd you smack her with?"

"That thing over there. It's a leg from the cot. Henry got it loose. He tried to use it on me."

"I told you not to go into this room, babe."

"He wasn't in the room. He was already out."

"No way."

"I swear. The door was locked, but he wasn't inside."

"If the door was locked, how'd you get in?"

"Well ... I opened it. But the room was empty."

"Sure it was." He snorted. "Old Henry probably walked through the damn wall, like a fuckin' ghost."

Sofia sulked. "I'm telling the truth."

"Well, he's a ghost now, anyway. Surprised this bitch didn't shoot you, too."

"She was only here for Henry. The thing is, I couldn't just let her leave."

"You did right, Mommy. She knows we been hiding Preacher. She knows way too much." Bonnie felt the toe of a shoe in her ribs. "Eyes open, Danger Girl. I can tell you're shamming. You ain't fooling nobody."

She raised her head, blinking in an oddly familiar electric glow. The lantern from the kitchen. He must have brought it upstairs with him, a necessary step because the hallway was now fully dark. Night had fallen.

"Where'd that purse go, anyway?" Sofia murmured, picking up the lantern. It threw shifting patterns of light and dark around the room. On the floor, six feet away, lay Henry Phipps, eyes open, mouth agape. The moving shadows lent his face an unsettling illusion of life.

Bonnie reached carefully for the waistband of her jeans, where she'd snugged the Glock. It wasn't there. She looked up at Jonah, and, oh hey, there it was. In his hand.

He gazed down on her, a tall, rangy figure with a prematurely grizzled face and cold humorless eyes. She knew his type instantly. He had done his share of killing, and he had a taste for it. And unlike her, there were no lines he wouldn't cross.

"What's your name, bitch?" he asked.

"Bonnie Parker."

"Seems like I heard that before."

"I run a PI office in Brighton Cove."

"That ain't it." He muttered her name under his breath three or four times, and then he had it. "Bonnie and Clyde, right? You're named after them."

"After one of them."

Sofia paused in her search for the purse. "Who are Bonnie and Clyde?"

Jonah looked at her in disbelief. "You fuckin' kidding me? Bonnie and fuckin' *Clyde*."

She shook her head, her eyes vacant.

"Damn." He expelled a disgusted sigh. "They was only two of the most notorious outlaws ever. Bank robbers back in the nineteen thirties, I think it was. They shot up a bunch of folks. Law officers, even." He squinted. "You seriously never *heard* of Bonnie and Clyde?"

"Why should I know anything about a couple of bank robbers from before I was born?"

"'Cause they was famous. Movies been made about 'em. Come to think of it, they was a lot like us. We're outlaws like them. Badasses."

"Seems to me," Bonnie said, "Henry Phipps was the badass, and you two were his entourage."

Jonah bent lower, scowling at her. "See here, missy, I got me some notches in my gun. Just came from wasting one of your pissant town's finest. Shot a certain Detective Phil Gaines right in the back of the noggin. Stone dead."

She met his eyes. "With Henry's twenty-two?"

"That's right."

"I see."

He nodded appreciatively. "Yeah, you see, all right. I'm on a crime spree of my own, but the Man in the Moon takes the rap. Nobody knows there's any connection between him and me. Nobody 'cept you."

"But how could she know about us?" Sofia's voice rose, colored with a tinge of superstitious awe. "How could she even be here?"

Jonah's face darkened as he worked it out. "Maybe she followed Preacher when he left home last night. After him and me met up at Domani, she tailed us here. Waited to make her move till I was out." He thumped his chest. "She didn't want to tangle with the Big Bad Wolf."

"Yeah," Bonnie said. "That's it, all right." She was willing to let him think so. She didn't want Brad brought into this.

"Well, you're up against it now, girl detective. You know what's gotta happen here."

"I have a pretty good idea." With her left arm she boosted herself to a sitting position. The pounding in her head grew sharper. Lights flashed across her field of vision. "But you're wrong about me."

"I doubt that."

"I'm no threat to you. I don't talk to the police. I'm not exactly on their side."

"You ain't on my side, neither."

"If I walk away, I won't say a word."

"You won't walk away."

She nodded toward Henry's corpse. "Anything I say about you implicates me. Just who do you think I'm going to tell?"

"Your boss, maybe. Mr. Big himself. And I don't want him knowing my name. I went to a lot of trouble to stay off his radar."

"There it is." Sofia had discovered the purse. It had slid into the closet near the door.

"Did you tell him I saved your life?" Bonnie asked the girl.

Sofia hesitated. "It's true. Henry was choking me. She made him stop."

Bonnie looked at Jonah. "That count for anything?"

He shrugged. "Maybe a nickel's worth. Against that, I never done no female of the species. You can't expect me to pass up the opportunity."

She studied the hard lines of his face, the lightless

depths of his eyes. Her credo was to never give up. Always play for time. Something might happen. Anything was possible.

But not here. Not with this man.

He wasn't interested in prolonging the moment. He wasn't imaginative enough to be bargained with. He only wanted to get it done.

Well, she'd always figured she would go out on the job. Her number had to come up eventually. And she was ready—as ready as anyone could ever be, when the hammer was about to fall. She wasn't even afraid, or if she did feel any fear, it was distant, unimportant. What she felt above all was an overpowering sense of her presence in that moment, as if the dark little room and the trio in it were the whole of reality, a private universe. Weird, really. She had never felt so alive.

"Okay, then." She sat up straighter, looking down the barrel of the Glock. "So get it over with, you dumb redneck motherfucker."

He smiled. Steadying the gun, he planted the muzzle against her forehead, directly above the bridge of her nose.

Bonnie waited for the gunshot she would never hear.

"Ooh. Look at all the money." Sofia was rummaging in the purse.

Jonah's eyes flickered. "What money?"

The girl extracted a thick wad of bills. "They're all hundreds, it looks like. It's, like, five thousand dollars, maybe more."

"Count it."

He waited while Sofia worked her way through the cash, making small exclamations of delight. "Ten thousand," she said finally.

"Ten grand." Jonah's voice was low and thoughtful. "I thought it just might be." His gaze swiveled downward. "That's Bradley Walsh's money, ain't it? The money he got from Mr. Big?"

Bonnie held her voice level. “I don’t know any Bradley Walsh.”

“Like fuck you don’t.” The muscles of his face twitched.

She said nothing. She only waited, unsure if he would follow through with the execution or not.

He didn’t seem to know, either. He stood mulling it over, his mouth working soundlessly, chewing air.

“Is Walsh alive?” he said at last.

The question took her by surprise, but she showed no reaction.

“Is he, bitch? Is that how you found out about me? Maybe you didn’t tail me, after all. Maybe he fuckin’ gave me up.”

She just watched him, keeping her face unreadable.

“Shit.” He turned away, breaking eye contact. “I gotta know. And if he’s alive, you gotta tell me where he is.”

“I’m not telling you a goddamn thing,” Bonnie said.

The gun wavered, then dropped lower, signaling a reprieve.

“Oh, you’ll tell,” he said. He nodded and went on nodding like a bobblehead toy. “My lady here’s got all kinds of ways to break the ice, conversation-wise. Don’t you, Mommy?”

Sofia didn’t answer. Intent on counting the money, she stood there cooing like a child.

31

THE WORLD HAD gone dark by the time Dan Maguire reached Phil Gaines's house. The last daylight had leaked from the sky, and only an immense unsmiling blackness remained.

He left his car and tramped through the accumulating snowdrifts in a blur of dancing flakes, wet and heavy, peppering his face like cold kisses.

Jensen and Quinera were already on the scene, and Guilfoyle and Wallace had been called. The state troopers, too. In the meantime no one was to touch anything. The crime scene would be left undisturbed for the state's Special Investigations Section and their forensic team.

There was nobody who could have processed the scene for Brighton Cove anyway. Phil Gaines was the only detective the department had.

"Shit," Dan muttered, blowing into his frozen hands as he neared the front door.

Jensen and Quinera had found the back door ajar, the house chilled by winter air, and Phil Gaines dead in the kitchen with a bullet in the back of his head. The size of the entry wound, and the absence of any visible exit, suggested a .22 round. Ballistics would have to match it to the slugs taken from Henry Phipps's other victims. But really, there was no doubt.

The Man in the Moon had killed again.

Dan nodded curtly to Quinera, guarding the door. The media hadn't shown up yet, but they would, and they had to be kept at bay.

"So he's done seven," the patrolman said.

"Maybe," Dan answered gruffly, thinking of Rosa Martinez. "Where's your partner?"

"Watching the rear."

"You guys find anything? I mean ... anything else?"

"No sign of forced entry."

"Doesn't make sense. Why would Phil open the door for him?"

"Why would he go after Phil—I mean, Detective Gaines—at all?"

Dan had an answer for that one. "Because the detective was in Phipps's house. It was all over the news. I'm guessing Phipps took it personally."

"Gaines was just doing his job."

"You can't reason with a crazy person, son." Dan shook his head. "Phipps saw Phil in his house, and it pissed him off, and he decided to do something about it."

"If that's true ..."

Dan knew where this was going. "Yeah?"

"He might target anyone who was there."

"Like us, you mean?" The same thought had already crossed Dan's mind, which was why, on his way over, he'd called Bernice and told her to lock all the doors and set the alarm. "Yeah, he might. I'd advise you to stay alert until Phipps has been brought in."

He left Quinera to think about that and proceeded through the living room, heading toward the kitchen. It occurred to him that he'd spent very little time in this house. Phil had been his friend, divorced, childless, probably lonely, yet Dan had seen him almost exclusively on the job. The realization made him sad. How many times might he have invited Phil out for a beer or over to the house for dinner, or maybe to Milano's on Route 71 for some pizza and chopped antipasto? He'd never thought of it.

And all the time—all those long nights—Phil had been

here, alone, in this dusty house where cobwebs made complicated traceries in the corners of the ceilings. Alone and ignored.

Dead now. Dead in his kitchen. On Christmas Day.

Dan found the body, sprawled on the floor. Cheap linoleum. That was what he noticed first, before the corpse itself fully registered. Linoleum from the 1960s or earlier. Awful yellow stuff, cracked and peeling. That made him sad, too.

The TV was on, tuned to News 12, which was still fixated on the Man in the Moon. Well, they would have a new excuse to play their breaking-news music now.

He was tempted to switch it off, but he supposed he really shouldn't touch anything until the state troopers got here. He couldn't see why it would matter—the TV, that is—but he was taking no chances. He felt numb and stupid, emptied out inside. So he just stood there awkwardly, looking down at his friend, listening to the newsreader drone.

He wondered how it had happened. No sign of forced entry, Quinera had said. Maybe Phil had left the door unlocked. Maybe he'd opened up for Phipps, not knowing who it was. He would never have expected an attack. That was something that just didn't happen in Brighton Cove. Even now, in the wake of the Man in the Moon killings, people didn't expect to be murdered in their own homes.

"Damn it, Phil." The words came involuntarily. Dan looked down at the ragged terrycloth robe and flannel pajamas and fur-lined slippers. Phil had gotten to bed late last night, having spent hours at Phipps's house. He would have risen late also. A tall glass of something purple, one of Phil's disgusting fruit smoothies, sat on the counter. He hadn't been awake long when the killer showed up.

Outside, blue and red lights flared as another squad car arrived. That would be Guilfoyle and Wallace. Dan didn't care. There was nothing they could tell him, nothing they knew about a situation like this.

It occurred to him that if Parker really had killed Rosa Martinez, she could have done this job, too. But there would be nothing in it for her. And the bullet, unlike the one in the Martinez case, would still be identifiable for ballistic comparison.

He was close to getting Parker. But at the moment he couldn't feel anything about it. There was a word he'd come across—*desolated.* He'd had to look it up. *Crushed*, it meant; *devastated.* That was how he felt now.

He thought of the things he would miss about Gaines. The annoying quirks and odd mannerisms. The stupid sound effects he employed to dramatize his theories of a case. His habit of wearing mismatched socks, which Dan was sure he'd done on purpose, though he denied it. The way he put mayonnaise on everything, and how he claimed to hate cats but always stopped to pet one. All the dumb, trivial, ridiculous things that gelled together to make a human being.

And the cases they'd worked together. That torture setup in the bathroom of the motel everybody called the Roach House, which Dan still thought Parker had something to do with. The rash of burglaries last year, and the fingerprint Phil had found in the dirt on a windowsill, the only clue, but it had been enough.

Nothing but memories now—memories, and the dead man on the kitchen floor.

Outside came the tramp of boots in snow. Guilfoyle and Wallace had arrived. Dan met them in the living room. He knew they wouldn't have anything for him. They hadn't had time to canvass Parker's neighborhood.

But they surprised him. "Chief," Wallace said, his droopy, hangdog face looking even glummer than usual, "I don't know if it matters right now, but we got something on the limo."

Dan blinked. “So fast?”

“Just dumb luck,” Guilfoyle said. “We started at Parker’s duplex. Her neighbor was home. Gloria Biggs. Elderly lady, not a huge fan of the PI next door.”

“We took her statement.” Wallace had taken up the story. “She saw Parker leave with two men in suits around eight this morning. In a black stretch Mercedes.”

That was it, then. The last piece. All he needed for a warrant.

Dan nodded and turned away, feeling a sudden burn of tears in his eyes. He was going to do it, really do it. He was going to take down Bonnie Parker at last.

And the only thing he could feel about it was that Phil should have been here when it happened.

32

JONAH HAD TO hand it to Bonnie Parker. She knew she was beaten, and she had to have an inkling of what lay in store for her, but she didn't look scared. More like pissed off. He could respect that.

She was a pro, and he was taking no chances with her. He'd had Sofia hold the Glock on her while he tied her hands behind her back with strips of Henry's bedsheets. He'd seen her wince when her right arm was wrenched backward, and remembering that Henry had talked about finding her blood in his house, he'd patted down the arm and found the lump of bandages under her coat sleeve. Gunshot wound.

That was useful information. It meant that he could hold her by her right arm as he guided her down the stairs, squeezing a little harder whenever he thought she might be about to bust a move on him. He wouldn't put it past her, even with her arms secured. She was a fighter, this one. Even when she'd told him to go ahead and get it over with, she'd fixed him with the evil eye. He had a feeling she'd sink her damn teeth into him, like a wildcat, if he ever turned his back.

With the lantern strapped to his neck to provide illumination, he took her all the way down to the cellar, where they could make noise without worrying about the neighbors. Descending below ground into the feverish heat and the furnace's flickering glow was like taking a trip into hell. He was okay with that. He thought if there was a hell, he would probably make out pretty good there.

As they touched bottom, he said, "So tell me, girl detective. You know Officer Bradley Walsh, or not?"

The lantern lit up her face as she glanced his way. Her skin was already moistened with sweat from the furnace's heat. Her eyes never wavered. "Should I?"

"I dunno. Can't see how someone in your line would be close with a cop. Then again, Walsh ain't your ordinary boy in blue. He's got a drug habit. Maybe he's got other bad habits, too."

"Why do you care about him?"

"'Cause he's the only one that could connect Henry and me. If you didn't tail me here after tailing Henry, then you talked to him. Except that don't make no sense, neither."

"Why not?"

"Because your boss would've told you all about Henry. You wouldn't have needed to talk to Walsh until after Henry ran off. And that would've been too late."

"Too late for what?"

"Too late to ask Walsh any questions. I sold him some poison pills last night. You suck one down and you're a goner. The way he was jonesin' for a fix, I gotta believe he yielded to temptation without delay."

And yet there had been nothing on the radio. No news about a local cop found dead of an OD.

"So what are you worried about?" she asked.

He gave her a hard squint. "You, Bonnie Parker. I am worried about what you know, and how you know it, and who you told."

"That's a lot of worries."

"It surely is. But before long, you will relieve my curiosity on all these points and ease my mind." He unslung the lantern and set it down. "Kneel."

"Why?"

Jonah was not, as a general rule, inclined to explain himself. He replied to her question by kicking her legs out from under her, driving her to the floor. She hit the rug hard on both knees.

"Down you go," he said calmly.

While she knelt, he cut the bedsheets off her arms with a pocketknife, then made her shrug free of the coat and toss it aside.

"Can I get up?" she asked.

"No."

He didn't want her up. Her hands were unencumbered now, and even though he had the gun and the light and every advantage, he would give her no opportunities. She was the type who would take advantage of any slip. He had to play it just right.

Sofia appeared on the stairs, awkwardly toting the chair from the kitchen, which he'd told her to fetch. That item would have been a damn sight easier to handle if she'd folded it first, but his girl, let's face it, didn't have the brainpower of a fuckin' parakeet.

"You know," Jonah said to Parker as Sofia set up the chair by the furnace, "you kinda messed up my plans by killing Preacher when I still had one more corpse to make. Preacher being my name for the late Mr. Phipps."

"One more corpse? So ... three in all?"

"Three little piggies. That's right."

"Who's the third?"

"I told you, you got too many questions. It's my turn to ask things. How'd you get that ten grand?"

"Won it on a horse."

"Funny girl."

He leaned down and delivered a solid punch to her right arm, targeting the bandages under her shirt sleeve. Her face seized up with pain, and she fell on her left side, her mouth locked tight to suppress a scream.

Across the room Sofia looked on, fascinated.

"Where'd you get it?" he said again.

"Selling Thin Mints."

He drove his fist into her arm a second time. Blood

spotted her sleeve. The bandages had come loose, and the wound had opened.

She writhed on her side, her left arm pinned under her, her eyes shut against a spray of tears.

"Where'd the money come from?"

"Santa Claus."

He punched her again. Her sleeve was dark with blood now.

"Hurts, don't it, bitch? Make me stop hurting you." He hit her again. "Make me stop."

She opened her eyes and looked up at him through a sweaty tangle of hair. "Fuck you, Cletus."

He almost gave her another one, but there was no point to it. He hadn't really thought he could break her that way.

"Okay," he said. "That's how you wanna play it. Fine by me. Stand up."

With halting effort she managed it.

"Don't do anything stupid, Danger Girl." He thought she was too weak with pain to pull any tricks, but you never could be sure with someone like her. "You're gonna sashay over to that chair and sit down. And that is all you are gonna do."

It was a distance of less than six feet. He kept the gun on her the whole time. Even so, he was on edge until she reached the chair and sat.

"Arms on the armrests," he ordered.

She placed them there.

"Palms up."

She rotated her wrists and waited.

No funny business so far. Maybe he'd knocked all the orneriness out of her.

"Babe," he said with a glance at Sofia, "get me the rope from that bundle of kindling."

He sidled up next to the chair while Sofia untied two short lengths of rope and brought them over.

"Now," he said to Parker, "while I truss you up, my

best girl here is gonna be training your very own Glock on you, so I'd advise you to make no sudden moves." He handed Sofia the gun. "Like you done before, Mommy."

Bonnie Parker looked straight ahead, unblinking. Jonah knew that look. The thousand-yard stare.

Yeah, she was all hollowed out. Whatever fight was in her had been used up, spent.

He set to work applying the ropes. Sofia watched, her face lit from below by the lantern on the floor, blonde hair backlit by the furnace's fireglow.

"She's pretty," Sofia murmured dreamily. "So precious. That's what I'll call her. Precious."

"Don't name her," Jonah said. "You'll only get attached."

He finished tying the knots, making them tight, pinching her skin. It had to smart, but she showed no reaction.

He was satisfied now. She wouldn't be getting free. There was nothing she could do. And she knew it. He could see it in her face.

"You're dead already, ain't you, Bonnie Parker? You done given up."

She didn't answer.

"I'll bet old Preacher put up more of a fight than you, and he was just itching to die. He was forever saying this world's a prison and death's a jailbreak."

"You didn't buy into that," she said quietly.

"I thought it was bullshit. All that God talk. It was just some crap he came up with to make himself important. And to give him a reason for what he was gonna do anyway."

"Killing, you mean."

"Damn straight. People come up with reasons, but reasons ain't got nothing to do with it. Sometimes you just gotta draw blood. That's all. That's the whole of it."

"Interesting philosophy."

"You know it's true. Take me, for instance. I'm all set to draw blood right now. I could make it real easy on you.

Bullet in the head—bang. No muss, no fuss. All you gotta do is tell me what I need to know. Like, who's the Mr. Big you're working for? And does he know about me?"

"I'm working for Armin Petrossian. Whatever I know, he knows. If I go missing, he'll come after you."

For the first time Jonah found himself disappointed in her. This ploy was too obvious. It was like saying she'd written everything down in a letter to be opened in the event of her death.

"I don't think I buy that," he said.

"You don't believe it's Petrossian?"

"That part rings true enough. The Armenian, right? Yeah, he could be the man behind the curtain. But you keeping him up to date—it just feels a little too convenient, you know?"

"So kill me, and see what happens."

That was more like it. That was the stone-cold bitch he liked to see.

"Oh, you're gonna die, Bonnie blue-eyes. Believe you me. But first I'm gonna see to it you tell the truth, the whole truth, and nothing but." He turned to Sofia. "What've you got that'll make her open her yap?"

"Heroin. It releases inhibitions."

Jonah wasn't exactly sure what that meant, but he wouldn't demonstrate his ignorance by asking. It was his opinion that smart people never asked; they just knew.

"Okay, get some. Enough for two doses. First dose to make her talk, and the second so she can OD." He looked at the prisoner in the chair. "You ever do heroin, Bonnie Parker?"

"No. I could go for a shot of bourbon, though."

Jonah was feeling likewise, but he thought he'd better keep his head clear for now. "Sorry. This ain't that sort of hostelry."

Sofia hadn't moved. Her idleness annoyed him.

"There a reason you're not fetching the needle?" he inquired.

A fey, slightly goofy smile lifted a corner of her mouth. "I'll bet her titties get nice and hard."

"Get going," he ordered, putting some mustard on it. With a sigh, she started to glide away. "Hey, wait a sec. You got that cash on you?"

"It's in the purse." And the purse, he observed, was hanging from its strap on Sofia's shoulder.

"Give it over." He didn't trust her with the money. He wished she'd never found out about it. Damn girl spent every cent on her meds. She'd run through nearly all of the inheritance her grandma had left her. All of it, up her nose or in her arm.

Sofia surrendered the purse. He took out the wad of bills and stuffed it in his pants pocket, then tossed the handbag on the floor by Parker's coat.

"See you soon, Precious." Sofia's sandaled feet padded up the stairs.

"Your girlfriend seems to bend both ways," Parker said.

"Lady, she bends *every* way." He studied her. "You're a pretty cool customer for someone in your position. You get that we're putting you under, and you ain't never coming out?"

"What am I supposed to do, beg for mercy?"

"Wish you would. I'd like to see that."

"Don't hold your breath."

"Yeah, I know. You're not the type. Some beg and cry, and some just sit there and take it. Your arm hurtin'?"

"Like a bastard."

"Good." He chuckled. "You're gonna die, Bonnie Parker. But before you do, you will answer every one of my questions and inform me of everything I need to know."

"Maybe you won't like what I have to say."

"Don't matter. Whatever's happened, I will deal with it. Because that's what I do. I deal, and I adjust, and I survive. Like old Clyde, who ran with your namesake—I survive."

"Clyde Barrow died in an ambush," she said, still staring fixedly ahead. "He was shot to pieces."

Jonah grinned, unfazed. "But not until he'd danced with the devil a good long time."

33

BONNIE CONSIDERED HER situation—the chair, the ropes binding her wrists, the cellar, and the pair of lowlife crazies who'd made her their gimp.

Terrific. Her life was officially a grindhouse flick.

She was seriously ticked off at herself. Last night she'd let Henry get the drop on her. Today it was Jonah Stroud's turn. She was starting to think she'd lost her mojo.

But she wasn't done yet. Stroud could have pulled the trigger on her in the upstairs room. He hadn't, because there was something he wanted from her, and that meant she was still in the game. She just had to hang on. Hang on and breathe and wait for any opening.

Stroud had handled her pretty well so far. He might be a trailer-trash rube, but he was shrewd. He'd seen a lot of people in their last moments, and he knew how to play it smart. He'd made just one mistake, and because of it, she had a hole card—if she could find a way to play it.

On the stairs, a patter of sandals and the low hum of a familiar tune. "Scarborough Fair," it sounded like. Sofia descended, carrying a paper plate piled with small items. She set down the plate carefully on an apple crate that served as a table. Still humming, she arranged the items one by one with ritualistic care. A package of brown powder, a hypodermic needle, a spoon, a ball of cotton, a bottle of water, a squeezable container of lemon juice, a hand towel, a shoelace.

Jonah wasn't watching. He was busy feeding the furnace. He stooped and dug a coal shovel into a bucket, drawing up a heap of sooty black crumbs which he slung through the feed door. The flames jumped higher. The furnace roared.

Bonnie wished he would quit it. The heat was getting to her. Sweat had already soaked through her shirt. Well, most of it was sweat. Some of it was blood.

"Don't you think you've got enough of a fire?" she asked.

"Need to get the furnace hot. It's got work to do. See, since Preacher died too early, I need to make sure his mortal remains never turn up."

"You can't fit a body in there."

"Sure I can, if it's cut up. And I ain't guessing, neither." He thrust the scoop deep into the furnace, rooting around. "Proprietor of this establishment disappeared some time ago. Poor Mrs. Bailey. Sweet old gal. They never did find her."

With a grunt of satisfaction, he hoisted something out of the ash pit, balanced on the scoop's flat blade.

A jawbone. Charred and toothless—the teeth had popped loose in the heat—but unmistakably human.

"Guess they didn't look too hard," he said.

So the two of them really had played Hansel and Gretel. They'd even put the wicked witch into the oven.

Jonah shook the bone off the scoop, letting it drop into the soot at the bottom of the firebox.

"Plenty of room for another one." He looked back over his shoulder, a grin cutting his face like a scar. "Make that another two."

Sofia tapped some of the powder into the spoon, adding water and a drop of lemon juice. She stirred the mixture lazily with her finger.

Bonnie tried to find the irony here. She'd done her best to break Brad of his opiate habit, and now here she was, about to slam some heroin. It was kind of funny if you looked at it in a certain way. Not funny ha-ha, admittedly.

Okay, not funny at all.

She looked up at the unfinished ceiling, the exposed pipes crisscrossed amid whorls of cobwebs. Then down at the ancient short-nap carpet on the stone slab of the floor. And all around her, windowless brick walls like the walls in Henry Phipps's cellar. She'd thought she'd gotten out of that cellar, but somehow she was back.

The thought almost deflated her, but she fought off the feeling. While she still had the chance, before the drugs made her crazy, she tried to work out exactly what had gone on. Jonah had cultivated a friendship with Henry with the intent of misdirecting the blame for his own crime spree. His targets were Brighton Cove cops. One of them, the detective named Gaines whom Bonnie had run into once or twice, was already dead. Another, Brad Walsh—her Brad—should've been dead, too, but sobriety had come just in time.

There must be a third. He'd said there was one target left.

"What did the Brighton Cove PD ever do to you, anyway?" she asked.

He pitched another scoop of coal into the furnace. "Sent me away."

"For dealing?"

"Assault. I got into kind of a heated discussion with a client in your shitty little town. Sheldon Rice was his name."

"You beat him up?"

"Fuck, no. I chopped off three of his damn fingers." He dispensed another scoop of coal. "Was no big thing. They wouldn't never have made the charges stick if they hadn't flipped Rice. See, old Sheldon played it safe once he sobered up. Said I didn't have nothing to do with it. Said he cut off his own fingers by accident. Slicing an apple or some fuckin' thing."

"Standup guy."

"Nah, just scared. He thought I'd come after him if he testified."

"Did you?"

He shook his head. "I don't give a shit about him. We was both pretty wasted, truth to tell, and he'd already lost them fingers. I mean, they sewed 'em back on, but he can't move 'em or nothing. Nah, I don't hold any particular grudge against that guy."

Sofia had wrapped the spoon's handle in the towel. "Can I get to the furnace now?"

"All yours, babe."

He stepped back and let her hold the spoon just inside the feed door, waiting as the heat from the fire pit went to work on the tarry mixture. The furnace loomed over her, its multiple ducts climbing to the ceiling like tentacles.

"So who's the third little piggy?" Bonnie asked.

"The one that went to work on Rice, broke him down, turned him against me. Smooth-talking motherfucker. He flipped old Sheldon, and that's what did me in. Mr. chief of police hisself, Daniel J. Maguire."

"I know him. He's an asshole."

"Soon to be a dead asshole." He plucked something from his back pocket and dangled it before her. A pair of keys, clinking together on a ring. "I got me the keys to the fuckin' kingdom. I'll waltz right in and get it done."

"Is that how you got into Gaines's house?"

"Sure is. I'm a B 'n' E man in my spare time. I stole the keys to both houses. I am good to go. How about you, Mommy?"

"Just about," Sofia said.

The spoon's contents had liquefied now. Sofia replaced the spoon on the apple crate and put the cotton ball on top of it. The cotton puffed up like a blowfish, absorbing the mixture. She lifted the syringe.

"How much you giving her?" Jonah asked.

"Plenty."

"Don't overdo it. We can't stop her heart with the first dose. That comes later."

"I know what I'm doing."

"Okey-doke. Let's get this party started."

Slowly she drew the liquid into the syringe through the cotton, filling the hypodermic.

Bonnie sat very still as Sofia wound the shoelace around her right arm, just below the bleeding wound. She looked at the girl's long fingernails, curling like claws, painted the deep maroon of dried blood.

By now it was night outside, and in many homes people were sitting down to Christmas dinner or relaxing after it, amid a pile of unwrapped presents. A homey scene: a Christmas tree with plastic angels, Bing Crosby crooning on the radio, snow settling into deep drifts outside.

And here she was, in this personal hell, where her life would probably end. Frank had told her she'd made a wrong turn early on, and she needed to correct her course before it was too late. He'd been right, and she'd known it, even if she hadn't taken his advice.

Hadn't visited him today, either. Even though she'd promised. Well, shit, it wasn't as though she'd had a lot of free time.

"She's got good veins." Sofia looked over at her partner. "She's ready. We can start any time."

He nodded. "You gonna fly now, Parker. Like a fuckin' angel."

"'Tis the season," Bonnie said gamely.

34

SHE DIDN'T FLINCH when Sofia punched the needle in. She glimpsed a red squirt of blood from the vein, and then a wave of heat rushed over her, not heat from the furnace, but something alien and scary, like the sudden onset of fever. It was bad, but only for a moment. Instantly the heat diffused into a gentler warmth, an all-encompassing embrace that felt safe and loving, a return to the womb.

The cellar was gone. The furnace with its litter of bones—gone. Everything was gone, even the pain of the gunshot wound, and all of the pain she'd ever known.

The warmth receded a little, leaving her oddly somnolent, with no worries, no fears. From somewhere came voices. Two voices, or maybe three, and possibly her own voice was one of them. She didn't know. She was relaxed and contented, immersed in a soothing bath of good feelings, drifting in and out of awareness, maybe talking sometimes, or maybe not.

"How'd you find out about Walsh? How'd you get his money? C'mon, bitch, answer me."

"Talk to us, Precious. Tell us about the policeman."

"Brad ..." The word echoed off distant corners, endlessly repeated, losing its meaning.

"Yeah, Brad. Officer Bradley fuckin' Walsh. Was it the Armenian that gave him up to you?"

"Armin the Armenian ..."

"Was it him? Was it Petrossian?""

"The Fighting Rooster ..."

"Rooster? What's that supposed to mean? Quit giggling, you stupid cunt."

"You have to go easy on her, sweetie. You have to be gentle when she's like this."

"Fuck gentle."

"Rough won't work when she's on smack."

She floated higher. The air was thin up here, the sunlight strong. She was above the clouds, which lay below her like a carpet of down. Her body trembled with sweet vibrations, like a harp string—angels played harps—angels in the clouds ...

Was this heaven? She'd never quite believed in heaven. She has an automatic resistance to anything that sounded too good to be true. In the world she knew, everybody was on the make, and heaven had seemed like only another con. But up here in the brilliant light, so far removed from the grit and filth of the earth, heaven seemed not only possible, but inevitable.

Heaven is a state of mind, she thought. It's always within reach. I only had to know where to look.

"Okay, okay," the male voice said grudgingly. "Answer me this, little miss. How'd you track me to the halfway house? Did you tail me like I said?"

"A rooster has a tail ..."

"Fuck the damn rooster. Did you tail me, or did Walsh clue you in?"

"Rooster's a cock. A-doodle-doo."

If this was heaven, God must be here. She didn't see him, or her, or it. Didn't see anything but that wonderful shining light. But she felt the presence of something holy. Something kind and caring, vast enough to solve all problems, small enough to be held in her heart. It was probably God. If not, it would do until the real thing came along.

"Quit laughing, God damn it." That voice again, inexplicably insistent. "How'd you find out about me? Come on, how?"

A storm blew through her, threatening to upset her delicate equilibrium.

"You shake her like that, you'll just bring her out of it."

"What the fuck do I care if she comes out? She ain't givin' me shit."

"Only because you're not doing it right."

"Oh, so now you're the expert. Maybe you should go to work for the CIA at Geronimo Bay."

"I'm just saying, she needs to feel like she trusts you."

"Bullshit. This ain't working. She's day-trippin', and she likes it. Look at the stupid smile on her face. We're giving her a free ride."

"Maybe if you let me ask—"

"I'll do the asking, and she'll answer. Listen to me, Bonnie Parker. Did Brad Walsh tell you about me? Did he know I was squatting here?"

"Rooster," she murmured, stuck on that word.

"Hell with this shit. She's playing us, that's what." His breath on her face. "Did you get Walsh's name from Petrossian? Did you?"

"From Petrossian ..."

"Did you?"

"Yes."

"And Walsh gave me up?"

"Yes."

"Okay. Now we're getting somewhere. What'd you tell Petrossian? You give him my name?"

She hesitated, vaguely aware that it would be a mistake to tell him too much, though she couldn't remember why.

"Did you, you stupid bitch?"

"No," she said, forgetting her reservations.

"You didn't tell him about me? About Jonah Stroud?"

"No."

"He don't know about me?"

"No."

"Only about Walsh?"

"Yes."

"You lying to me?"

"No."

"I'm safe from Petrossian?"

"Yes."

She heard him breathing hard, like a man after a hard run.

"Okay," he muttered. "Okay."

She went off on her own, floating in the heavenly spaces above the clouds. Had she ever been this happy? As a child, maybe. Before her parents died. Before everything turned ugly and brutal and cold.

"Can you hear me? Hey! You hear me, Bonnie Parker?"

Reluctantly she came back a little bit. "Yes."

"How'd you track me here? Walsh know about this place?"

What place? Oh, the Gingerbread House, with the witch in the oven. Jonah Stroud's hideout. That was who the man was. Jonah Stroud.

"Last known address ..." she murmured.

"Oh, I get you. Smart girl, huh? Dog always returns to his fuckin' vomit. Okay, now how about Walsh? He gave me up, so he was alive last night. What about now?"

Again she felt a tug of resistance. There was a reason she couldn't tell him this. An important reason, probably.

"Talk to me, girl. Is Officer Bradley Walsh still alive?"

But she didn't remember the reason. And nothing was important, was it? Not when she knew the real truth of things, which was the light and heaven and God.

"Is he?"

No, nothing mattered. Nothing mattered at all.

"Yes," she said.

"He didn't take the pills?"

"No."

"He still got 'em?"

"Flushed them down the drain."

All but one, she thought. But she didn't say that.

"Fuck. Why?"

"He wants to be clean ..."

"Terrific. All of a sudden he's in fuckin' rehab. Where's he now?"

Yes, where was he? She had sent him off with somebody. Felix, that's right. He was with Felix, in the cabbie's little apartment in McKendree Park, over the paranormal bookstore.

"His place," she said, distantly astonished by the lie. "His apartment."

She had no idea why she'd said that. It seemed wicked to lie when in the presence of God.

"To his apartment?" Jonah asked.

"Yes."

"His place in Algonquin?"

"Yes."

"You ain't lying, are you, Bonnie blue?"

"No."

"She's telling the truth," Sofia said. "She has to be."

"Yeah," Jonah said. "I think so."

The voices dimmed, became murmurs, only partly intelligible.

"... all I need to know."

"You want me to ..."

"Just end her. Give her enough to stop her heart."

"It'll only take a minute. Shame, though. Poor Precious." Sofia released a sad little sigh. "Such a pretty mouth."

35

THE VOICES LINGERED only a little longer. Jonah said he needed to get busy; it was after dark, and two little piggies were still alive.

"You hang on to that Glock, babe. I got Preacher's gun in the van, and I'll take the Luger as a backup."

"Love you," Sofia called after him as the lantern floated off, his heavy footsteps climbing the stairs. Then he was gone, and Bonnie was alone with Sofia in a cellar now lit only by the dancing flames in the furnace. But really, Bonnie wasn't there either. She was far away, observing the scene from a great distance, blissfully indifferent to anything that happened.

Sofia occupied herself with pouring more brown powder into the spoon. Bonnie closed her eyes. She might have slept. She wasn't sure. Dreaming wasn't much different from being awake.

Slowly the clouds that carried her began to dissipate. She could see patches of ground below. Hard, stony ground, a long way down.

She opened her eyes, and she was in the cellar—really *in* it, this time. It wasn't some vision glimpsed dimly through smoky glass. It was her world, solid and actual, her brick and concrete prison. She was back.

She didn't want to be back. The crushing disappointment of it was hard to bear. Her head drooped. She groaned.

But she need not linger long. Escape was in sight, the final escape. She only had to let the next dose carry her away, back into the soothing light and the endless peace.

And yet ...

She wasn't ready. She wanted to hang on. She didn't know why. Maybe it was only force of habit. She'd made it this far by always hanging tough. She couldn't go soft now. She didn't know how.

When she lifted her head, she saw Sofia tying the shoelace around her arm a second time. The Glock rested on the apple crate, within the girl's reach if she needed it.

"All right, Precious." She readied the needle. "Time for you to go."

No more questions. Of course not. She had given Jonah Stroud everything he wanted, or so he thought. But she hadn't given up Brad.

And there was something else, something she'd almost forgotten.

Her ace in the hole.

Bonnie pulled in a breath, struggling to hold her mind in focus. "Another trip?"

"Your last trip—straight to the end of the line." The girl made a tsk-tsk sound. "Too bad. If things had been different ..."

"You're kinda into me, aren't you?"

"I'm into everything." She squirted a few drops of liquid from the hypodermic to clear it, then bent down, preparing to deliver the dose. "I believe in sampling every experience."

"So ... how about sampling me?"

The needle hesitated, poised over the bruised vein. "What are you trying to say?"

"I have a pretty mouth, you said. Want to taste it?"

"You playing games or some bullshit?"

"I just want to go out with a bang."

"Oh, you will. I'm giving you enough H to launch you to the moon."

"Not that kind of bang." Bonnie's tongue made a slow

circuit of her lips. "What do you say? One more for the road?"

Sofia appraised her with narrowed eyes. "You serious?"

"As a heart attack."

A wary smile lifted a corner of her mouth. "Okay, Precious. But you try anything, and I'll make it even worse for you."

She set down the syringe on the crate. In the moment when the girl's back was turned, Bonnie ducked her head to her left hand, where a small blue tablet was wedged between her thumb and forefinger.

The last of Brad's pills, the one he hadn't flushed, the one she'd confiscated just before Felix drove him away. It had been in her pants pocket until Jonah kicked her to the floor. While he'd whaled away at her right arm, she'd eased her left hand into her pocket and palmed the pill.

You suck one down and you're a goner.

She tongued the pill into a pocket of her cheek. By the time Sofia had turned to face her, she was upright in the chair, praying the tablet wouldn't dissolve too fast.

"Now"—Sofia let out a coquettish giggle—"let's see how good you taste."

Her lips locked on Bonnie's with a hard shock of intimacy.

Bonnie knew something about kissing, and she had to make this kiss last. She'd never Frenched a girl before, but she figured the technique would be the same regardless of gender. First, the slight pucker of the lips, the gentle forward thrust, the feathery caress of lip on lip. Then open wider, her tongue daring an instant of contact, then a coy retreat, then another dare.

And each time the small blue pill was nudged forward, until she slid her tongue under Sofia's and curled the edges, easing out, leaving the pill behind.

The furnace roared, and the blood roared in her head,

and the painful spot on the back of her skull pulsed in angry sympathy.

Sofia slowly pulled away with a drawn-out moan of pleasure.

"Nice. Very nice." She stepped back, an airy smile riding her mouth. "You have anything in mind for an encore?"

"Yeah." Bonnie raised her legs, bending them at the knee. "This."

She slammed both boots into the girl's solar plexus.

A blow to the solar plexus will paralyze the diaphragm, temporarily disabling the lungs. Sofia went down, hands on her belly, hunched over, sucking wind. For a long moment she could only make hoarse wheezing sounds as her face lost what little color it had.

Then her lungs unfroze, and instinctively she threw her head back and swallowed a huge gulp of air—and with it, the pill under her tongue. It went down with a visible jerk of her throat.

"You're crazy." Her voice was a croak. "You're ..." Coughing strangled her words.

Bonnie hawked up a generous gob of spit, doing her best to clear the taste of Sofia Windsor from her mouth. "I told you I wanted to go out with a bang."

"Then you fucking will."

Sofia lunged for the apple crate, a clumsy move that knocked it over, spilling the Glock onto the floor. It landed just out of reach. She fell on her belly and twisted forward, writhing, squirming, until her hand closed over the grip.

"Kiss this, bitch." She lifted the gun but was stopped by a new spate of coughing.

She would point and shoot as soon as she could, and Bonnie, still tied to the chair, couldn't do a damn thing about it. What the hell. If that was how it played out, taking a bullet would be quicker than overdosing on heroin. She was disappointed in the blue pill, though. It must've been a dud.

Sofia rocked back on her heels and raised the Glock again. She was bearing down on the trigger when the first spasm shuddered through her body. The gun dropped out of her suddenly boneless fingers, and she fell on her face, twitching like a broken toy.

When she looked up, her eyes were impossibly large, her skin mottled. "What'd you do to me? What'd you fucking *do*?"

She snatched up the gun, squeezed off a shot. The round blew past Bonnie's head, thudding into a wall.

A new wave of tremors sent her spinning onto her back. She made strange noises like hiccups. She thrashed and kicked.

Bonnie watched her, feeling no more than she would feel about the death throes of an insect.

The girl's eyeballs turned up inside her head. Foam lathered her lips. Her thin body jerked up and down, shoulders and hips slamming the floor.

Finally she trembled all over and lay still, her eyes white like eggshells, a pale ribbon of puke unspooling from her mouth.

"I offered to let you walk away," Bonnie said to the sprawled corpse in the gossamer grown. "You should've taken me up on it."

36

GETTING OUT OF the chair was easy enough, now that nobody was around to stop her.

She rocked the chair until it fell over. On her side, she frog-kicked herself close to the coal scoop leaning against the furnace. With effort, twisting her left hand against the cords, she was able to grab hold of the scoop. Its forward edge was a sharp, polished blade. She sawed at the rope binding her right arm. It took time, but she felt no urgency. The stuff in her system was keeping her strangely mellow.

Finally the rope unraveled and came apart, freeing her right hand. She transferred the scoop to that hand and went to work on the rope that was knotted around her other arm.

When that rope gave way also, she dragged herself out of the chair and stood. Her knees hurt—she'd banged them up pretty badly when Jonah knocked her down—and the pain of the bullet wound was back, and her head was still pounding. All in all, she'd had better holidays.

The open wound was the first priority. It was only oozing a little, but she took the opportunity to adjust the bandages, tying them down with the shoelace Sofia had used when finding a vein. She retrieved her purse, her coat, and the Glock.

Going upstairs was harder than she'd expected. Her balance was off. The world kept blurring out of focus, and a high hum played in her ears, reminding her of Sofia's rendition of "Scarborough Fair."

The ground floor was pitch dark. She groped her way to the back door, shrugged on the coat, and stepped outside, where there was more light but not much greater visibility. Snow was falling hard, obscuring everything in a whirl of white. The misty suggestion of a crescent moon swam behind tumbled clouds.

She crossed the backyard, navigating the deep drifts. The gap in the fence was where she remembered it. Her Jeep was still parked on the street.

She unlocked the door and fell into the driver's seat, breathing hard enough to fog the windshield.

What she needed was sleep, a long sleep, twenty-four hours of it. But her day wasn't done yet.

Stroud was out there, hunting Brad and Dan Maguire. She was in no condition to go after him, obviously. She would, anyway.

Unfortunately she didn't know which target was his priority. If it had been Dan, she might have waited until the job was done. Ha ha, only kidding. Maybe.

Rummaging in her purse, she found Brad's phone. She brought up the text messages from Jonah. She called his number and waited through five rings before he picked up.

"Walsh?" he said, confused by Caller ID. Noisy heavy metal music growled behind his words. He must be in the van.

"It's not Walsh." Bonnie fumbled a cigarette out of the purse and did her best to light it with the phone wedged under her chin. "It's me."

"What the fuck ...?"

"Yeah, that's pretty much what your girlfriend said after I pilled her like a dog. Walsh didn't flush his whole stash."

"You saying she's ... dead?"

"Give the hillbilly a prize." The cigarette was lit by now. She sucked down a voluminous draft of smoke. "Gotta tell you, she didn't go easy."

"Well, shit," he said slowly. "Shit."

"So now it's just you and me, cowboy. You up for a little high noon action?"

"*Mano a mano*, is that it?"

"Yeah, it's fucking Thunderdome. Two killers enter. One of them leaves." She took another drag. "If you got the stones."

"You think you can take me? You got a bum right arm and a shitload of smack bubbling in your veins."

"That's my problem."

"Jesus, lady, I ain't never seen nobody in such a hurry to die."

She needed to end this call. Even with the nicotine hit, she was having trouble holding up her end of the conversation. "Cut to the chase. You in or out?"

"You know Domani in McKendree Park?"

"I know it. Brad said you liked to hang there."

"Preacher did, too. It was his church, you might say. Meet me inside, and we'll get it on."

"Sounds good. By the way, before she croaked, your girl and me shared a soul kiss."

"So?"

"She said I was better than you ever were." She clicked off.

Okay, that last part had been a lie, but she wanted to give him something to think about.

Before starting off, she took out her own phone and located the photo of Henry Phipps, deceased, which she texted to Petrossian's number. There was no message. A picture was worth a thousand words, right?

She hoped so, because she didn't trust her fingers to type anything. Her hands were shaky and clumsy, and "Scarborough Fair" kept getting louder in her head, and the clouds in the night sky were somehow entwining themselves with the clouds in her brain, threatening to waft her away.

◉

Jonah had turned the van around as soon as he started talking to Parker. He was moving fast, blowing through scattered mounds of snow on Highway 35, nearly to the outskirts of McKendree Park.

His plan was to reach Domani before she did. It was his turf, he knew every inch of it, and he already had a plan for taking her out.

She was fuckin' crazy to go after him. She might be a pro and a stone-cold killer, but she was also majorly fucked up right now. Once he bagged her, he would return to the halfway house and dispose of Henry and Sofia in the furnace. He would put down the last two piggies, shoot them both with Henry's gun, then blow this burg and head south. Too cold up north this time of year, anyway. He would have the van, the Luger, and—once he killed Parker—that sweet little Glock, too. And ten grand in his pocket, a nice chunk of change to start a new life in a warmer clime. Georgia, maybe. He never realized until now how much he missed it there.

He could still do everything he'd planned. Okay, Sofia wouldn't be part of it, but he could always get another girlfriend. Truth was, he wasn't altogether sure he'd wanted Sofia to go on living, anyway. She would have blown his ten grand on meds. And she wasn't the type to keep her mouth shut about his little killing spree. Not to mention, she was kinda nuts, and it was never a good idea to stick your dick in crazy.

If you looked at it from a certain angle, Parker had done him a solid by taking her out. Saved him the bother, so to speak. On the other hand, she'd also cheated him of a tat. But he would earn one, anyway, when he took her out.

By now he was in McKendree Park, steering the van down the main drag. His music was back on, Slipknot screaming at him, the bleak hulk of Domani rising in his windshield behind the blur of the wipers. Snow poured down in a white waterfall. The roads had started to freeze. Turning up a side street, he almost went into a skid. He parked directly outside the vacant lot bordering Domani, leaving the van in plain view, which was just how he wanted it. He killed lights, engine, and music, leaving him in sudden silence except for the bagpipe skirling of the wind.

The .22 and the Luger went into his waistband on opposite hips, the Luger on his right because he intended to use that gun for this job. Pinning Parker's death on the Man in the Moon would raise too many questions. She must have made a lot of enemies over the years. No one would be too surprised that one of them had caught up with her.

The quarter-full bottle of cognac was under the passenger seat where he'd left it. He took it with him, not because he wanted a drink, although he did, but because he had a use for it.

Then he was out of the van, slipping through one of the many breaks on the fence, ducking under the billboard that told the world Domani was Italian for tomorrow. At a run, he crossed the field, glancing back now and then, afraid she would show up and blast him before he'd reached cover. There was a slim chance she'd beaten him to the scene and was drawing a bead on him even now, but he had to risk it. The blinding torrents of snow would make it hard to hit a target at a distance, anyway.

He passed between steel girders, into the cavernous space within. A spread of concrete enclosed by bars of steel, a giant cage, appropriate for the cage match to come.

Two killers enter, she'd said. *One of them leaves.*

Hardly a fair fight. He wouldn't be much of a man if he couldn't neutralize one female. And his daddy didn't raise no pussies.

He would get it done.

◉

Bonnie found the white van on the street and parked behind it. She thought she glimpsed a dark figure in the far distance, creeping inside the meshwork box that was Domani. But she might have been wrong. For all she knew, Jonah was still in the van, so she approached it cautiously, checking it out from all angles before concluding it was empty.

After that, she retreated to the Jeep and took a moment to rest. She was definitely not in prime condition. Her strength kept fading in and out like a weak radio signal. Her head sometimes felt as if it were detaching from her shoulders, about to float away like a helium balloon. How long did it take for heroin to leave your system, anyway?

"Fuck it," she muttered, pushing open the Jeep's door. She wasn't risking that much. When she cashed in, it wouldn't be because of some brain-dead *Deliverance* reject. She'd already finished off Henry Phipps and Sofia Windsor, working her way through two-thirds of her very own three little piggies. Only Jonah Stroud was left.

She stepped out into the cold, pulling the coat over her again, leaving the hat behind. At the moment, fashion seemed strangely unimportant.

Quickly she made her way toward the fence and, beyond it, the dark scar of Domani against the whirling sky.

◉

There she was. Crossing the field, stooping low against the wind and snow, blonde hair blowing at her back.

Somebody else, somebody not smart like him, might have tried taking a shot at her before she got inside the structure. In clear weather he would have chanced it. But tonight the wind would throw off his aim, and the snow would conceal his target, and he would be lucky even to wing her.

He didn't want her wounded. She was already wounded, and it hadn't stopped her. He needed her dead. Which meant taking her at closer range, away from the elements. It meant lying in ambush in the cold darkness down below, in the subterranean space that had been Preacher's church.

He knew that space. She didn't.

It felt right for her to die there, on that holy ground, in a baptism of fire.

The bottle in his pocket clinked against the gun at his hip as he descended the concrete stairway, taking care to leave good tracks in the snow.

◉

The ground floor of Domani was vast. Stroud could be anywhere. Bonnie moved from pillar to pillar, exploring the darkness. There was a flashlight in her purse, but she didn't use it. The beam would make her an easy target.

As before, the Glock was in her left hand. She couldn't count on accuracy from a distance. She had to get close to her quarry.

At a far corner of the structure she found fresh tracks, not yet obliterated by snow. They led to a concrete stairway descending into a deeper darkness. In the chancy light of the horned moon, emerging now and then from behind clouds, she saw a wall covered in crude spray-can art like cave drawings, and a hand-lettered sign reading KEEP OUT.

It seemed like good advice, but Jonah hadn't followed it. His footprints disappeared down the stairs.

He'd taken cover underground, knowing she would come after him. He would be waiting at the bottom.

She crossed the interior to the opposite corner, where she found a second stairwell. Possibly a safer approach. Or possibly not, if he had anticipated this move. Well, life was all about taking chances. At least her life was.

She planted a boot on the top step and started down. She had no idea what lay beneath Domani. A basement of some kind.

Henry had tried to get her into his basement. Jonah had taken her to the basement of the halfway house. Now here she was, once again venturing below ground.

Three strikes, you're out? Third time's the charm?

She wasn't sure which adage applied in this situation. All she knew was that she was seriously pushing her luck.

The stairway descended into flights breached by a concrete landing. She paused on the landing, halfway down, listening.

The faint light from above was nearly gone. From below there was no light at all. But she heard noises. Faint rustlings and scrapings. And mutterings, coughs, and cries. Human noises. Not Jonah, but others. People who lived down there, hiding from sun and sky. A colony.

Yeah, this was getting better and better.

She took the second flight of stairs, moving fast, the gun leading her. Without stopping, she pivoted through a doorless entryway into the larger space beyond. She still couldn't see anything, but she felt the room opening up around her. She sensed a high ceiling and distant walls.

It felt like it was a single large enclosure, not partitioned into separate rooms. The floor sloped gently toward a central point. A parking garage, probably. There would be an entry ramp somewhere, sealed up now.

Motionless, she stood just inside the doorway. The whispery background noises continued. She had no idea how many people were down here. The darkness felt weirdly thick with unseen presences. There were bad smells—mold, rotting food, human waste—and strange unidentifiable scrapings, the sound of things shifting in the dark, like ballast in a ship's hold.

And it was cold, bitterly, brutally cold. Many degrees colder than the upper world—the real world, as it seemed to her. In this place where light never reached, there was a permanent chill, a frigidity that had settled deep into Domani's concrete bones. She shivered.

This was a dead place, and the things living here were more dead than alive, more ghost than human.

Okay, quit it. She was freaking herself out. Or maybe it was the crap still circulating in her bloodstream, spinning her mind in all sorts of crazy directions.

She took a step and heard the faint crunch of broken glass, the shifting of gravel. The floor was a concrete slab strewn with debris. Impossible to move quietly.

She needed to find cover. A parking garage would have support posts at regular intervals to hold up the ceiling. She crept forward, moving blindly, her boots crushing bits of refuse.

And there was gunfire.

The darkness lit up with purple muzzle flashes. Three shots landed near her. In the flickering glare she glimpsed a pillar two yards away. She dived for it, hitting the floor, cutting her palms on sharp stones and glass fragments.

She folded into a crouch behind the post and blinked away the afterimages burned onto her retinas. Her ears rang. The shots had been loud, echoing from every corner like a clamor of bells.

As her hearing returned, she heard the babble of voices, more of them, and louder now. A dozen or more people in many parts of the cavernous space, chattering like a troop of monkeys in a rainforest.

She hugged the pillar, feeling the deep chill of the concrete penetrate her coat, as the voices rose in a chorus of gibbering and howling, the soundtrack of a kennel—or an asylum.

She'd thought Jonah's cellar was hell. But it was only halfway there, which made sense for a halfway house. Hell's anteroom.

This place was hell. This icy darkness crying with the

voices of the damned.

Jonah Stroud belonged here.

Maybe she did, too.

37

JONAH HADN'T TAKEN her out with the Luger's first volley, but that was okay. He'd never counted on finishing her that fast.

There were two stairways to the parking garage, and he'd known she could take either. As a compromise, he'd positioned himself in the middle of the parking garage, with a clear shot at either entrance.

He couldn't see for shit. But he didn't have to. Having been down here before, he knew that the floor was carpeted in debris swept down the stairwells by rainstorms or pitched down by people hanging out above ground. Nobody could cross that minefield of trash without making noise.

When he'd heard the crunch of her footsteps, he'd opened fire. In the strobing half-light of his muzzle flashes, he'd seen her slide behind a concrete post fifty feet away. She was still there, cowering like the scared little bitch she was.

He had the edge on her. He knew her position, and she didn't know his.

The mole people were settling down now. That was how he thought of them. Ragged people, caked in dirt, wrapped in soiled bedrolls, living in cinderblock shanties. They had furniture—folding chairs scavenged from dump bins, milk crates swiped from behind grocery stores. Other possessions, too—shopping carts brimming with hoarded junk, bags of old shoes, stacks of useless CDs or waterlogged, coverless paperback books.

He didn't mind them, or the world they'd made. Truth was, he kind of liked it down here, in the friendly dark.

When the room had quieted, he began to advance on his belly, slithering like a hognose snake in the Altamaha's boggy muck. No footsteps. No noise. No mistakes.

He covered a good twenty feet before stopping. Now it was time to execute the second part of his plan.

He'd already prepared the cognac bottle, stuffing a rag inside after soaking it in alcohol. From his pocket he took out a matchbook. With his back to the pillar, he struck a match against the cover, making a small blue flame, then touched the flame to the rag corkscrewing out of the bottle. Capillaries of red traced bright new patterns in the weave.

Pivoting on his hips, he pitched the bottle in a high, looping arc.

◉

Bonnie was thinking of making a move for another hiding place. It was a risk. Jonah might hear her again, as he must have heard her when she'd walked across the floor. But she might have to chance it.

In the flareup of gunfire she'd seen a line of pillars, evenly spaced at intervals of roughly twenty-five feet. Each was a concrete rectangle, unpainted, wide enough to conceal her as long as she hugged it close.

She was bracing for a run when the darkness was broken by a pinwheeling blur of fire. A torch or a lantern, flung in her direction, plunging toward the floor two yards to her left.

It landed with a crash of breaking glass and a shout of flame. A Molotov cocktail.

The voices whooped and shrieked in a new outbreak of gibberish.

She watched the flame sputter and smoke. If it was meant to flush her out, it didn't work. She held her ground.

But maybe it had a different purpose. Not to spook

her into moving, but to light up the area around her. The guttering fire cast its glow over yards of concrete. Not a lot of light, but for someone whose eyes had adapted to the dark, it would expose her if she left concealment.

The fire would burn itself out before long. But Jonah didn't need a lot of time. His shots had come from pretty close. With the firelight pinning her down, he could circle around, approaching from an angle. If he stayed beyond the reach of the light, he would be invisible. He could line her up in his sights.

Shit.

The son of a bitch had her trapped. If she ran, he'd gun her down. If she stayed put, he'd take aim from the shadows beyond the fireglow. She couldn't move, and she couldn't sit still.

Bonnie wasn't much of a chess player—she never could get the hang of that little horsey thing—but she knew when she was checkmated.

Already he must be moving into position. The kill shot could come from any direction, at any time.

Jonah was close. He'd crawled straight as an arrow toward the pillar where she hid, using the glow of burning alcohol as cover. He knew she couldn't see past the scrim of light, and what with all the crazies jibber-jabbering around him, she couldn't hear him, either.

He could see the pillar, though. See it well enough to know she hadn't stirred.

Maybe he'd hit her, after all, when she'd dived for cover. Maybe she was bleeding out, or even dead already.

You dead, Parker? he asked the darkness. Did I close your bright blue eyes?

Funny thing. He couldn't recall the color of Sofia's eyes. Couldn't remember the sound of her voice. All he could bring to mind was the lacy swish of that gossamer gown of hers as she sashayed around. She had a sexy walk, like a model on a runway. He would miss that.

The fire was nearly out. Darkness was settling over the basement again. That was all right. He didn't need the light anymore. He was less than four yards away.

Parker wasn't as smart as she thought she was. She shouldn't have come down here. It was like walking right into an open grave.

◉

For at least the third time Bonnie ran through her options. The nearest new cover was another pillar twenty-five feet away. Even in an all-out sprint, she couldn't reach it before he took her down. The stairs were nearly as far in the other direction. A run in either direction was suicide.

There was no way to guess where Stroud was. All she knew was that he was closing in—from somewhere.

She was completely vulnerable. He could get her in his sights at any time. Her only hope was to expose his position before he was near enough for a clear shot.

There might be a way.

◉

The voices began to quiet down. Jonah slowed his crawl. The idea was to get right up close, then open up with the Luger. At short range he wouldn't need to aim. If he squeezed off five or six rounds, he was bound to get her before she could even react.

He would gun her down in the dark and leave her carcass on the floor, where it might rot forever, like the mummified cadaver of a dog he'd stumbled across on one of his other trips into the lower depths. Hell, it wasn't like anybody here would be calling 911.

It was kind of a kick, almost like he was lighting up the original Bonnie Parker, the one Sofia had never heard of. And what the fuck was that all about? Who the hell didn't know about Bonnie and Clyde?

He wriggled a few feet closer. Near enough now. She had to be ten feet away, or even less.

By now the fire was out, the darkness total. He could no longer see the pillar, let alone anyone hiding behind it. But she had to be there, low to the floor, positioned at a forty-five angle to where he lay.

His first shot would outline her in purple, and his next rounds would finish the job. The whole business should take only a few seconds.

He lifted the Luger, propping his right arm under his left, ready to earn one more swastika, his best one yet.

◉

In her purse, she found it.

There wasn't much time. The Molotov cocktail had burned out. He must already be in position to shoot.

She turned it on and punched one button.

◉

Jonah was tightening his pull on the trigger when a blast of noise and light erupted from his pocket.

His phone, his goddamn *phone*.

The angry chords of "The Devil in I" gnashed their metal teeth, and the home screen lit up, shooting its white glare into the space around him.

He wasted a precious half second trying to silence the phone before giving up and trying to fire on the pillar.

Too late. A spray of gravel was ripping up his face and shoulders and arms, cutting deep.

Not gravel.

He heard the delayed coughs of the Glock in her hands.

◉

Bonnie emptied the gun, then risked using her flashlight for the first time. The beam cast a wavering yellow oblong on Jonah Stroud. A good part of his face was gone, which was no real loss.

He wasn't dead, though. Not quite. She heeled another magazine into the Glock and approached him, keeping him pinned in the circle of light. The Luger wasn't in his hand, and he showed no inclination to reach for it, but she was taking no chances.

As before, the rainforest chatter of unseen witnesses surrounded her. Some brainless creature was laughing hysterically. Other voices prayed loudly or issued orders for the intruders to leave.

She ignored all that. She stopped at his side and stood over him, staring down. Blood bubbled out of his mouth, smearing his chin.

For the last time their eyes met. He glared up at her with the bottomless hatred of the damned.

"You fucked it all up," he mumbled. "Cunt."

"Yeah, Merry Christmas to you, too."

His eyes flickered. Went dark. He was gone.

He'd gotten closer to her than she'd expected. He could have picked her off at that distance. Probably he'd been about to. It had been a close-run thing.

But that was her life. Every day, a spin of the wheel. So far she'd come up lucky. The house would win in the end, but in the meantime she was racking up a pretty good score.

Kneeling, she pried the phone out of his back pocket. She didn't want it found on his body. If the police recovered the phone, they would check the log and find Brad's calls, which he'd been stupid enough to make from his own cell.

Until Jonah's phone lit up, she hadn't been absolutely sure he'd had it on him. He could have left it in the van, in which case hitting redial on Brad's cell would have accomplished nothing, and she would be dead now.

But she supposed a drug dealer could never afford to be without his phone.

She put his cell in her purse, adding the Glock and the Luger to the mix. Not the .22, though. Henry's gun needed to stay where it was, wedged at Jonah's hip. Having never touched it, she had no need to wipe it down. In his pants pocket she found Dan Maguire's two keys on their keyring, and the wad of bills. All of that went into the purse also.

She stood, cleared her throat, and addressed the invisible multitude around her. "Hey! Nutcases! Shut the fuck up!"

Her shout boomeranged back at her from four corners. The crowd quieted.

"Okay, here's the deal. Cops are gonna be all over this place in about an hour. You freaks might wanna make yourselves scarce."

No one answered. No one moved. She didn't know if they would take her advice or not. She also didn't care.

The stairs led her back to a world of sky and snow and air. She left Domani and stood facing the wide, overgrown lot that concealed so many hidden, hopeless lives.

Her fingers dug in her purse and found Brad's ten grand. She didn't want it. Drug money. Blood money. Brad didn't want it, either. He could never spend it, not without risk and guilt.

She riffled through the wad like a deck of cards, then held the money high over her head. When a cold gust kicked up, she let it go.

The bills scattered among the snowflakes, flying everywhere throughout the field. The money would be found, a few bills at a time, tomorrow and the next day, and for days and weeks afterward. For the next few months, every day would be Christmas—for somebody.

"God bless us," Bonnie told the night, "every one."

The last scraps of green paper spun away into the dark.

38

DOMANI WAS ONLY a few blocks from Felix's apartment. Bonnie figured she ought to stop in and check on Brad. She had something she needed to talk to him about, anyway.

On her way over, she pulled into an alley and chucked Jonah's phone and Brad's into a trash bin, but only after whacking both items several times to scramble their circuitry.

Felix opened his door after one knock. Bonnie smiled at him from under her Cossack hat, which she'd replaced on her head, because her survival had put her in the mood to be stylish.

"Hey, amigo. How's it been?"

"Pretty rough. But"—he eyed her up and down—"it looks like it has been rougher for you."

She hadn't given much thought to her appearance, but now that he mentioned it, she probably did look like shit, even with the hat. "Yeah, well, the holidays are stressful. He give you any trouble?"

"It got a little hairy. He really needed a fix around four o'clock. When the sun goes down, that is when they start to feel it."

"What happened?"

"I kept him under control."

"He didn't hurt you, did he?"

"*Bandida,* I am tougher than I look. I think we are past the worst part."

"He do any throwing up?"

"Much throwing up."

"Add it to my tab."

"I have. This will cost you. But love is worth it, right?"

"Right." She forced a smile. "He asleep?"

"He woke up a few minutes ago."

"I'll say hello, then."

She found Brad in Felix's bed, just lying there, staring at the ceiling with a befuddled, vaguely angry look.

"Yo, Walsh. How's it hanging?"

With visible effort he focused his attention on her. "Still alive," he said, his voice thick with phlegm and weariness.

"Detox doesn't kill you. It just makes you wish you were dead." She sat on the edge of the bed. "I chased down your supplier."

"And?"

"He's no longer in business."

"How about Henry Phipps?"

"I found him too. Problem solved."

"The way you always solve problems."

She wasn't crazy about his tone, but she cut him a break. He was going cold turkey, after all. "Yeah, that's right. He won't kill any more dog walkers or joggers."

And Jonah Stroud won't kill any more cops, she added silently. But she didn't want to get into that.

"So how you doing?" she added. "Seriously. No bullshit."

"It's been hell. I think I vomited, like, a million times. Every part of my body hurts. Don't ever do Percocet. I mean it."

"Nah, I'll stick to heroin." She said it lightly, and he took it as a joke, which was fine. "So I've been thinking about something. You told me you kept getting headaches and muscle tension—bad enough that you needed painkillers?"

He shrugged. "Yeah."

"Why?"

"I don't know. Life, I guess."

"Try again."

His head dropped back on the pillow. "All right, it was us. I was always afraid of getting caught. I wasn't sure how much Dan knew or what he guessed. I was just, I don't know, nervous around him. And I thought he could tell. Which only made me more nervous. I had to work really hard to keep it together at work. It took its toll."

Bonnie felt more tired than before. "That's kinda how I figured it. But you never said anything."

"I didn't want to be a burden. I thought I could handle it on my own."

"By getting hooked on opiates."

"It was the only way to decompress."

"I get that." She shut her eyes. "So it all comes back to me."

"I'm not trying to put any of this on you."

"I know. But I think maybe—maybe I put you in a situation you weren't equipped to handle. See, lying and sneaking around comes easy to me. Sometimes I forget not everyone is built that way."

"I chose it. It was my call. I went in with my eyes open. I knew the risks."

Stupid words. Clichés cribbed from bad movies. Sometimes she forgot he was younger than she was, and he'd seen a lot less of life.

"Yeah," she said. "You knew the risks."

The risks. But not the cost.

She looked at him, but he had nodded off. Carefully she raised herself off the bed and left.

"He's dozing again," she told Felix.

"Is there anything more you want me to tell him when he wakes up?"

Goodbye, she thought. Tell him goodbye.

"Just say I'll check in tomorrow," she said.

◉

The metal detector in the lobby of the Brighton Cove police station allowed her to pass, because she'd had the foresight to leave her purse in the Jeep. She'd assumed the whole force would be working late, and she was right. The station house was lit up, the whole place a hive of frantic worker bees.

"Wanna see Maguire," she said to the duty officer, whose only answer was a scowl of recognition. As an inducement she added, "Tell him I can help out on the Phipps thing."

This worked. She was buzzed through.

She climbed the stairs to the second floor. Dan was at his desk, and he was smiling as she entered.

"This is good timing, Parker. I just received a judge's sign-off on a telephonic warrant to search your person, your vehicle, your office, and your residence." He waved a piece of paper at her. It looked very official. "I'm going to put you away. Merry Christmas."

"Happy New Year." She dumped herself into an armchair facing the desk. "I heard about Detective Gaines. I'm sorry. He was a friend of yours, I know."

"Yeah. He was a friend. And you aren't. I don't need your sympathy, and neither does he."

She puffed up her cheeks and blew out a whoosh of air. "Oh, Dan. Wherever did you learn your manners?"

"Save it. I'm not in the mood for your crap."

She just laughed. Good old Danny boy.

He leaned forward, squinting at her. "You feeling okay? You seem a little off."

"It's been a busy night. I visited heaven and hell."

"Parker, are you high?"

"On life, Dan. On life. Are you in the mood to close the Man in the Moon case?"

"To do what?"

"You heard me."

"Are you telling me you know where to find Henry Phipps?"

"There's that steel-trap mind of yours, cutting straight to the chase."

"So what's the story? You come here to make a deal?"

"Maybe. What's it worth to you to clear both the Phipps case and the Phil Gaines homicide?"

"It's the same case."

"Wrong-o, Danno. Phipps didn't kill your friend, even though it was made to look that way."

He pursed his lips. "And you know who did?"

"I do."

"And you can deliver him?"

"On a platter. It's a big opportunity for you. They'll make you police chief of the year, or *People* magazine's sexiest cop."

"You could be telling the truth. It's possible." His fingers drummed the desk. "But I still think I'd rather take you down."

"Petty and spiteful to the end, huh? Fair enough, but there's one more thing you ought to know. Phil Gaines wasn't the only Brighton Cove cop who was targeted today. You were number two on the hit parade."

She was keeping Brad's name out of it. She didn't want Dan trying to get in touch with him right now.

His mouth curved into a scowl. "You're saying you saved my life, is that it?"

"It wasn't exactly my top priority, but it did work out that way."

"Bullshit."

"Eloquent as always."

"Even if someone did intend to come after me, how would they get at me? Here in the station, with dozens of officers around?"

"Nope. At home."

"I've already told my wife to keep the doors locked and the security system armed. Nobody's getting in."

"He had these." She tossed the keyring from Jonah's pocket onto the desk. "They're from your house. I'm guessing the funny-shaped one turns off your alarm system."

Dan stared at the keys on his blotter. His voice was much softer when he spoke. "How could he get the keys?"

"He broke in and stole them. He was planning this for a long time."

"I'm not missing any keys."

"That's probably what Phil Gaines thought. There are always spare keys lying around, Dan. Nobody ever notices if one or two disappear."

He checked one key against a key on his own set, lining up the serrated edges. "It's mine," he murmured.

Bonnie smiled. "If not for me, you would've received a nasty surprise when you got home tonight. And your wife ... well, the first rule of the killing game is, no witnesses."

"You would know," he whispered.

She ignored that. "I realize we're not exactly compadres, but keeping you and your missus out of the morgue ought to earn me a few Brownie points. And you know what they say—peace on earth, goodwill toward PIs."

He looked up at her from his desk. "You were in Phipps's house last night, weren't you?"

"Yeah."

"He shot you."

"In the arm." She patted her sleeve.

"You went there to kill him, on Armin Petrossian's orders."

"I did."

"For money."

"No. I didn't take any cash. Petrossian proved to me that Phipps was the guy, and I agreed to do the hit. As kind of a public service."

"Public service." His face went through a complicated variety of expressions, settling on contempt. "You should go away for that. And for all the other things you've done."

"Then send me away, Dan." She watched his eyes. "And kiss your wife when you get home."

He held her gaze in a brief staring contest. He was the first to glance away.

"God damn it." He picked up the warrant, gave it a long, mournful look, and tore it in half. "Tell me everything."

She did. It wasn't a long story, though it would have gone better with a cigarette. Lacking her purse, she soldiered on, smoke-free.

Jonah and Sofia, squatting in the Gingerbread House, where they'd held Phipps prisoner while Jonah went after the cops who'd wronged him. All dead now. Henry shot in an upstairs room. Sofia in the cellar, victim of a drug overdose. Jonah in the basement of Domani.

"And where were you when all this happened?" Dan asked wearily.

"Up on the housetop with old Saint Nick."

"Ha ha."

"Get with the season. You're supposed to say ho ho ho."

"Seriously, how the hell am I supposed to explain three dead bodies?"

"Easy-peasy. Henry was shot with an unlicensed Glock, one of those ghost guns the media's always warning us about. Jonah was killed with the same gun. I'm thinking Sofia was good for both murders. She was a crazy addict, and she killed her prisoner and then went after Jonah and killed him in Domani. The witnesses down there, if you can get them to talk to anybody other than their imaginary friends, will tell you a woman did the shooting."

"And why is Sofia dead?"

"She went back to the Gingerbread House and ate something that disagreed with her. The coroner can tell you what it was. Maybe she was grief-stricken over killing her boyfriend. Maybe she was on such a high, she didn't know what she was taking. You'll find evidence of heroin use. It could be why she got herself so scrambled."

"How about the Glock? Is that in the cellar too?"

"It is now." She'd planted it there after leaving Domani. By this time the snow would have covered her tracks.

"And how do I justify knowing about Jonah Stroud and his girlfriend in the first place?"

"Tip from a CI. That's CI, not PI, capisce? Oh, and by the way, the lady who ran the Gingerbread House—you'll find what's left of her in the furnace. Stroud put her there. That's another case you can close. You're on a roll, Dan."

He shut his eyes. "All right, Parker. I'll play ball with you. Just this once."

"Great." She pushed herself out of the chair. "One more thing. Brad's future."

"He hasn't got a future."

"I want you to let him keep his job."

"No way. Absolutely not. I can't have an officer in my department consorting with—"

"Yeah, I get that. But it's not an issue. I'm breaking it off."

"Are you?"

"I haven't told him yet. But I will." She took a breath. "I have to."

"What accounts for this sudden change of heart?"

"Call it a Christmas miracle. Will you let him stay?"

"You already fooled me once ..."

"No fooling, this time. I'm not good for him. I see that now."

"You're not good for anybody."

She couldn't argue. She was too tired, and besides, the son of a bitch was right. "Can he stay on?"

Dan puffed up, ready for a fight, then abruptly

deflated. He was tired, too, she realized. Tired and shell-shocked and grieving for his friend.

"Aw, hell," he muttered, "I guess so. He's a good cop, otherwise." He made a halfhearted attempt at wagging a finger. "But if you two start sneaking around again ..."

"We won't. It's over." She turned away. "Everything's over."

Back in the Jeep, she thought about what she still had to do. Ditch the Luger in a convenient body of water. Redress the bandage on her arm. Sleep for a million hours. But first—visit Frank Kershaw. It still wasn't too late, and she'd promised to be there on Christmas.

Her phone chimed with a text as she was starting the engine. The message was from Petrossian, and it consisted of three words.

See me. Now.

Shit.

39

THE GATE TO Petrossian's estate opened for her as before. Her two friends, Donner and Blitzen, were waiting on the front steps in the tumbling snow.

Before climbing out of the Jeep, she checked the time on her phone. Nearly ten. Late for a meeting. But drug kingpins did tend to be night owls. It kind of went with the job.

The two men greeted her with grunts. They didn't seem happy to see her, maybe because they had to work on a holiday, or maybe because since their last encounter, she'd taken out two of their colleagues.

They led her inside, past the too-modern Christmas tree, through the ever-present strains of Vivaldi, to the elevator at the end of the hall. The guy with the sawed-off shotgun was still on duty on the second floor. She wondered if he had ever left.

At the door to Petrossian's study, Donner turned to her. "This time we take your weapon. No argument, please."

It was hard to say the word please as a threat, but he pulled it off.

She put up no resistance. She'd expected as much. After her impromptu performance in the limousine, Petrossian would be taking no chances.

When she'd been disarmed and, for good measure, patted down with conspicuous thoroughness, Blitzen rapped on the door. It opened at once, and she went in.

Petrossian sat at his desk, in the same dressing gown, nursing what might have been the same glass of brandy.

She heard the door close behind her, leaving them alone together, as she took her seat.

She was trying hard not to be afraid. In a situation like this, fear was counterproductive. A man like Petrossian could smell it.

"Bonnie Parker," he said pleasantly enough.

"Mr. Petrossian." She did her best to sound respectful and not ironic. It wasn't easy. She wasn't good showing deference to authority.

"I was surprised and gratified to receive your photograph of the late Mr. Phipps."

"So ... we're good then?"

"More than good. I'm most favorably impressed with your skills."

"That's not the song you were singing this morning."

"You've redeemed yourself since then. Shall we celebrate with a drink?"

It took all her willpower to say, "I'm okay, thanks."

"You're not a teetotaler, I'm sure?"

"Tonight I am. We done?"

"There's just one more thing."

She waited warily. His tone had shifted ever so subtly. At least she thought it had. She could be imagining it. She was operating on limited sleep and even more limited food, with a bullet itching in her arm and the residue of heroin swimming in her veins.

"My decision to select you for this assignment wasn't random," he said. "I've been interested in you for some time."

"Have you?"

"For the past two and a half months, more or less. Ever since my wife hired you to kill Rosa Martinez."

Bonnie sat very still.

"The Man in the Moon killed Rosa Martinez," she said.

Petrossian nodded, smiling. "That's how it was meant to look. You and I know better, don't we?"

"Just what exactly do we know?"

"We know that my wife paid you forty thousand dollars to assassinate Rosa Martinez on a Tuesday morning in October. We know that you took advantage of the spate of killings attributed to the Man in the Moon to camouflage the job. You were aware that Rosa jogged alone in the morning. She was fearless that way. It was a simple matter for you to lie in wait by the railway. And to shoot her from behind as she crossed the tracks."

It had been simple. He was right about that. She had tried to think like the killer. To *be* him. And it hadn't been difficult.

"The next train crushed the skull and destroyed the bullet, ruling out comparative tests. There was thus no way to prove that it came from a different gun from the one used by the Man in the Moon. Everyone merely assumed he had done it. As they were meant to. And that"—Petrossian spread his hands—"was that."

Yes, indeed. That was that.

It occurred to her that her plan had been essentially the same as Jonah's—to use the serial murders as cover for an unrelated homicide. She didn't care for the thought. It made her more like Jonah Stroud than she wanted to be.

"What makes you think your wife hired me?" she asked.

"I know more of Kira's activities than she imagines—though I'd never thought she would prove to be the jealous sort."

"She isn't. And she didn't come to me. I went to her."

"Why?"

"Because Rosa Martinez contacted me. She wanted to arrange a hit on your wife."

He steepled his hands. "Ah."

"I didn't go for the idea. Moral standards, remember? So I went to your wife and gave her a heads-up. We both knew Rosa would find someone else to do the job. Kira hired me to execute a preemptive strike."

"That makes sense."

"You're not surprised your girlfriend was shopping for a hitter to take out your wife?"

"Rosa was ... ambitious. One might even say delusional. She was something of a fantasist. I believe she imagined herself at my side, as my second wife, enjoying luxury and a glamorous international life."

"When in fact ..."

"In fact I was already growing tired of her."

"So you didn't love her."

"Bonnie, I've never loved anyone. This includes my wife. But I wouldn't want to lose her. She's far too valuable. It's upon her father that all my good fortune depends."

"You never gave a damn about avenging Rosa."

"Actually, her elimination spared me the trouble of an unpleasant breakup."

"And you never cared about killing Henry Phipps."

"There you're mistaken. I did care, very much. Had Phipps been taken alive by the police, he might have denied any involvement in the Martinez killing, and the authorities would have been obliged to wonder if it was a copycat case. Their investigation could have led them to you—and through you, to my wife—and therefore to me. So yes, I did want Phipps silenced. And so, I think, did you ... for the same reason."

"I suppose."

"Your motives in this matter weren't entirely altruistic."

"They never are."

"I was counting on that. I knew your self-interest would provide you with additional encouragement to finish the job. When it appeared you'd failed, I found it prudent to eliminate you before Phipps was caught. I couldn't have the police taking you into custody, or the whole matter would come out. Luckily that scenario did not come to pass." He smiled. "I'm gratified that things worked out as they have."

"Yeah. Me, too. Does Kira know you're on to her?"

"She does not. But she remains upset about the affair. It's why she took our boy to spend Christmas with his grandfather in the old country."

"You worried she'll tell her daddy?"

"She won't. She likes her life in the United States. If my father-in-law found out, he would recall me, and she would have to live in Armenia again. There's one small detail, however. The news stories say Phipps kept press clippings."

"He did. I saw them."

"If Rosa's murder isn't among them, it will raise questions."

"I worried about that, myself. But it's there. Even though he didn't do it, he still kept the articles. I guess he kept anything that mentioned him."

"My sources say there's a mapbook also, with the locations of the killings marked, but with Rosa's page untouched."

"Guess I missed that." She shrugged. "It's no big deal. There are always loose ends in investigations."

"True. In investigations—and in life." He fixed her with his stare. "You're a loose end, Bonnie."

She didn't like the sound of that. "Am I?"

He nodded. "To be perfectly frank, I'd hoped I could persuade you to work for me. It was another reason I approached you. I could use someone with your skills, someone outside the organization. You could be very valuable to me."

"We've already been over this."

"So we have. But I'm curious, if you don't object to a personal inquiry." His tone implied that her objection would be of no consequence. "You speak of moral standards, yet you are, at heart, a killer. We both know this. You take lives for money. You could make money with me. Yet you resist. Why?"

"You're not trying to get me to change my mind?"

"I'm honestly curious."

She thought he meant it. She gave him a straight answer.

"I had a talk with a friend a while back. He told me life is all about lines. There are lines you can cross and lines you can't. The first kind, you can cross back over and go on like before. The second kind, there's no coming back." She let her shoulders lift and fall. "Working for you is a line I can't cross. Not unless I want to stay on your side of the line forever."

"You accepted the assignment last night."

"It was a one-time thing. Special circumstances. I could come back from that."

She expected an argument. Things might get ugly. But he surprised her.

"Thank you for your answer," he said. "It was well spoken."

"You're not pissed off?"

He smiled. She thought it might be the first sign of genuine amusement she'd seen from him.

"Excuse my bluntness, Bonnie, but you're not important enough to piss me off."

She found herself smiling in return. "Don't sweat the small stuff, huh?"

"Exactly. I have, as the expression goes, bigger fish to fry."

"I get it."

She did, too. All at once she saw herself as he must see her—a small-town PI driving a broken-down Jeep, renting a fleabag office, living in a crappy duplex, subsisting on fast food and cheap rum. She was nothing to him. A diversion, a curiosity. Like a bug on the windowpane. As easily ignored. As easily squashed.

Somehow this train of thought didn't leave her unsettled. On the contrary, she found it reassuring. He didn't seem like a man who would go to the trouble of squashing a bug.

She got up, reasonably confident for the first time that she would actually be allowed to leave. He opened the door with a wave of his hand. At the doorway she looked back.

"I won't hear from you again," she said. "Right?"

Armin Petrossian smiled. "If you do, Bonnie, it will be only because you got in my way."

40

SHE WISHED SHE could crawl into bed. She was dead tired. Better than being just dead, she guessed.

Even so, she would go see Frank. It wasn't too late. It was still Christmas.

She took Highway 18, heading southeast. She thought about Rosa Martinez. Dan's words from last night came back to her: *You're a born killer. You have zero respect for human life. You and Phipps could be twins.*

It had bothered her at the time. Not because she cared about his opinion. But because he'd blundered too near the truth. It wasn't Henry who'd lain in wait in the shrubbery as Rosa jogged closer. For a few minutes in the early morning light, she had become the Man in the Moon.

And it had been easy. As easy as it had been for Jonah Stroud, when he copied Henry's MO to blow Phil Gaines away.

So yeah, she could beat herself up about that. But she wasn't going to. There was a difference, a big one, a difference that maybe even Dan could see now. Her targets were neither random nor personal. She wasn't killing innocents or settling scores. By killing Rosa, she'd saved Kira Petrossian. By killing Henry, she'd saved the next victims he would have picked. By killing Stroud, she'd saved Dan Maguire and maybe Brad. And by killing Sofia, she'd saved herself.

So let the world call her wrong. She was okay with what she did. Sure, she got paid most of the time, but a girl had to make a living. And she wasn't working for Armin Petrossian. She'd stepped back from the abyss.

And she'd survived. Again.

At Maritime she cut inland. She drove past the hospital where she'd found Brad this morning. A minute later she hooked right, climbing a side street up a sloping hillside. Near the summit she eased to a stop on the side of the road. She killed the Jeep's headlights and engine, listening to the crazy knock of the motor and the rattle of the exhaust pipe. When the vehicle had fallen silent, she got out, braving the cold one last time.

The cemetery was closed, but she had no trouble with the lock on the gate. She trudged among the monuments and headstones and scattered wind-bent trees, her boots sinking into pillowy piles of snow, not yet iced over.

She found the spot where the bronze plaque had been newly set in the earth and toed the snow with her boot until she uncovered the marker itself. She had to use her keychain flashlight to read Frank Kershaw's name.

Their Thanksgiving conversation was their last. He'd slipped into heart failure a week later, lingering unconscious in the ICU for a few undignified days. She hadn't been there when he died in the middle of the night, but she'd paid for his cremation and interment, and for the plaque.

There was no funeral service. He had no family. His friends, to the extent he had any, were back in Philly; if she'd ever known their names, she'd long forgotten. He must have had other friends in Ohio, where he'd lived as Frank Hatch before circumstances required a change of identity. But to anyone from his Ohio days, Frank Hatch had died decades ago.

Once or twice, Brad had asked if Frank was like a father to her. No, she always said. This was true. They'd never had that kind of relationship. Neither of them had wanted it.

And yet he'd been the closest thing she'd had to a real

father. He filled the bill, however reluctantly and imperfectly, far better than Tom Parker ever had. She owed him, and that was something she couldn't say about many people. More important, he'd never called in her debts.

And she did miss him. She missed their talks. She missed his advice, which she seldom followed. She missed the steady susurrus of his breathing as they sat together on the porch at Green Harbor.

She wasn't in the habit of talking to graves, but she decided to talk to this one, just a little.

"Merry Christmas, Frank," she said.

It didn't feel as weird as she'd thought it would.

"I crossed a pretty big line," she said, "but I got away with it. I made it back. You'd be proud of me, I think. I made it back."

Gazing down at the bronze rectangle, at the name encircled in a wavering spotlight and half obscured by a mist of flakes, she felt suddenly, desolately alone.

She had lost Brad. She had lost Frank. There was no one left.

The truth of it hit her with a new kind of pain, worse than a needle stick or a bullet wound. Pain that was raw and deep, drilling down to the bone, to the root of the nerve.

She ought to cry. To shed tears—tears for herself, tears for the dead. She wanted to.

But she didn't know how.

Author's Note

AS ALWAYS, READERS are invited to visit me at www.michaelprescott.net, where you can find links to all my books, news about upcoming projects, contact info, and other stuff.

Tears for the Dead is the fifth book featuring the intrepid Bonnie Parker. The series began with *Cold Around the Heart* and continued with *Blood in the Water*, *Bad to the Bone*, and *Skin in the Game*.

Many thanks to Diana Cox of www.novelproofreading.com for another meticulous proofreading job. And thanks to all you good people who keep buying—and reading—my books, even in today's hyper-competitive marketplace.

—MP

ABOUT THE AUTHOR

AFTER TWENTY YEARS in traditional publishing, Michael Prescott found himself unable to sell another book. On a whim, he began releasing his novels in digital form. Sales took off, and by 2011 he was one of the world's best-selling ebook writers. *Tears for the Dead* is his most recent thriller.

Made in the USA
San Bernardino, CA
03 March 2019